". . . marks a large de[...]
out secularism of most c[...]
has no inkling that peopl[...]
religious faith. In this way it also marks the rehabil-
itation of an important truth."

Russell Shaw

"Fickett offers a fast-moving historical saga that invites but does not demand multiple levels of atten-tion. *First Light* is a romance by a writer whose sense of the genre encompasses the medieval tradition of *Sir Gawain and the Green Knight*. Here, as in *Gawain*, the marvelous and the miraculous are reported with-out fuss in the course of a narrative grounded in the realities of everyday life."

Christianity Today

". . . Fickett will continue doing what he does best, and that's writing good fiction."

Publishers Weekly

". . . one of the rare historical romances that does right by its genre, taking the characters, plot, time period, and readers seriously."

World

". . . artfully written. Full of surprising plot twists, unusual characters, and sound wisdom, it's a rare narrative that could become a classic."

Bookstore Journal

OF SAINTS & SINNERS

———

First Light
Daybreak

OF SAINTS & SINNERS

HAROLD FICKETT
DAYBREAK

BETHANY HOUSE PUBLISHERS
MINNEAPOLIS, MINNESOTA 55438

F.
Fic

Fiction

Published in association with the literary agency of Alive Communications,
P.O. Box 49068, Colorado Springs, CO 80949.

This is a work of fiction. Except for publicly recognized historical figures,
the characters, their names, the events, and dialogue are products of the
author's imagination and should not be construed as having a relation to any
person, living or dead.

Cover by Dan Thornberg,
Bethany House Publishers staff artist.

Published by Bethany House Publishers
A Ministry of Bethany Fellowship, Inc.
11300 Hampshire Avenue South
Minneapolis, Minnesota 55438

Printed in the United States of America.

Library of Congress Cataloging-in-Publication Data

Fickett, Harold.
    Daybreak / Harold Fickett.
        p.   cm. — (Of saints and sinners ; 2)

    1. United States—History—Colonial period, ca. 1600–1775—Fiction.
I. Title. II. Series: Fickett, Harold. Of saints and sinners ; 2.
PS3556.I324D39   1995
813'.54—dc20   94–40301
ISBN 1–55661–176–5   CIP

For Karen

Be ye therefore perfect, even as your Father which is in heaven is perfect.

—Matthew 5:48

There is none righteous, no, not one.

—Romans 3:10

CONTENTS

Part V • Evil Loves the Night

Part VI • Let There Be

HAROLD FICKETT is the Executive Director of the Milton Center at Kansas Newman College. He is the author of four books, including *The Holy Fool* and *Flannery O'Connor: Images of Grace*, and has written for a host of publications including *The New Oxford Review, The National Review, Publishers Weekly*, and *Christianity Today*. Coming from a family that has been at the heart of the evangelical Protestant experience for generations, Fickett's life has been shaped by countless saints and sinners. In this series, OF SAINTS AND SINNERS, he has embarked on a historical tribute to the spiritual heritage of American culture.

DAYBREAK

*T*his is the story, as I know it, of our family, the Whites, a clan of men and women whose souls, like mine, distilled Calvinist rectitude from Highlander savagery. A story of saints and sinners, the two so inbred that only the Lord, who looks on the heart, truly knows who's who. But I have written this account—for myself and my children—so that we will not forget the redemptive power of memory or the magnificent gesture of the past toward what lies beyond us all.

PART I

—

The Spirit Is Willing

CHAPTER 1

———

When She Told Him

A day and a thousand years are said to be the same in heaven, and
happiness in marriage may be an instance, in human terms, of
what this means. In the mid-eighteenth century, the founding couple
of our family, Abram and Sarah White, enjoyed almost a decade together after their newlywed troubles ended. Sarah designed and dec-
orated Copper Beech House; Abram made a success of his shipyard,
White Star. The two made their new town, Newburyport, Massachusetts, home. Yet they hardly recognized these years as happy. That's
how fast they went—as quick as willing, as easy as true companionship, as tranquil as satisfied passion. Like one late, long, cool summer
evening watching the stars glitter out in the eastern sky.

Then, almost suddenly, they lost this earthly sense of paradise.
They began thinking what to do and making up their minds.

In April of 1765, after a gala at Theophilus Parsons' home, Abram
and Sarah stepped from under the wisteria-twined portal, and Abram
went forward quickly to a lamplit open carriage waiting in the street.

Then he turned back to Sarah and extended his hand. She stood for a moment, looking straight ahead, holding herself back. He feared the restraint she had shown all evening, her humming replies to the dinner conversation, the terrible patience of her refusal to be drawn into conversation, even by their host, Theophilus Parsons, who knew everyone she knew and better. Abram wished he could see her eyes. But then, just as he despaired of provoking her interest, she caught up her ball gown and took his hand. Her shoulders and back rested in his arm as he ushered her to the carriage.

Abram came round from behind and swung up and into the seat beside her. He took the reins off the postern and slapped the back of a horse whose coat was as black as a crow's feathers and had the same starchy sheen under the moon and stars. He did not turn toward their home, Copper Beech House, but kept going down Water Street through the poorest fishing neighborhood, Five Points, with its gull-toned and weather-beaten shanties. They traveled past the clamming area, Joppa Flats—dry now at low tide—and rolled on around the curve of the estuary toward Plum Island.

"You aren't too tired?" Abram asked. "You always get that second wind at the end of a party and can't sleep. I thought we'd enjoy your high spirits together."

Sarah said nothing as the carriage rolled farther along the sandy lane, her hands clasped on her crossed knee, which increased the difficulty of balancing.

"You haven't done this for a good while," she said finally.

"No," he said. She had guessed at his strategy, as he knew she would.

He glanced over but could not see Sarah's face in the shadows. He remembered another time, her face hidden but with a burnished outline—a day's late sun on a courtship walk firing a band of gold embroidery around her head and shoulders. Swimming through memory, he recalled a similar effect as they traveled together before sunrise in the coach to their wedding. He had made her change into her wedding gown in that coach, and his first look at her in the gown was like seeing the sun rising early. Then memory called up the stiff suspension of another coach, the one that had brought them back from the home of Jonathan Edwards as they considered what they had learned from the New England divine and his wife. Years earlier, as she awoke after he had taken her away from her family estate Elysia, Sarah had asked, "How long will it be?" A question that still hung over them in many ways.

Yes, he remembered. Did she?

Soon they had reached the point where the marshlands wedged out on the right from the high ground of Newburyport and the road swung left toward Plum Island, which was really an outer bank that guarded the shore—a tiger shark's head of sand, dune grasses, scrub pine, poison oak, and beach plum vines. The marsh's thick smell of corn grass and decay overwhelmed the brine in the air. Spring had come early to New England this year, and in this last of April nights the freshets of wind chased the touch of humidity in the air. After winter's raw weather the effect of such a clement night was like being received into the world's arms.

At the tidal flow that dug a moat around the back of Plum Island, Abram brought the carriage to a halt and hobbled the horse. He escorted Sarah down on his arm to his longboat, which his workman Bachelder had portaged here earlier, along with the provisions in the bow.

Abram rowed them, with the banks of the highest marshlands at first above their heads, out toward the little bay that separated the southern tip of the island from the town of Ipswich. Sarah seemed tranquil as she sat with her arms folded, her head leaning to one side, her shifting slow and easy, at last relaxed.

The water lapped easily, too, against the boat, and he swung the oars in their metal rings with a shallow stroke. He took her out several hundred yards from the shore into the bay, and the full moon surrounded them with silver wavelets.

"It's the night for this," she said.

"It is just as I had hoped," he said and looked to see how she would receive this. She did not return his glance.

"You are gone so much during good weather," he said. "In all our years here, I haven't shown you much of what I enjoy in this place."

Sarah let her hand trail in the water, then shook it quickly against the icy cold and worked her two hands together to get the warmth back. She bounced her shoulders and hugged herself tight to show him what a mistake she had made.

After a while she said, "You have worked hard here for a decade, and yet there's still something of the sea captain about you. I sometimes wonder whether you know anyone well here."

"I talk more with the townspeople than you realize."

He began to turn them back in toward shore.

She noticed immediately. "I remember you describing your brother-in-law Hugh to me. How you admired his sense of being an Irishman. How you admired even more his ability to make Ulster County his new Ireland. I'd like you to be more at ease, that's all."

Abram paused his stroke. She was trying to be kind, and he didn't want to be angry. "I can row the estuary blind. Later in life, the friends you make, they have mostly to do with business."

"You think too much about me," she said.

She had landed them at what he wanted to say, or close to it, but too soon. "I always think of you," he said and wheeled them around toward the beach.

He made a fire in the shelter of the scalloped dunes and set the provisions out: roast chicken, scones with last year's beach plum jam, a ham, pickled cabbage, and roasted potatoes that he quickly warmed at the fire.

"We will never get up tomorrow," Sarah said. "The coach goes at noon."

"It's always an hour behind from Portsmouth."

She nodded, a sign that she would let the matter of the late hour pass. "This is a lovely supper," she said.

"You never eat when you go to a ball."

"Those long groaning boards with their pyramids of macaroons stuff me before I've taken a bite."

He broke off a wing from the roasted chicken. "What do you do at all those parties in Boston? This must be the secret of your youthfulness—to dine where you must starve." He tried to laugh.

She took an especially large bite out of her chicken leg, wiped her mouth with her serviette, and spooned jam onto her scone. "I know where this conversation is leading," she said. "But my cousin is expecting me."

Abram took a breath. "I'd like you to consider not going this spring," he said.

"To stay here and torment you?" Sarah asked.

"I still take great pleasure in your company."

"Great pleasure? What little there may be would soon dissipate if I stayed. I depend very much on my visits with Submit."

"For what?"

"For what neither of us can find here. Friends and relations. Society. I need such a world, even if you do not."

He cleared his throat. "I could be more thoughtful of that here. Accept more invitations. Theophilus and his circle are of the same class." He gestured to their midnight setting. "And the two of us could use our powers of invention to better effect in enjoying ourselves."

"We have been married for thirteen years," she said, this time a little prickly. "Can we really change so much now?"

Abram covered his eyes and worked his hand down over his chin.

He exhaled, heavily. "We . . ." he said.

"We?"

"We are not living . . . not fully . . . as man and wife. I would be happy for you to see your cousin; I do not begrudge you her society. But I am not happy now. It has not made the difference I thought it would."

"And this difference?" she asked.

He stood up and walked a few paces away. He found the air much less comfortable away from the fire and circled back. He tried to begin again but then felt awkward standing over her. He sat down once more and leaned toward her.

"The carriage tonight reminded you," he said. "It must have."

"Truly," she said, "it did. Of many things. Many of them unpleasant." She turned her head from one side to another, as if not knowing where to look, and pursed her lips. "You knew that it would," she said.

"The morning we journeyed to be married?"

"When we came to this town," she said, countering, keeping her eyes down, holding herself still.

"And that memorable occasion with the Edwardses. I promised to love you for yourself then, Sarah, for what you are to God. I thought by letting you enjoy your cousin's company, the society of Boston, I was doing so. Your actions tell me that I have still not loved you as I ought. What is lacking? We have become such a small thing!"

She moved to his side and touched the back of his neck, keeping her hand there.

He did not move but sat quietly, his legs sprawled out, bent slightly at the knees. He spoke into the fire. "What do you desire? What remains?" He half raised his hands and then dropped them. "To see you as a . . . a companion, a friend of longstanding . . . that is not marriage. If I am in need, I am in need of a wife, not friends and relations. I want what we intended long ago."

She kissed his cheek and massaged the muscles high up on his neck where the ribbon bound his hair. "Life itself may be smaller than we once thought. How could our courtship have lasted? The flesh is never equal to the spirit."

He shrugged away from her and stood up once more. "We are betraying our vows, Sarah, and the God who gave us to each other."

"I have not betrayed you," she said, keeping calm.

"I did not say you had. But let us remember what we were to each other—what the Edwardses told us we could be."

Now Sarah stood up and brushed the sand from her ball gown,

working at it, sending showers flying. "That Mrs. Edwards was such a spiritual enthusiast. She *hopped*," she said, disgusted.

Abram watched his wife as she looked out over the bay and then upward to the clustering stars and the steamy whiteness of the Milky Way. After their years together, he thought he could hear the debate she was having with that sky's Author. He truly believed that his wife's deepest desire must still be to see the family that had appeared before her in a vision—which was to be their family, generations hence, a family noted for its Christian service. Sarah Edwards, wife of the great Jonathan Edwards, had prophesied it.

Did his own Sarah see that family, at this moment, gazing down at them from the ring of eternity? "You thought she spoke the truth at the time," Abram said. "You thought you saw that family before you."

"A young girl with all her life before her—what wouldn't I have seen?"

"You don't believe in this anymore?"

She turned and looked at him, and in her firelit face he could see an adamant calm that refused to hope. "We have waited," she said. "You and I, we *have* kept faith with that promise."

"There is yet time."

She clasped her hands before her as if she were about to begin a public talk. "No. Not as I would have it. Because the years have not passed for us in the same way. You have enjoyed the waiting and trying as pleasure. I have been used cruelly by it. With each cycle, each month, I have been given another chance, renewed hope, and then denied. And denied and denied and denied and denied and denied. Thirteen years of twelve cycles. So many months of mockery. Prayers answered with a bloody course as if I had to be wounded for my hoping. With the denial not enough, but as if the Lord himself did me injury. And you expect to take me out under your Lord's sky and woo me back into more years of ridicule. I would rather not allow the possibility of hope. That is the only measure I can take against God's humiliation."

Abram looked down—could not meet her eyes. Her suffering demanded respect, even honor, and yet how could her anger against God help? "So our relations are at an end?"

"That is what I wish to say," she said with irritation, as though speaking to one of slow understanding.

"What does this mean for us?"

"To be what we have become and are."

"And only that?"

"This is how I choose to act."

"By not behaving as my wife?"

"By being who I am and that only—barren and without hope. If there be any dignity in renouncing pretense, I would gain it. It is little enough." A bullishness came into her eyes as they grew large, flat, and fixed, and her mouth clasped down so hard it drew her entire face into a mask of anger and pain.

"I must go to Boston now," she said. "I must be away. I know this to be only diversion, but I cannot hope any longer for what will not be. You have been kind in permitting me these months away while not fully knowing my feelings. Now that you know, be no less kind to me."

Did he know? It seemed just then that nothing should ever surprise him; and yet, as he thought it best at times to keep even his own memories sequestered, he wished, too, that some judgments could be kept forever in abeyance. At last, he said, "I have known. I have."

She went to him, reached up, and clasped him with both hands around the neck. She kissed him with hard, closed lips, sealing his mouth and his appeal.

She walked away from him, down the strand, and he became aware of their islanded circumstances and all they would have to do to get back.

CHAPTER 2

———

A Serious Call to a Devout and Holy Life

Because his sister Dorsey's farm in Ulster County, New York, proved too demanding, Abram's aged French Huguenot mother had come to live with Abram and Sarah five years earlier, in 1760. At seventy-three, Abram's *maman* sat in a spindle-backed rocker in his front parlor most of the day, a book in her hands, a piece of sewing or knitting or needlepoint by her as a badge of her matriarchy, though she might spend months darning a sock. She read aggressively, in spurts, as Abram did, and through these last years he had come to see how much of his inquisitiveness came from her. She sat close to the parlor's beveled window to see the street, and rarely allowed the Chinese screens to be used, or even the draperies pulled despite the long chill in New England from October to May.

Two weeks after Sarah had left for Boston, on a Saturday morning,

Abram decided to talk with his mother about his unhappiness, the malaise that had come to him. He found his maman in her chair, dressed, as she usually was, in black bombazine with lace trimmings. The dress made her look regal. But, incongruously, she always wore a simple white cap with it, rucked close with a drawstring—a servant's cap. She liked elaborated finery almost as much as a Spaniard, but the cap signaled her democratic prerogatives.

"Ça va, Maman?" Abram asked as he stepped over and kissed her on the forehead. "Qu'est-ce que tu fais, aujourd'hui? You were reading Mr. Edwards yesterday as if preparing for an examination."

"Should I not be preparing?" she asked. "'Study to show thyself . . .'"

"In that sense, so should we all, my dear Maman."

He popped his head back out into the hall and called to Jezreel for the parlor fire to be replenished and then went back in and sat on the green damask settee opposite her chair. The black servant, dressed in dove gray waistcoat and breeches, came in and carefully placed two more quarters on the andirons and used the bellows until the charred logs recaught.

"Abram must have a touch of ague," Maman said, in apology for the summons.

"Jezreel knows his duties. He's charged with looking after you, Maman. Not you with him," Abram said as he repositioned the fire screen in an L, behind the settee and along the outer wall, making sure it did not block his mother's view of the window.

"This is my own particular concern, mum," Jezreel said, his bass voice rumbling. "What will you be needing then? I'll fetch you some tea."

"You see how helpful he is," Maman said.

Abram looked at the servant suspiciously. He liked the tall, princely West Indian well enough, except for his tendency to court his mother. (He did miss his old manservant Hodges, though, who had established his own family soon after their move to Newburyport—Hodges only courted him.) Abram did not look forward to their talk being interrupted by the serving of tea. Jezreel liked to serve with a great deal of ceremony, showing off a punctilious niceness.

When the servant had left the room, Abram said, "I do suffer from an illness, Maman." Seeing his mother's expression, he added quickly, "No, no, no, not of the flesh but of the spirit."

"Your wife is gone again," Maman said.

"Yes," he said, "I am lonely for Sarah. And there is something more."

"You are lonely, *mon petit,* for what Sarah should be giving to you, even when she is here."

Jezreel opened the door and wheeled in the cart. Abram stood up quickly, took command of the cart, and said, "*Merci,* Jezreel. I will pour so that *Maman* and I can continue."

Jezreel nodded in a self-satisfied way and left the room.

Abram said nothing more until he had poured the tea for them.

"*Maman,*" he said, beginning again, "I have my doubts of Mr. Edwards. I have my doubts of what the questions of this exam truly are. Those of the catechism you taught me so long ago?"

"You remember their answers?" *Maman* said.

"I remember that I am to love God and enjoy Him forever. I am not sure that I love God. I feel no such love. I feel as if dead—a whitened sepulchre indeed."

His mother's cheeks fell with disapproval, but Abram could not unsay what he had, and he was glad at having spoken from his heart. His mother would settle into the talk in another moment.

"This is what you wanted to say to me?"

"Yes."

"Tell me the rest."

What would he do when he could no longer be her child? The luxury was too close to being at an end. "Sarah no longer believes that we shall have a family."

"Sarah is still so young."

"She has lost faith in the possibility."

"*Mais,* you love her?"

"Yes . . . yes. But I cannot give her what she most wants. The one thing she needs. And I, I'm older, less in need if still needful, and I cannot sustain her love with memories. I know that I love her, but not how to renew our life together. I would try with everything that I have if I knew how."

His mother's head quavered with irritation. "You both have put too much faith in that Edwards woman's saying. That is not your true hope."

Abram tried to ease back into the settee, which remained as stiff and unaccommodating as always. "There must be a means of realizing such a hope in this life."

"To live as God intended," *Maman* said, as if prompting an answer he should know all too well.

"But more particularly."

His mother's hard amber eyes flashed out at that.

"Consider now," he went on. "What have I done in life? Brought the family to America, made my place—my fortune. Was this for God? I thought so. Now I cannot be sure that I have done anything but what I wanted."

"And it is necessary that you have another idea? Even a prophecy?"

"You see how really selfish I am," he said, and smiled to himself.

"*Et là*, so your faith has disappeared."

"I wonder about God's care. The French encyclopedists claim He sets the world running like a timepiece and then watches the ticking of human initiative."

"But you are this clockmaker's ideal!" she said, a mock cheering in her voice. "A little boy who runs away from Ireland and makes a fortune. What they talk of now as the new man of the Americas. Are you not satisfied with this glory?"

"Be kind."

"You are too intelligent for such notions."

"Too miserable. I am at a time in life when I should be at peace with my lot, and I am far from that. I feel, so much, that sickness we spoke of, its useles craving . . . and for what? As you say, another idea or grand purpose?"

She hit her knees with both hands repeatedly and leaned forward. "What are you doing for others?"

"My shipyard employs a great many."

"What about alms?"

"I tithe."

"That is not my meaning. I speak of alms. What Mr. Whitefield and the evangelicals call acts of mercy. The Reverend Parsons is a supporter of Mr. Whitefield, you know."

"I have been meaning to read Mr. Whitefield's journals."

"You have not?"

"No."

"And Mr. Law, his *Serious Call To A Devout And Holy Life*?"

"Not yet."

"Then you must. But answer my question now."

He looked at her and realized that for years he had thought only of the welfare of his family circle.

"You must find something—maybe quite a small thing—something you do for others who cannot help you in return. Who cannot, perhaps, even give you friendship. Something only God can know about, and so when this foolish act, this offering, brings life, you know from whom the life comes."

Abram sipped his cooling tea. "Faith," Abram said, almost with a start, discovering the joke he had played on himself.

"Yes, faith," *Maman* said. "More absolute. More pure. *Ça veut dire, plus dur.*"

" 'Hodder,' as our Bostonians say."

"More hard," *Maman* said, and nodded. She waved her hand, indicating the stack of books by the side of her chair. "Now, Mr. Whitefield, Mr. Law. Take them."

He went down on his knee, found the two books in the stack, and paused to give her a kiss as he rose.

───────

After services the next Sunday at South Presbyterian Church, Abram stood with the Reverend Jonathan Parsons. The pastor had such a thatch of silver hair, still threaded with darker strands, that he wore no peruke. The sun was high and hot, and Parsons' brow and the deep-grooved runnels beside his mouth ran with perspiration, which he dabbed at with his huge linen handkerchief during their exchange.

"Thanks be for your sermon, Mr. Parsons."

"I give my hand to you and your thanks to the Lord, for what virtue there was in it, if any, belongs to Him."

"I would have a word."

"Speak, sir."

"My mother asked me the other day what I was doing for others."

"Yes?"

"I am looking for a charitable enterprise."

The Reverend Parsons swabbed his face once more but with greater care. "I must speak then of parish needs to you, Captain White."

"I'm afraid I know them. I mean within the town."

Rev. Parsons put his handkerchief up in the side pocket of his greatcoat. "Do you know of the Acadians?"

"I know of them," Abram said, remembering the many French neutrals who had been forcibly exiled to New England sea coast towns, Newburyport among them, during the French and Indian War of the 1750s. "Surely they have made lives here by now."

"The lives of beggars," Parsons said. "Joseph Dorsett and his kin have petitioned the town council for relief."

"I thank you then, sir, to know of this."

"Just so. Good sabbath to you and my greetings to your mother."

───────

Without Abram speaking further of the matter, he soon received the calling card of Tristram Dalton, a young Harvard graduate who owned a shop in town importing finished goods from England. Dalton also had lands from his parents, as Abram understood it, in Essex County. The penciled note on the back of the card simply said "Acadians" and proposed a visit on the following evening. Abram sent word he would be happy to entertain him.

Abram received the young official into his parlor, from which *Maman* had removed herself at the mention of business, even charitable business. Tristram Dalton was a Beau Brummel, turned out in a silk greatcoat and ivory waistcoat. His shirt was done up with a high cravat collar, and its cuffs were almost foppishly long and butterflied out with the least gesture. He wore a brown peruke and a little face powder, emphasizing his already doughy skin, but his large and yet keen eyes and the tip of his prominent nose gave his whole expression a pointed shrewdness. He had a buckled courier's pouch under his arm.

Abram found himself amused when he dealt with such ambitious characters these days—younger men, with their sincerity, their eagerness.

"Mr. Dalton," he said, "if you accomplish all your duties with such promptness you'll soon be governor. How did you know I was interested in the Acadians?"

He saw the intended effect as the younger man bucked his head back and prepared to explain.

"I am only too glad," Abram said quickly, "that Rev. Parsons spoke a word in good season. Let's see what you have for me. This chair, if you please."

"I have brought you the full text of the Acadians' petition," Tristram Dalton said, without a single pause for pleasantries, as he seated himself, opened his courier's pouch, and handed across the document. "We want to return the French neutrals to their homelands. I am here as a representative of the Overseers of the Poor. We have no funds for such special petitions, but we would grant it."

"You would?"

Dalton handed Abram another paper with estimates. Funds would not only be needed for transport but also for subsistence while the French neutrals reestablished themselves. Abram knew the estimates were short, on the basis of what it took to establish his immigrants in Ulster County.

"You will need a greater sum," he said.

"Will you then supply it, sir?" Dalton asked, his eyes level, completely established, if a little clenched in the jaw, in his purpose.

"I will."

Abram could see the exaltation, although the young emissary suppressed the shout inflating his chest.

"You will be remembered, sir," Tristram Dalton said, and buckled up his courier's pouch. (Abram thought he might go without speaking again, so laconic was he proving to be.)

"Tell me," Abram said, "about the Overseers' charge."

"Poverty can have its dignity," Dalton said. "Need, though, often proves a useless lash." His speechifying voice finally slowed. "A seaport, as you must know, has its influxes of population and coin, and these attract those who disdain more stable employments and think only of ready money."

"Those who like their rum, our dipsomaniacs, prostitutes, sly boys?"

"You live here."

"Are they very many in number?"

"They breed a good many children and are careless of them." The young man's voice became urgent. "Haven't you seen them scouring the wharves for food with the rats?"

For the first time, Abram saw that the young man could be genuinely moved.

"And I suppose there are additional causes of distress. The fishing runs are unpredictable," Abram said. "The prices they attract much more so."

"Indeed."

"I've seen what lean times do to the gangs who work in the yards."

"You have it right, sir."

"I have not thought enough on it, though, I will confess. You can tell your committee they have a friend."

"We have already counted you as one."

———

This conversation cast light on the reading Abram did over the next month as he took up George Whitefield's *Journals* and William Law's *A Serious Call To A Devout And Holy Life*. He also engaged the local bookseller, Daniel Bayley, to bring to hand as many works about these gentlemen as he could locate.

The two authors complemented each other. Until this time, Jonathan Edwards had been Abram's lodestone, as the great New England divine was so concerned with understanding religious affections—experiences like Abram's childhood inspirations, his wife's second sight. Abram also had a taste for speculation, and he liked how Edwards was able to encompass some of the new thinking of Locke within a sturdy Calvinism.

Such sentiments and speculations were easy ones, though, asking little of him. Mr. Law asked a great deal and seemed to know nothing in the Gospels but the command: "Be ye perfect."

Mr. Law believed in the strait gate, the absolute word to the Rich Young Ruler, and the apostle's advice to imitate him even as he imitated Christ. Reading William Law inspired Abram with the demands of Christ's teaching, its impossible practicalities and its clear call.

At the same time, Abram was enough of a theologian to see that William Law thought man more guided by sheer reason than the Scriptures allowed. "The heart is deceitful above all things, and desperately wicked: who can know it?" said the Word. Yet Law thought the heart more foolish than deceitful, and he proposed that the heart's remedy came too much, perhaps, through merely human knowledge.

In contrast, the evangelist Whitefield strove after Mr. Law's personal sanctity, while keeping in mind his own need for grace—which his obvious egotism kept in Abram's mind as well. His journals showed that the evangelist had drawn the entire colony of Georgia together in a new way through his acts of mercy—his visits to the sick, his ministrations of charity to the poor, the soft answers he gave to every wrathful indictment.

Abram knew that Whitefield performed these acts partly because he had another end in view, the conversion of souls, which qualified the famous evangelist's charity.

Still, as he read the journals and writings about Whitefield, Abram saw that the man loved others as much or more than his own grand mission. His travels through the British Isles and back and forth to North America, where he spoke in the open fields to tens of thousands, supported the humble and yet financially draining orphanage Bethesda. Whitefield took up collection after collection of hundreds of pounds and it never seemed to be enough. He lived his whole life raising funds, while keeping himself on a small chaplaincy.

More personal aspects of the two men also spoke to Abram. Law advised voluntary poverty, virginity, and devout retirement as aids to the spiritual life. He himself never married, and lived for most of his life (he had died in 1761, four years before Abram's readings) in a small village, King's Cliffe, with his aunt, Miss Hester Gibbon, and a pious widow, Mrs. Hutcheson. They managed on a tenth of their fortune's earnings, gave the rest away, and spent their days in a perpetual round of prayer and good works. They started a school and alms-houses.

Whitefield could hardly be accused of "devout retirement," with his peripatetic ministry, and yet he had undertaken similar renunciations, including a strict married chastity—his wife, Elizabeth, lived at the orphanage in Georgia, and he saw her even more rarely than Abram saw his Sarah. As Abram soon found out, both Whitefield and John Wesley had a view of marriage that so emphasized promoting the kingdom of God that they looked on their wives chiefly as fellow laborers.

Abram remembered how he had enjoyed every conjugal pleasure, and he wondered at the temperaments of these men. The "virginity" that he himself had been obliged to undertake had hardly been voluntary. And yet, he thought, the examples of these men might serve more purposes than he knew.

Mr. Boardman wrote away for back issues and current ones of newspapers featuring stories of Whitefield, and Abram added a hobby to his spiritual exercises: tracking the evangelist on his missionary journeys. Of the first accounts that came to hand, Abram liked the one which came from Whitefield's most recent journey through Pennsylvania.

The Pennsylvania Gazette, October 12, 1763

The Reverend George Whitefield preached to some thousands in the vicinity of Swarthmore this past Sunday after his own attendance at the local parish. This correspondent found occasion to record verbatim the following anecdote from his remarks, a fine story and most indicative of the field preacher's manner.

"I am told [Mr. Whitefield recounted] that people say I bawl, and I will bawl—I will not be a velvet-mouthed preacher, I will not speak the word of God in a sleepy manner, like your church preachers—I'll tell you a story. The Archbishop of Canterbury, in the year 1675, was acquainted with Mr. Butterton the player. One day the archbishop . . . said to Butterton . . . 'Pray inform me, Mr. Butterton, what is the reason you actors on the stage affect your congregations with speaking of things imaginary, as if they were real, while we in church speak of things real, which our congregations only receive as if they were imaginary?' 'Why, my Lord,' says Butterton, 'the reason is very plain. We actors on the stage speak of things imaginary as if they were real, and you in the pulpit speak of things real as if they were imaginary.' Therefore," added Whitefield, "I will bawl; I will not be a velvet-mouthed preacher."

The Overseers of the Poor collected Abram's contribution and made arrangements that finally saw Tristram Dalton, Ebenezer Little, Captain James Hudson, the bookseller Daniel Bayley, Stephen Hooper, and Abram standing on the dock at Newburyport harbor on July 16, 1767, waving goodbye to the Acadians as they left on the ship *Constance*.

Abram found less satisfaction in this project than he had hoped, mostly because Tristram Dalton, Esquire, & Company had handled all the arrangements with the petitioner Joseph Dorsett and the other French neutrals. Abram's limited involvement eventually directed his attention, however, to the poverty that was as close at hand as his actual neighbors. Although it took more than two years of study, he was finally determined to act on his own.

———

So that next year, in the late spring of 1768, Abram began visiting Five Points, a neighborhood bounded by back lanes that ran at laterals to its crosshatch of four streets—filthy trails that starred it as a capital slum. The bottom two points of the star, at the corners of King and Water, and Malboro and Water, each had its distillery and bottle shop. Less formal affairs than Wolfe's Tavern on State Street, these shops sold drinks by the bottle and provided benches for those who preferred not to do their drinking at home.

The walls of the Points' weather-beaten shacks sagged inward, topped by tar-paper roofs that slewed downward at collapsing angles. These dwellings were usually little more than clam shacks, and not half as well fitted out as Abram's shipyard shanty. When these hovels had an upper story, they were sure to harbor two families, each with many children, who usually did as much as their parents to provide the family's daily bread.

Abram started in by visiting one family at a time, shack to shack, door to shaking door, day after day. He always brought a basket of food with him, especially fresh vegetables from his summer garden, tomatoes, summer squash, rutabaga, kale, beets, and a chicken or ham. He made these visits during the mornings, when their work occupied the older children, for his first evening visits brought out interfering swarms of them, calling, running after him, reaching into his pockets, hanging on his arms. Their threadbare, cast-off jackets, tattered breeches, and bare, heavily callused feet recalled his own impoverished childhood—made him uncomfortably aware of it, in fact. He suspected he had smelled, as did they, of sour milk and soiled undergarments, and wore the same grime on his cheeks and around his mouth, so thick and permanent that tears and drool lines patterned it. He always carried a walking cane with him, as protection against the dogs, and when the children came near, he found himself gripping it.

By his fourth visit, Abram had become wary. Everyone he met with had been suspicious. This time, the slattern at the door—a frequenter of the bottle shops, it seemed, from her stoop and circling shuffle—complained to him of his late arrival.

"His 'ordship started at the McJimsey's. They be next door. So we wait. We was waiting on Tuesday, and then you crossed the lane. You crossed the lane! Who would have known you was going to do that? You might have said—oh! you might have said. Come out of nowhere and then crossed the lane. Haven't known what I would give the young ones. I've been mysteried." With this, she collapsed into the room's lone chair and hung on to its back, twisted half-around, as she labored to get her breath after that speech.

He left the basket on her table, and then watched her to see if her glassy eyes were recording his leaving. Her eyes remained stuck on the side wall, her open mouth wounded and unsatisfied.

Five Points was certainly proving better, in his mother's reckoning, than the Acadians' case, since the chronically poor seemed so reluctant to repay him with gratitude. He hadn't really expected this, and he found it harder not to resent than he expected. Many thanked him, yes, but this could be worse, since their fawning appreciation came across as bribery. "The good Captain White! What a man of mercy!" He suspected they were taunting him. Whether through indifference or mocking formality, they told him at every turn that he had no right to think himself their better.

One morning he ventured into a shack, when no one met his knock, to find a clean spare room. The family's few plates, cooking utensils, and spoons were up on pegged shelves. The wood by the stove was neatly stacked. The room smelled, almost pleasantly, of boiling potatoes.

A child, the lone occupant of the room, woke up on his straw pallet in the corner. He stood, frightened, wearing only a homespun nightdress. He looked to be about four or five years old, his head shaped like a thumb, with a huge cuticlelike forehead that flattened it. A chawlike knot at his jawbone on the left side swiveled his mouth and small chin into a permanent gnarl that exposed two rows of spiky teeth. His wispy hair had gathered itself into five or six short tufts.

Abram raised the basket he carried, showing him the reason for his visit. The little boy still looked shocked and uncomprehending, breathing heavily through his wet, red mouth. He wiped his runny nose on his sleeve, smearing the mucus across his cheek, and as the color of the pressed cheek came back, he suddenly looked fevered, his cheeks boiled.

Abram thought to go, but he knew his sense of failure in the enterprise would grow if he were to be scared off by an idiot child. He took out an apple and set the basket down. Reaching out, he offered it to the boy.

The boy reached out for the apple with both hands and grinned horribly—more of his spiky fish teeth showing. He kept staring at the greenish treasure. He took a quick, slashing bite, as if to test its being real, and then another, and another. He put his hand over the side of the apple he wasn't eating as if caressing it. Without looking up, still eating the apple, he took a few hesitating steps toward Abram. He put up one hand, never taking his gaze off the apple, as if he wanted to be picked up.

The boy was not only simple but diseased. He probably had pneumonia, even malaria. Abram had given him the apple; he did not mean to give him his health. Then Abram remembered Mr. Leach and the man's kindness to the young boy he had been when he found himself belowdecks, kidnapped to America. Mr. Leach had cared for Abram and everyone else around him through the smallpox epidemic, even in the midst of losing his own wife and daughter. Abram took a breath against the child's piled britches and picked him up. The child felt much lighter than he should have for his height and age.

The boy took a few more bites and then nestled his snotty face into the crook of Abram's greatcoat. Abram raised his right hand tentatively and started to stroke the child's head.

Then the boy half turned his face, and with the same snatching movement with which he had taken the first bite of the apple, he bit Abram's wrist, his spiky teeth drawing blood.

Abram grabbed his hand away and went to strike the child, when he caught the reflex, opened the fingers of his striking hand, and drew the child's flattened head back to his chest. He looked at the pink ring, like a crown, the child had tattooed on the inside of his wrist.

"Where's your mother now?" he asked. He stroked the child's head and repeated the question. Despite his brief attack, the boy began holding Abram and hugging him, burrowing his runny nose all over Abram's chest.

In another few moments the mother came in, her mouth opening in a way that resembled her child, although nothing else about her did: short and well-proportioned, she had dark hair, large, widely spaced gray eyes, and a cleft chin. Her widow's peak and the cleft made the heart shape of her face as prominent and attractive as the boy's was odd and unnerving. If she would smile her cheeks would bunch, Abram was sure of it.

"David," she said, and reached out for her son.

Abram gave the boy to her and introduced himself. "Let me offer apologies for entering uninvited," he said, "but I did want you to have the basket. The fruit should help the boy's ague."

"He came to you? He's often afraid of strangers."

"He wanted to be held, I thought, but then he gave me a nip. Nothing I didn't deserve, for entering without his mother's permission."

"Oh, *David*," she said, and rocked him against her chest. "He's mute," she said, apologizing. "He's . . ."

Abram nodded once, receiving as much as she wanted to tell.

"David spoke for a while, a year or more. 'Momma,' he said, 'Momma.' " She half turned away, put the boy down, and wiped her hands on her apron.

"He's often sick," Abram said, guessing.

"An ague, a fever, his stomach. He has rarely been well. I almost expect something to take him away. He's strong in his way, I guess."

"His father?"

"He's away to the outer banks with the fishing fleet." The woman smiled. "He's a good man, Thomas. He keeps us. He loves his little boy."

"Your home," Abram said, and debated how to finish what he meant as a compliment, "your home shows care."

"As do you, sir, in your charity. We thank you for it."

"These are my first visits to Five Points," Abram said. "I will be coming back. I mean to establish the help that people need. I have so rarely been able to ask the question, though." He stopped, wishing he could explain so much about his visits to this woman. "Your ambitions. What would they be?"

"Should we have ambitions?"

"You should."

"I begin to feel that such as we are should not."

"Your Thomas wants to carry you to heaven, I would wager."

"He wants a good run of cod," she said, and laughed.

"If he can do any carpentry, he may come to see me at the ship-works. As they go on, my skilled workers do a little better. Or if he only would come and talk, I could speak for him when I had the chance."

"Do you have so many ships to build that you can say this to all the neighborhood?"

"No," he said, "no indeed."

"We thank you, then. We do." She lifted up her large gray eyes to him and could not fight back her wide smile. Her cheeks bunched like a cherub's.

———

That day changed Abram's feelings about "acts of mercy." Indeed, it eventually changed the way he greeted the day. The question remained gratitude, not of those to whom he ministered but his own. At some point he had indeed begun to consider himself the ideal of that clockmaker God, a paragon of self-initiative, when another accounting of his life, the one he was inclined to make now, revealed that life as singularly blessed. From his mother and sister, through the Mr. Leaches he had encountered at every critical juncture, to advantageous events such as Captain Hawks' contracting smallpox when the man's cruelty threatened to release his own destructive powers. Even his difficulties with Sarah required the apt recognition that if he had been given a troubled love, he had also been given something genuine. He still believed Sarah's greatness of soul had yet to be realized, and he wanted to trust it would be. He had only been put in the crucible, not abandoned. Compared to everyone in Five Points, his life was felicity itself.

So Abram took on extra day-help to prepare provisions and make up clothing for those he visited. He recruited his mother into the effort, putting her in charge of the newly hired girls. And when *Maman* looked up at Abram from her administrations, her quavering old head shook with a fierce approval.

CHAPTER 3

But the Flesh Is Weak

On a Monday, as he continued his efforts in Five Points for a third week, Abram noticed that he had arrived two doors away from Mrs. Anne Farmington's house. He would be seeing her on Wednesday, if the weather held. His charity to her predated his work in the Points by two years.

When any of Abram's workmen suffered an incapacitating accident, he supplied the family with a pittance until the man could work again. Carpenters often suffered serious cuts, to the extent of self-amputations, in fact, and men sometimes slipped off the scaffolding and broke their legs or backs. The heads of two households had become paralytics. But Anne Farmington's husband, Allen, who fell during a mast-raising on an icy March day when his foreman advised against proceeding, died.

The woman's one-story shanty leaned against its taller neighbor at such an angle that it seemed to be staggering. He remembered the place from his trip here to deliver the bad news about her husband.

He wondered how the woman had fared. Except for momentary glimpses in the street or at church, Abram had not seen the woman since he had broken the news. He sent a man round with the monthly allowance.

Come Wednesday, when the midsummer day broke with an early sweat of humidity, Abram decided to skip his early morning visit at the shipyard and make his charity rounds hours earlier than usual. Five Points' shacks, with their tar-paper roofs, turned into fish smoking sheds on such close days.

As he walked down the slope of King's Street, he fingered the buttons of his ivory satin waistcoat, halfway unbuttoning the garment as the heat and his walking caused beads of sweat to track through his sideburns.

Mrs. Fiddich, sweeping her steps, waved to him and called out.

"Good morning to you!" he shouted, waving, and then cupped his ear. He hadn't caught her last words.

"What brings you out, then, before the morning's started?" she called, this time in such a loud voice the next street must have heard.

Abram glanced up toward the sun, instantly blinded himself, and half-disoriented, he added, "I thought to finish the business before the sun finishes us all for the day."

"Whether the day's a smithy furnace or an icehouse, women must be doing," she said, and gave her step a last straw-cracking spank. "And who is it today?"

He thought whether to answer. She would see him; she could watch him from there. "Mrs. Farmington," he called back.

"Our Queen!" she said. "You'll have no reward in heaven for visiting Anne, though she needs it as much as any."

He did not call back but waved as he continued down the street. He knew Anne Farmington was famous in these streets—the "Queen of Five Points"—the most attractive woman within memory to reside in the neighborhood.

To Abram her looks did not matter, exactly, but what he had felt on the tragic occasion of their first and only meeting. Even as he had told her that her husband had fallen from the mast and was dead, he remembered the time, years before, when Sarah had come into her father's drawing room to entertain at the harpsichord. This provided such an unexpected torque to the occasion that his stomach still twisted with shame. Abram would hardly act on this attraction, but his anticipation of this visit told him that it could play havoc with his mental devotion to Mr. Law's voluntary virginity.

He knocked at the low side door, and Anne Farmington opened

it to him, her eyes questioning, her shoulders hunched warily.

He held the basket up and said, "I've been visiting the whole neighborhood. This is for you today."

She opened the door more fully, inviting him in. He noticed that, like the idiot boy's mother, this woman managed to bring a singular order to her home—the small pewter vase on the pegged shelves at the end of her cracked and chipped but spotless crockery, the faux-Chinese scarves over the settee to disguise, he presumed, its tatters, a few rhododendron floating in a jade green ceramic bowl. He remembered the same cooking smells from his last visit, oats from the morning's stirabout and lingering traces of what must have been her favorite spices, basil and mint.

All this time he governed his eyes, glancing around here and there and at the knotted-wood floor, but not at her, so that when he felt the fingers of his left hand touched, the shock traveled up his arm and into his shoulder before the sweaty hand grasping his own came to mean her child. Her child was now a toddler, a slip of a boy with a sweep of strawberry blond hair across his forehead and big eyes.

He bent down and picked up the child. The neighborhood's thronging children had taught him that their mothers could not give them all the affection they craved, and eventually Abram had accustomed himself to making up for this lack as well. He propped the child in the crook of his arm, put his hand on his tummy and jiggled it, which caused the child to smile and giggle and grasp Abram around the neck in an embrace meant to fight off the laughter.

"No-o-o!" he said, and laughed, and pulled hard at Abram's gathered ponytail. "No!"

"Very well, then, Master Farmington, I'll put you down."

"Noooo!" the child protested.

Abram stopped his tickling and looked at the child's mother. She stood with one foot forward and her arms half-raised, preparing to take the child from him. He saw in the way she looked at her son the deep pleasure of a mother whose child is instantly likeable.

"What would be his name?" Abram asked.

"I call him Theo. Theodore."

"Here, Theo," Abram said, "go to your mother."

The child nearly jumped out of Abram's arms into his mother's, and she took him the one step to his pallet in the corner and directed his attention to his alphabet blocks. "Build a castle," she said as she stood and looked at Abram.

"You looked alarmed when I came in," Abram said finally.

She half turned away, and he noticed strands of her auburn hair, coming undone from beneath her simple red cap, coiling down her neck onto her shoulder. The ear turned to him was tipped out. Her only flaw, he thought. Her skin was cream, with peach highlights. A beauty mark, actually a twinned mark, a planet and its moon, accented one cheek, as if nature condescended to fulfill the fashion of the time. The mark made him aware of the corner of her pleasingly wide mouth and the incisive and touchingly delicate line of her jaw. When she turned back to him, she kept her chin ducked down so that her large blue eyes, as if concealed by this shy attitude, could search his own.

She had an hourglass figure of such striking dimensions that it kept a man wondering. Her dress of homespun had the lines of more fashionable wear, with a square expanse of décolletage and a fitted bodice.

She was clasping her hands as if in prayer, one of her dark sable eyebrows buckling down in a V, and she spoke reverently. "You have been so kind, sir, and I have not shown any gratitude. Theo and I would have starved but for what your man brings us each month. Now you've come with a basket yourself. Your generosity has already visited this house so many times. I only wish I had thanked you before this."

Her response renewed his impression of the woman's spirit. He remembered the way she had put her face in her hands and wept at the news of her husband's death. He had seen many people grieve, but he had never seen anyone grieve so simply, without apology or embarrassment. Her tears on that occasion had almost comforted *him.* She had an innate dignity, which seemed to express itself through the way she stood on her feet—so upright, tall, composed.

"You have been under no obligation," he said.

She clutched her apron and wiped her hands on it as if preparing to do some work. Her wide mouth tightened. He noticed a tremor wimple her cheek and a splotchy red and milky rash break out along the left side of her shoulder and neck.

Before she could speak, he said, "You extended me every courtesy in receiving my charity. For my thoughtlessness caused your husband to slip from his high place. I am not your savior. I have meant death to you."

The words exploded from her in response to this as the rudeness of her class came out. "So say my neighbors. But that, Allen said, was his duty. He told me of it and would not ask for other duties, though I bade him do so. He scorned me. He might have come home violent if you had not carried on with the raising that day. He relished the danger."

The passion in her voice made Theo look up and stare at his mother.

"Allen was a brave man," Abram said, his voice even. "When his fellows mentioned his wife, he smiled at the treasure his home contained. You ought to blame me. Men who are ready to sacrifice are too few, too valuable, to grant them their wish."

Now the young widow was shaking. She took a quick breath, held it, then took another, holding herself tightly with both arms wrapped around her body, her eyes squeezed shut, as if she would trap and subdue and break her emotion.

As Abram watched this struggle, he felt too close and too far away. He could neither suffer with her, nor alleviate her suffering. He might have held her if she looked like another housewife.

"Is what my man brings you enough?" he asked, to divert her attention to other matters.

She looked at him as if she had communicated a thousand things and he had failed to comprehend one.

"Does the amount keep you?"

"We have nothing else to keep us," she said simply.

"Your family?"

"There be fourteen children in that blighted family. Allen would not farm, and we came to find work here. The family had more happiness than trouble in saying goodbye."

"You must know . . ." Abram began and paused. "You must know the whole town speaks well of you. When you are ready, you'll have husbands standing in line."

She shook her head. "The men as come here are all talk and teeth. Or they have another manse in the Points that needs a slave."

"They are rough, that's surely true, but you'll be better able to distinguish their spirits in time."

She moved to her table and picked up a sugar bowl and glanced inside. "Is there a term to your charity?" she asked, and swiveled the sugar bowl lid around the rim until it fitted. "I . . . I understand if—"

"Mrs. Farmington," he said quickly, "you may count upon it until the need passes. I came rather to see if you lacked anything. Is there anything? I find it a great pleasure to be able to help, and you must only say the word if you require any addition."

She settled once again into her composed, square, forthright posture. "We are well," she said. "You see Theo. Is he not a healthy creature?" The warmth and pride in her voice made Abram proud of her—and himself, for helping.

She went to the child and picked him up again, and Abram watched the tension in her back and shoulders flow into her embrace of the child. As she swung the boy back and forth, she cooed, "Theo is a big'm lad, a laddy boy—my lovems child, mommy's sweetness, her own buzzy wee."

"Is there . . . any addition?" he said, repeating.

She shook her head for emphasis. "We are most grateful, sir. I suffer the grieving still at times, but we are truly well. We live only because of your charity, and we thank God for it every night. I would that the angels had countered our rude behavior and whispered to you of our prayers. But then He has given us breath and speech to thank Him and our benefactors, and so now, if not before, I do thank you."

She put Theo down. "Bless you, sir," she said. "In the Points, they call you 'The Missionary.' Did you know?"

Abram did not answer but said, "I will send another five shillings. The boy's at an age where he needs a bed. We will see to this, and . . . your welfare. Whatever is needful. I'll be going now."

As he went out, he kept trying to shut the door properly, which had swung wide and half-off its loose hinges. He had to try three times to close it, finally lifting it with both hands on the wooden catch as he set it back into its frame.

CHAPTER 4

See No Evil

One Sunday morning, late in June of 1768, *Maman*, Sarah, and Abram were standing under the horse chestnut tree on Federal Street in front of South Presbyterian Church, waiting with their neighbors to go into Sunday services.

Sarah had come home from her usual Boston sojourn two weeks before. She looked magnificent, and for a little while, as she always did, she would carry the high and witty and worldly wise temper inspired by her Boston social schedule. This always set his mother off, as, Abram suspected, it was meant to. Thus, Abram's attentions had turned to keeping peace between the two. His visits to Five Points stopped, almost abruptly. All the charity he could muster was needed at home.

"He can surely pick up my cloth from Bosworth's," Sarah would say.

"No, no, he has to be at the shipyard," *Maman* would say. And Abram would assure them that he would attend to both duties, although he might send one of his men for the cloth, which he could see from the way Sarah shut her eyes satisfied her not a whit. She continually prodded him for attentions and courtesies, while living with him as if she were his sister.

As they waited on that Sunday, Abram felt rather than saw someone watching him and turned to see Anne Farmington standing next to him, quite close, as the crowd hedged them in. She wore a new dress, at least a different dress of light navy blue cotton, that clung like a summer nightgown. She also had on a fancy white cap embroidered with ginger stitching around its rim. He felt with his foot behind him to step back and clipped someone's heel.

"Your wife has come home," Anne said.

Abram glanced over at Sarah, saw she was already curious, and took her arm, laced it through his, and turned them together to Anne. "This is Mrs. Farmington, Sarah, whose husband suffered the tragic accident at the shipyard."

Sarah unlaced her arm and extended her hand.

"My wife, Sarah Nicolls White," Abram said. "Mrs. Farmington."

"You have suffered a great loss," Sarah said. "I hope my husband has not been stinting in his charity."

"Your husband has been our savior," Anne said, her tone subdued.

Sarah looked up at Abram and lengthened her lips in an even, discriminating smile. "Your savior, Mrs. Farmington? I suppose he can appear that way. He once did to me."

Maman turned in to them, enclosing the ring. "And who is this?"

"*Maman*, Mrs. Farmington."

The two women smiled politely at each other.

"My son has told me of your great *tristesse*," *Maman* said. "Your grief this year. You will start to live again now—yes? A new life has been planned?"

Abram was astonished at the readiness of his mother and his wife to bring this woman into their thoughts and advise her.

Anne's good spirits had left her, and she stood mutely before them like a frightened, hunted animal.

"What can you do?" Sarah asked, in a voice at once commanding and practical.

"Keep house? Sew?" Anne said.

"I kept my family for years in Ulster with my wheel," *Maman* said.

"From her dress, *Maman*, I would say that Mrs. Farmington likes to do more finished work," Sarah said.

"I did make this up," Anne said, her voice brightening.

"So does every woman in this town make her own dresses,"

Maman said, "though not our Sarah. She likes to have her dressmaker in Boston."

Abram thought he would soon find himself in a mood that he would be unable to carry into church. He started looking down toward his shipyard on Water Street and thinking of excuses. He could quote "the ox in the ditch."

"I know that every woman must have her accomplishments, to make a dress, play on the pianoforte, and see to her family's receipts," Sarah said in a singsong voice, wagging her head all the while at her mother-in-law. "But those who have been shown God's favor must surely show it to others through useful employment. This is what the use, the *long* use, of wealth has taught my family."

Abram looked at his wife, and before he could help himself he showed his dismay.

She looked back for a moment too long. "What I need is someone to mend the dresses I have made up, to keep me in the fashion that I feel it is my place and duty to maintain. Especially here in this town. Abram still finds servants a mixed blessing and so hires as few of them as he can decently allow. But I have long felt the want of a handmaid. I have, most especially. And I would like you to consider, my good Captain White, whether this pretty young woman might serve us in that capacity."

With that, Sarah took her spreading skirts in one hand, nodded to Anne Farmington, and stepped into the line waiting to go into the open doors of the sanctuary.

Abram looked at his mother, who was so upset that she refused to return his inquiring glances.

"My wife's wishes shall guide my thoughts . . . as always," he said.

His last hope that the family had not just hired a servant in the street disappeared with Anne Farmington's murmured thanks.

"It remains to discuss terms," Abram said. He turned decisively from her, then quickly looked back to say, "We must all be at our prayers about this now." And at that he nodded his farewell and pushed on into the congregants, with his mother by his side.

———

Abram and Sarah were alone in what was ostensibly still their bedroom after their midday dinner when the subject came up again.

"You see," Sarah said, holding up a dress that had been tossed over a spindle-back chair, indicating a snag in its satin weave. "With the furniture that's not been dovetailed, the carriages and this hurly-burly of traveling, my garments are shredded in a trice. *Maman* says she wants to do these things, and then keeps them in her hands for months. I should have had my own girl from the beginning. I would have been so much happier here, I'm sure."

"Mrs. Farmington has a child," Abram said.

"I would expect so. The poor are always breeding. I do not see why that should make for any difficulty." Sarah stopped for a moment. "Why didn't you tell me of the allowance you have been giving her?"

"I told you of the accident. You know that I provide for the families in such cases."

"You never spoke to me of Mrs. Farmington."

"You were away when all of this transpired. I did write of the accident. You hardly pen a line of what transpires in Boston."

"I am telling you now that my life requires a handmaid."

"You have Lucinda and Jezreel."

"Lucinda is occupied with the cooking. *Maman* dominates Jezreel."

Abram went over and sat on their bed. "How can she travel with you if she has a child? And where would you keep them?"

"How old is the child?"

"A little boy just talking."

Sarah stepped over to the windows that opened onto the back of their property, where their garden lay beyond the chestnut trees, surrounded by a fence of tall stakes. A servants' cottage—meant for Jezreel and the other slaves they had once planned on making freedmen—lay to the left, at the bottom of the house's vast lawn.

"This woman and her child could live in the old quarters. She need not travel with me for another year or two."

Abram blew out his cheeks.

"I admit I *don't* want the child in the house. I want the woman. Not the child." She flicked her hand toward the distance. "The quarters will keep the mouse far enough away, I'm sure."

Abram walked over to Sarah and tried to take her in his arms. She made herself as clumsy in them as furniture, so he left her alone and said, "How I wish I could rid you of this demon that will have a thing, *must* have a thing, and will not be satisfied unless it does. You care not for the thing, Sarah. It's the having. The fine point is that Mrs. Farmington is not a thing. She may be a poor pauper of a woman, but she is a woman."

"A woman," Sarah said. "A woman most fair."

Abram would not talk to her directly of this.

"You cannot be prejudiced against granting her employment because she is fair," Sarah said. "Are you uneasy? Has something transpired between you?"

Abram looked straight at Sarah. "She is most fair. We should leave her to find a husband. She has a destiny that more properly belongs outside our own."

"What I say is, we might as well have some benefit from our allowance. It's poor stewardship otherwise."

Abram saw that Sarah would not be talked out of this plan. He made his last point by glaring at her, and then left the room.

———

Sarah was still lying in her bed the next morning, eating toast from her breakfast tray, when a knock came at the door.

"The breakfast suits me fine!" she called, trying to forestall the intrusion.

Jezreel came in and stood with his eyes up, as if he were about to announce a visitor. "Mum wants a word with you," he said.

"Is she coming up here?"

"She be having you in the drawing room."

"Halving . . . or quartering?"

Jezreel stretched his neck and reset his shoulders. His big, expressive face relaxed into a calculating watchfulness.

"Tell her I shall be there presently," Sarah said, choosing determined action. She put the tray aside and swung her legs to the outside of the bed, which sent Jezreel back through the door.

"Sarah!" *Maman* called.

She was about down the stairs, and although she had walked out the door many a time, not heeding her mother-in-law's cries, this was not her intention today. But she would not arrive as if summoned. She slowed her pace.

"Sarah! Sarah!"

Sarah turned the corner into the room. "*Maman*," she said.

Maman tapped her fist on her rocker's armrest. "You sit and we will talk. We must talk now."

"I am here."

"Abram says you will hire Mrs. Farmington."

"Your son is the head of this household. But he may choose to grant me this favor."

Her mother-in-law gave her a look that said she would not be finessed and ridiculed. "You have no need of this young woman. Not in this home. Send her your garments. That will be enough. Send them to her."

"A handmaid is not only a seamstress. I have other uses for her. She must be trained to them."

Maman leaned forward and started shaking her finger, but did not speak. She seemed to be using that shaking finger to make herself angry enough to say what she had on her mind. "You have no uses for the woman other than the devil's. You want to destroy Abram."

"Destroy him?"

"She is a young woman," *Maman* said and rapped her chair arm.

"Egad, *Maman*, every person has a sex."

"*Personne* has . . ." the older woman repeated, then her old, lined cheeks blushed an oxblood red.

"My relations with Abram are between us alone," Sarah said.

"You are sending him to this woman!"

Sarah had thought about this, of course, and she found it had a perverse attraction. "Perhaps I am. Mrs. Bredforet boasts of lending her servants to her husband. She can't be bothered."

Maman blew out her cheeks like Abram.

"*Maman*, you cannot pretend such things do not exist. The King of France has just built *Le Petit Trianon* for his favorite mistress, Madame Du Barry. A palace next to his own. On the Continent, true feeling seems confined to such arrangements."

Maman was so angry she actually shook her fist at Sarah. "That is not why the king built this palace. *Non*."

"It certainly is."

Maman started waving her hand for Sarah to wait as she struggled to strangle out her reply. "You think you do not love this husband anymore. You will find out how much you love him as soon as you have accomplished this evil thing."

The thought of Abram *not* failing had its own magnetism, too. "My intent is not evil. I have sought my own life more and more—and found what suits me. Abram seems to be doing the same. He is stronger than you give him credit for."

"But you ask him not to be strong."

"I doubt he will fail, although it might be better for him if he did. He deserves some comfort."

"You want your marriage to be at an end?"

"Part of it has come to an end."

"You would like to think so. Now. For the moment."

Sarah was surprised at how calm she felt, and she pitied this shaking old woman. "*Maman*, enough. I will think about what you have said. I mean no harm. In truth I really mean only to hire a handmaid."

"What you mean, what you mean! You think life is about what you mean?"

————————

Toward the end of the week, Jezreel called her to the door, and when Sarah opened it she found Anne Farmington and a child standing at her knee. Great storage bags—the kind sailors used—were piled around them. The young child had his face turned up to hers, but he was switching his blue eyes back and forth. The woman wore an old velvet hat. Her chin was ducked down, her eyebrow severely buckled.

Sarah had thought better of her perversity, but now these two were on her doorstep. The homeless travelers, frightened and in need.

"Madame?" Anne asked quietly.

"Come in," she said.

CHAPTER 5

—

Habits of the Heart

Through that first summer of the Farmingtons' residence in the back quarters, Abram avoided his wife's handmaid. He even kept his eyes averted when he happened to pass her in the house. Her greetings or occasional questions brought only curt responses from him.

The woman could undo him eventually, he knew, so he began recruiting his deliverer—he would find her a husband. He spoke a word or two to several of his carpenters and loaders. One replied bravely but did nothing.

Then he went to the Reverend Parsons, who said, "I have seen you zealous in many good causes, Captain White, but your charity in this seems . . . how shall I say, *fevered*. Not to put too fine a point on it, but she is not . . . *proud*, is she? Has some bumpkin run off and deserted her?"

Next Abram took the risk of visiting a rival's shipyard. The owner, Beniah Lynch, was a nasty, dwarfish man who made the mistake of taking any order that came his way. Always behind in his deliveries, his crafts often disappointing in their workmanship, he had ceased to attract the more lucrative contracts, which consistently fell to Abram or the Curriers or the East Boston yards.

Abram waited until he knew his rival had taken the Portsmouth coach and would be away for some days. Then he walked down to Lynch's yard, where the workmen had a double-masted tub in progress, and looked about for a likely fellow. He thought he found one in a strapping blond young man, Roger Baseforth. Heavily muscled, Baseforth had granite blue eyes underneath his swatch of fair hair and a strong jaw above his pedestal neck. When Abram opened the subject, a look of sheepish embarrassment came upon the man. "I've been meaning to find a wife," he said with shuffling humility, "and so I thank you for the road map."

The evening Roger Baseforth paid Anne a call, Abram watched from his bedroom window; the shadows of the two crossed the lighted window. Too soon, however, he heard the clop of the door being closed hard and latched, and saw Baseforth's overly long strides as he went away.

Abram wondered what the men in the shipyard might be saying about his efforts.

Abram directed his attention back to the Points. He remembered his sense of mission as he made his fortune, the gratification of fulfilling his pledge to his family. Acts of mercy brought a similar excitement, the return of his old energy, if modulated for his age. It taught him again that a line runs through human action, as had his encounters with his old mentor and nemesis, Captain Hawks. This time the line had little to do with him, though. For the present the line guarded and defended the weak; it was meant ultimately to encompass the world within a unified domain of justice. Until then, there were sides, and it counted what side he was on and how actively he fought for that side. However rich he had personally become, he needed the poor to avoid poverty of spirit.

With his renewed service, Abram could almost bear his estrangement from Sarah. Through the friendships he had made in Five Points, those with the Overseers, and at South Presbyterian Church, Abram emerged, much to his surprise, as a public man.

Still, when Sarah left again for Boston and the social events leading up to Christmas, Abram began to watch Anne's cottage from his bedroom window, the curl of its smoking chimney rising and corkscrewing in the gusty wind.

On a cold, snowy morning in December, Abram had to meet with ship architect Herman Bowditch, who was coming up from Marblehead. Bowditch was a descendant of the famous seventeenth-century navigator whose navigational guide Abram had first read in Captain Hawks's cabin. Once a year, this highly competent scion of the family provided Abram with shrewd, practical advice about his own designs for the coming spring's schooners and brigs. Bowditch helped Abram remember the commercial values of a ship, as the former mariner tended to design exclusively for speed and maneuverability. Bowditch could find the needed cubic feet in storage without turning Abram's schooners into Lynch's tubs.

Abram needed to make the most economical use of the man's talents, as he would only be staying the two nights. At the same time, *Maman* and he were determined to bring Christmas cheer—and fight the ague—in every Five Points shanty. Knowing that he would not have time to make deliveries of baskets and blankets this day, Abram went into the kitchen, where Lucinda was reaching into the hearth's beehive oven with a long-handled pallet.

Dark-haired, her complexion scarred with welts of acne, Lucinda could not be called fat, but she did look stuffed: her cheeks, her hands, her arms, her legs—everywhere, she bulged. She had the habit of placing her hands lightly on her hips and looking down as if measuring her gains. Her dark eyes rolled white when she felt under too much strain.

Abram thought he might see those eyes as he said, "Mr. Bowditch and I will be working in the front parlor today, Lucinda. But *Maman* and I would not have our brothers and sisters in Five Points praying in vain for this bread. Would you be God's hands in this? The McElroys and Dancy Topsfield and her children are to receive delivery today. You know their shanties? Together, on the shadowed side of King Street?"

"Dancy's boys have legs under them," she said, and swept the log pallet from under the loaves so quickly that they dropped onto the cooling table without tipping. "Let them come here for their bread."

"The boys are using their legs in their family's service," Abram said. "And while they are careful enough lads, it suits me better to serve them in their own home. We hope Copper Beech House is full of charity, and yet it would not do to have our neighbors mistaking it for the almshouse."

"After lunch, then?" Lucinda asked, in a bargaining voice.

"This morning, if you will."

He turned and felt her staring after him as he left the kitchen.

————

Bowditch bent over his drawings, his double chin and his high collar not quite throttling his tuneless humming. Each year Abram forgot about Bowditch's musical breathings, and each year he found himself desperately thinking of questions to ask. He was about to turn his attention to the narrow prow of one design when he noticed Anne Farmington walking out across the front lawn. She carried the Five Points provision basket, the blankets they were sending that day stacked on top.

He thought to rush out and stop her, but he did not want to embarrass himself with Bowditch. Abram did, however, excuse himself and go into the kitchen to look for Lucinda. She had disappeared, perhaps into her room, and Abram refused to chase servants around the house. He would have a talk with Jezreel.

He spoke to the West Indian about the matter at their midday dinner, even though Bowditch was in attendance.

"Lucinda probably thought you not want them peoples to wait. Anne be around and stirring for a walk."

"I gave her particular instructions," Abram said.

"Thems in Five Points be particular fond of Anne."

"You are a saucy slave," Bowditch said. He looked at Abram, his grizzled jowls inflating like a frog's set to strike. "If you'll let me give him the lash," Bowditch said, "I'll cut my fee."

"Jezreel no slave," the princely black man said.

"*Maman* and I freed him," Abram said. "We know what it is to be owned." Though these were some of Abram's deepest sentiments, he felt ashamed.

Which may have been the reason, when the two men had ended their day's discussions, Abram purposed to visit Anne and Theo in the servants' cottage.

He went out the back of the house into the thickening blue light of the late snowy day. Just enough snow had fallen to cover the leaves, whose crunch was amplified by its rime. A strong wind blew against him from the south, and the two hundred yards down to the cottage began to seem like a much longer distance. The cold irritated him, as did she. Her presumption, he thought, her maddening way of pushing in, her holding on—he had somehow come actually to live with this, and now she was taking away his means of escape.

He thought of just walking in but did not. He knocked at her door and heard a racing of small feet before the door bounced open, almost striking him.

Anne stood back by the hearth, in that same dress and apron he had seen at their second interview, with its striking décolletage. Theo came swooping by, his arms out, riding the southerlies Abram let in. Abram caught him as he passed the second time, and leaned down and said, "I'm going to be having a word with your mother."

The child's arms dropped and his eyes went to Abram's forehead. The tall captain turned him by the shoulder and gave him a gentle pat in the direction of the corner where his blocks lay.

"I think this would be your first visit with us here," Anne said and tried to smile. "You are most welcome—if that's my place, anyone's place, to welcome . . . the owner."

"You went to the Points today?" he asked her.

"Lucinda asked me to take the provisions down to Dancy and the McElroys. Dancy was so very grateful. Her Stephen's been almost dead and gone with the ague."

"I asked Lucinda to take the provisions."

"She—"

"She disobeyed my instructions. You helped her in this."

"I helped her. Yes."

"You are my wife's handmaid. If she is not here to give you instructions, then you take them from me."

Anne looked at him, her mobile eyebrow crimping. "The greater quarrel, if there be a quarrel, sir, must be with Lucinda."

"I would not have you in this business in the Points."

"I thought this business was charity."

"It is."

"The giving of charity belongs to the rich and poor alike. There's much charity among the poor that is unknown to the gentry."

"As I know. I am not that long removed from a starving family."

"You seem to be still starving, though, sir."

"Your meaning?"

She paused a moment, then said, "You are jealous of the privilege."

"I am jealous . . . of command in my own home."

Anne turned and, keeping her skirt clear with one hand, leaned down and stirred the hanging pot in her hearth with a long-handled spoon. Without looking up, she said, "I have friends in the Points, sir, and Theo and I have . . . a quiet life in this cottage—for which we are most grateful."

She stood up at last and clasped her hands. "We are truly grateful.

But my mistress needs me so little, you not at all, and today Dancy and the McElroys shared their rejoicing with me. It has been so long that I have had such a cause of my own—not since I came here, to speak plain. The boon of others gave me new hope."

"I know of what you are saying," Abram said, bitter.

"If you would let me serve in this way," Anne said, "while my mistress is away . . . that would lessen Lucinda's share, who has more than enough to do, and give me more occupation."

She wanted only to share her new fortune with her friends and enjoy their company. That was the greatest part of it, not acts of charity but friendship and neighborliness.

"The carrying of those provisions and the visiting remains my concern," Abram said, "for I am in want of what this supplies. Yet when Mr. Bowditch and such like take my time, I will send you rather than Lucinda. I am sure your former neighbors would enjoy this."

He saw her wide smile but could not bear any expressions of gratitude. He turned quickly and left the cottage.

As he walked back to the main house, the snow and leaves even more brittle, the air sharp, he wondered at her ability to change his mind. The late afternoon had grown so dark that indigo lines of the tree limbs were no longer distinguishable above the first branchings.

———

Two Sundays before Christmas, Abram paused outside South Presbyterian Church and watched as Anne, who was turned round toward the street at the foot of the church steps, received a string of Five Points residents. He heard a wash of their conversations: "Henry's so . . ." "That weren't ever his manner in . . ." "The poultice would be the thing." Enough to know that Anne was serving as a confidante.

Abram thought of crossing over to her, since these people's welfare had become his business, their conversation something he enjoyed, in small doses. He turned to go in, though, and as he did, he thought of the rented pew that awaited him in front—like the big, creamy white, rich man's square pew that the landowning Garritys had enjoyed in his childhood church. The place seemed almost the public stocks. He would sit there, alone—as *Maman* had felt too frail to go out—and be on view to Anne and her neighbors in the balcony.

Later that week, on Tuesday evening, before the first of the two midweek services, Abram saw the Reverend Parsons in the church's foyer. The minister's hoary head reared back and an almost jack-o'-lantern grin flashed before he whispered, "You are doing more service than ever, Captain White, though with fewer steps." The minister bent closer to him. "I know your charity to Mrs. Farmington, and the Lord is blessing it. You have found an even better means of helping her than providing a husband."

Abram stood up tall and raised a questioning brow.

"I said to her," Parsons repeated, " 'So you have joined your master in this good work to the Five Points,' and she said, 'For that, I am only performing a duty, but I do hope that I join my master in its purpose.'

" 'Which is?' I questioned. To which she replied, 'A knowledge, a saving knowledge, of God,' quoted she.

"Of course, I remonstrated with her on her Pelagianism, and reminded her of our Lord's sovereignty in electing us from all eternity, but I did congratulate her as well on these most evident signs of God's mercy towards her."

"We have spoken very little . . . of holy things," Abram said.

"And perhaps you best not with a young woman so comely," Parsons said, and gave that knowing grin again. "But you have spurred her devotion, and in that you are to be commended."

Evidently Abram could not conceal how troubling he found this commendation, and the minister added, "Do not deny yourself any holy friendship, good man. If you find yourself saying a pleasant word to her, be not overly troubled. Her more frequent attendance at this house allows me the same pleasure."

Abram thought to respond, and then experienced such confused feelings that he seemed to be searching for his reply in another tongue. "I take your point," he said finally, defeated.

———————

The next day Jezreel announced, "Mrs. Farmington wanting to have a word about them peoples."

Anne came in and sat demurely on the edge of the green damask settee, leaning only slightly forward, her hands in her lap, her chin tilted at a sharp, appealing angle, addressing *Maman* and Abram with studious concern.

"Mrs. Wickham has the ague so that she can hardly rise. Her son Trevor does his best, but the younger children would be better off if the eldest were a girl."

"And what of Mr. Wickham?" *Maman* asked.

Abram gave her a look and shook his head in a way that meant the man was dead.

"*Quel dommage!*" *Maman* said. "*Si tragique.*"

"I'll send the doctor down tomorrow," Abram said. "What about Franny Heppelwhite? Would she care for the children for a day or two if someone put a coin in her hand?"

"Franny's been asking me if you had any more 'appointments' for her," Anne said.

Abram noticed how bright with pleasure her eyes grew—the satisfaction she took in working out a problem for her friends.

When she left the room, *Maman* said, "She has a good heart, that one."

Out of the corner of his eye Abram caught her judging his reaction.

Then she said, "When Sarah brought this woman here, I did not care for it. *Eh bien,* now I find myself caring for her. She has a good heart, if less sense than this world demands."

"Her wits are keen enough for her position," Abram said.

"Wits and wiles, she may have," *Maman* said. "What she wants is something of her own. You must urge this to her."

"I would not involve myself overly much."

"Yes, this is very right. But you may still speak to her. And you must."

His mother had been gesturing at him, waving her hand at him, her double chin swaying with the movement as she sat forward in her chair, straining toward an ancient version of Anne's tilted-chin presentations. Anne was moving into his mother's soul.

———

Sarah came home for Christmas but stayed only two weeks. While there, she kept Anne at work mending and refitting her gowns.

"Haven't you finished on that gown yet—the wine-colored one?" Sarah would say.

"Yes, madame. It's been put back with the others. Shall I help you find it?"

"No, no. Just get on with the next, then."

Sarah left to go back to Boston with so little ceremony that she and Abram never said they would miss each other.

A few weeks after Christmas, Abram knocked on the cottage door. Hearing Anne's call, he stooped through the low frame and entered.

"I stopped by the house," he said. Usually when he made these early evening visits to have a word with her, a habit he had fallen into as Anne carried on more and more of the work in Five Points, he stopped at the cottage straight from the shipyard, then went into the house to clean up and have his supper with *Maman*. In the last two days, though, his mother had taken a chill and was confined to her room, so tonight he had gone to see his mother first, made sure she was comfortable, and then cleaned up, as he saw that his hands had resin all over them from a varnishing demonstration he had performed, in anger, for his workers. His long, thick, dark hair—now with silver twining through it—was still damp, tied back with a blue silk ribbon.

Theo scrambled up and ran straight for him, holding up his arms to be caught and lifted. Abram swept the child up, put his hand on the boy's tummy, and jiggled until the child was squirming and laughing and striking out at his head with both arms windmilling.

"I've got you, you mongoose," Abram said, tickling and scratching the child along his ribs.

"Get you!" Theo sang. "M'goose."

Abram caught his arms and pulled them around his neck. He kept the child's arms clasped with one hand, while he patted and rubbed the boy's back with the other, soothing him, calming the excitement he had caused. When he finally put the child down, the boy clung instantly to his thigh.

His mother came over, kneeled down, let the child feel her presence there by him for a moment. Abram looked down upon her crown of auburn hair and became aware, not so much of the clinging child, but of her bent figure and her skirt on his foot.

"Your supper is ready, Theo," she said. "Nice porridge with as much molasses as you want."

The child let go his hold and was persuaded to sit at their rude wooden table. His mother tied a cloth around his neck and sat beside him.

"Did you visit the Points today?" Abram asked as she began spooning the child's supper into his mouth. "The Sheffields?"

"Oh yes," Anne said, hurrying to speak as she was reminded. "Davis has signed on with *The Magdalene* for the spring, and the family shall have his first wages and then be set right when he comes back from the outer banks."

"That plan failed to prove out this year."

Anne paused in her feeding. "Some seasons the sea is stingier than others."

She never corrected him, and yet she could always tell him what he needed to hear. He tried not to compare her manner to Sarah's, but entering this cottage at the end of the day he could look forward to rest and contentment, not a battle.

"And the McDonoughs?" he asked.

"I've not been to them today. I'll go tomorrow, if you like. I know you'd prefer me not to take all the work for myself, but truly I have never found such a satisfying thing before."

"It's better to give than receive," Abram said, and then quickly wondered whether he had insulted her. "I mean to say—"

"You know this yourself," she said, smiled, nodded. "The Lord could have said, ' 'Tis more pleasant to give.' "

She turned back to the child, and Abram sat and watched Theo eat his supper. He noted the rhythm of the spoonfuls, how the mother slowed the pace as her child satisfied himself, how she made a game of tidying up his mouth with the spoon in between mouthfuls. The child's eyes were closing, and before the end of the meal, he was forgetting to swallow.

Anne took him out of his chair and laid him on his pallet. He woke up with a start when he found himself in his bed, and started to crawl out from beneath the covers in protest.

"Theo will want you to sit by him awhile," Abram said and stood to go. "Jezreel is waiting supper for me."

Anne was putting him back down, tucking the cover under his chin, and smoothing his hair back. The child kept his big smoky blue eyes open, with his lips buckling into a cry, and then he said, "Sing to me! Cap' zing."

Anne turned her head, smiled ruefully, and shook her head. "He means you. 'Captain sing.' If it wouldn't trouble you overly much, do you know any lullabies?"

Abram had not done much singing, except in church, since entertaining the tipplers in Bailey's as a prelude to getting himself kidnapped as a lad of eleven.

He stepped over to the pallet and crouched down beside her. "I remember one," he said.

> Wee one a wee,
> Wee one a lay,
> My babe, now sail away.
>
> Wee one a wee,
> Wee one a lay,
> So night becomes the day.

"Close your eyes, Theo," Anne said.

"Zing," Theo ordered again and closed his eyes tight.

"Wee one a wee," Abram began.

"Both," Theo said and reopened his eyes.

Abram and Anne exchanged glances. "Wee one a wee," Abram sang, and Anne joined in, her voice light and breathy.

" . . . so night becomes the day," they finished.

Anne put her hand on her son's forehead, smoothed back his hair once more, and shushed his final protest.

Abram stood up to go to the door.

Anne stood with him and whispered, "Bless you, sir. We are so grateful." Her large eyes began to well up with tears. "I would the world would know such kindness. I wish it knew you for the man you are."

He stopped thinking about Jezreel, the supper awaiting him. He stopped wondering about *Maman*'s health. His thoughts about Five Points vanished.

Then she took his right hand in both of hers and kissed it, rubbing it against her cheek. He felt her breath on his wrist and the pressure of each of her fingers. He left his hand in hers.

When he embraced her, in turn, he gave a groaning gasp.

The only thought he ever had was whether the child would wake.

PART II

Little Boston

CHAPTER 6

Pharaoh's Court

Submit Singleton Chauncey, her husband, Gaylord, and Sarah White jounced over Boston's cobblestone streets in the family's coach-and-four to the Isaac Smith's home on Beacon Hill. The humid night air streamed through the open cab windows, and here in the oldest part of the city, light from the houses, close on each side, kept peering into the carriage like an excited crowd running after dignitaries.

Submit leaned over to Sarah, across the puff-pastry layers of their billowing skirts, and whispered, "Liza trussed me up like a guinea hen when she tied my corset tonight. I'm putting a pillow over the lad's face, I'm sure." She put her hand over her stomach and glanced down. "Could you help me breathe again when we arrive?"

The women's eyes met in agreement, and then Submit noticed Sarah glancing beyond her to Gaylord. He was looking out the cab's window, one hand to his mouth, his legs crossed, letting the whispering women be. The touches of light from the houses stroked his cheek and jaw, while his eyes remained in darkness. Still, she could imagine their knowing squint. She thought of brushing her own fingertips over his cheek, along the line of his jaw, clean-shaven, lightly powdered, with perhaps the two or three whiskers just by the lobe of his ear that he often missed.

Gaylord was contenting himself with his own thoughts, as he always did, and enduring, with remarkable good humor, her friendship with Sarah, who had virtually come to live with them in these last months. She should tell Gaylord about her condition. She had told Sarah. It would make him more than happy. But not quite yet, she thought.

If she could only get some air into her lungs, the night should be a magnificent occasion. Boston society reserved this night, the Saturday following Easter Sunday, for Mr. and Mrs. Isaac Smith's annual spring gala, long before receiving their gold-lettered vellum invitations. Many of the town's first families, the Quincys, the Hancocks, the Boylstons, the Jacksons, the Wendells, the Storers, and the Perkins, were related to the Smiths, if only by marriage. The Adams were also relatives, but as they did not get along with the Quincys, they rarely came. Everyone else paid Isaac Smith court as a wealthy merchant and moderate Whig Justice of the Peace, which positioned him, in increasingly factious times, as the representative of his class to the Crown's governor.

This year the invitations had included a mysterious bit of verse:

Although our time may be brief in life's measure,
The splendid night see in the day too soon,
Your hosts expect to unveil timeless treasures,
Art's witness to the Ages of Boston's boon.

The meaning of these lines had occupied teatime discussion, until Mrs. Josiah Quincy, or if not Mrs. Quincy then Mrs. Ellen Storer—or Mrs. Fayerweather—until someone let it be known that the Smiths had commissioned full-length companion oil portraits by Mr. Copley.

Since his success in England with "Boy With a Squirrel" at the Royal Academy's annual exhibition three years before, John Singleton Copley's portraits had commanded attention. The promise of these new unveilings greatly enlivened the prospect of the Smith's annual gala. Even Sarah had entered into the talk of what the portraits might be like and seemed eager for this night to come. This cheered Submit, who had been worrying about her cousin. Sarah insisted on accepting every invitation that came their way, and yet on most occasions she appeared tired of the festivities before they began.

The carriage finally hit the smooth sandy stretch at the back of the Common and rolled into the pastoral landscape of Beacon Hill. It stopped before a long two-story house with many gables, a lit candle in each.

Immediately upon entering, Submit and Sarah stopped in the front parlor, where the women repaired the inevitable damage to their coiffures, powderings, and paints inflicted by carriage rides. The two women further closeted themselves behind a Chinese screen that allowed for the more extensive adjustments that Submit badly needed. With the loosening of her whalebone corset, which had been pinching her up under her arms as well as denying her air, she felt momentarily nauseous as her breath came back in a rush.

"You *were* smothered," Sarah said. "Your color's brightening."

Submit looked at Sarah in her pearl-colored stomacher silk gown, a cloud of sheer lace about the décolletage, perpendicular scrolls of pearl buttons setting off the bodice, with the waist fitted down onto her spreading skirts and marked by a heavy pleat. The gown contained her fine figure like a well-turned vase, and its silvery hue set off perfectly her dark looks. In Sarah's maturity, the arched framing of her icy blue eyes had become more prominent, her nose a touch sharper; her look had gained in watchfulness, gravity, and its power to attract attention. The luxurious swirl of her rich, dark hair crowned all this. Few men could be in the same room with her without staring.

Submit sometimes played a game and dropped several paces behind Sarah as she made her way through a crowd. Even in a huge place like Faneuil Hall, the crowd would always part, heads turn, and conversations drop away. For this reason, Submit had nicknamed her Moses.

Sarah, still peering into her hand-held mirror, slicked down the tail of her eyebrows. She glanced Submit's way and then returned once more to these ministrations.

Submit knew her cue, and she went to take Gaylord's arm and be announced in the ballroom. Sarah would follow almost immediately. She insisted on being announced alone, though, a practice she had pursued with great insistence until Boston society granted her this idiosyncracy—for the sake of her relatives, it was said, and because the men enjoyed her presence, others whispered.

After Gaylord and she were announced, they parted, and Submit stood back with a few other women on the distaff side of the ballroom. Its great wood floor gleamed under the huge chandeliers, shaped like evergreens. The chairs that lined the walls had lozenge round backs, round cushioned seats, and gold trimming. A string ensemble, at the middle of the room on the men's side, was playing a sprightly concerto.

But everyone's attention—on both sides—was directed toward the companion portraits stationed on easels at either side of the far end. Parties of men and women staged themselves at one side or another, and then approached the living subjects and a youthful figure of a man in a short white wig.

For all the attraction of the portraits, when the footman announced, "*Mrs.* Abram White," putting a questioning spin on her marital status, the men's heads turned back in virtual unison like the sails of a tacking regatta. Josiah Quincy came up to Sarah, and she spoke no more than a word or two with him before they headed straight down the middle of the ballroom, men and women cresting on both sides.

Submit called across to Gaylord and flashed such a panicked look that he stepped out toward her as if he meant to catch up to a departing carriage. They fell in behind Quincy and Sarah, who noticed and half turned round.

"Mr. Chauncey, madame, shall we take a closer look together, then?" Josiah asked politely.

"You haven't greeted our hosts and the artist already?" Gaylord asked.

"I have. I have indeed. But I would very much like to see the pictures at close hand through Mrs. White's eyes. If likeness makes for recognition, she might be expected to know a thing of beauty." Josiah was a handsome old blunt-nosed man in an overly elaborate periwig, and when he grinned, as he did at Sarah just then, you could still see the young blade he had been, the successful rake. "Which applies, of course," Josiah caught himself up, "to Mrs. Chauncey as well. These are cousins like unto two species of rare orchid."

Gaylord flashed a quick, worried look at his wife, who saw this and said, "Like unto the orchid and its compost, I do believe—although you are the one scattering it, Josiah."

Quincy sniffed and then grinned. "Submit, you are a naughty girl."

"I was a very good *girl*," she said, "and we've heard all about your youth, Josiah, but I never tire of hearing the stories repeated. You had such powers of scandalous invention."

Josiah turned completely round toward her now. "I have always endeavored to amuse my friends, madame. The world's palette, as we might say on this evening, would be very pallid indeed, if not for

those of us with scandalous invention, whether in words or deeds."
He kept to the warm manner of a doting uncle as he said this. "You
are much quoted, you know. I can think of no one whose raillery is
more recited. Chapter and verse."

Submit felt the heat in her face, and she suspected that with her
light freckling she looked like a strawberry, outer seeds and all. But
she would have to be dragged away from having the last word in this.
"If Scripture were more in our minds and hearts, Josiah, we might
leave off our profane translations. I would be other than I am."

"Not for the w-o-r-l-d," Josiah said, his voice as expansive
through that last word as its meaning.

"Not even for your Creator," Gaylord said, stepping into the conversation suddenly. "Not for your Creator who gave you a mind as
exaggerated as a parable." Gaylord pulled his head back as he realized, as did they all, that he had said something better than he knew.

"To the other parables, then," Sarah said, "these interesting pictures."

The Storers, who were with the Smiths and the artist, glanced
back over their shoulders, noticing them coming up from behind.
"You will want to greet your other guests," Mr. Storer said, half bow-
ing and taking his wife's gloved hand.

The portraits stood before them, on canvas and in the flesh. The
merchant Isaac Smith had the eyes of a reptile, tight lips, and jowls
and a double chin that suggested he'd just swallowed a nourishing
rodent. In his portrait, the artist had caught the man's scheming nature through a crossed look, the fully lighted eye of his three-quarter
profile looking outward, the one in shadow turning slightly toward
it, as if he were reflecting on how to make the best business use of
the opportunity he had just fixed on.

Mrs. Smith had the droopy-eyed, red-rimmed look of a worn-out
spaniel. As she greeted her guests each year, her flaccid cheeks and
wooden expression suggested she was suffering their company. This
evening, her eyes kept closing as she smiled to herself. When her eyes
opened again, though, she returned to her flabby-cheeked blankness,
and even revealed the suspicion at the core of her brown eyes. The
artist showed her sitting back in a studded upholstered chair, and her
body might almost have suggested a languid and graceful ease, if not
for the way her head came forward, as if straining to rise out of this
imposed comfort. The strain at the back of her neck, one imagined,
must be shooting into her forehead, and the same suspicion escaped
her rimmed eyes. One of her crossed hands held on to a bunch of
grapes that trailed down in her lap. The window by which she sat

looked out onto a pastoral scene of fields, a gathering of trees by the shores of a lake, with a distant mountain beyond.

"What handsome figures you make," Josiah said, and peered closely at Isaac Smith's portrait and then equally close at the old gentleman himself. "This one could use a bit of touching up, eh?" His sideways grin broke out and he grabbed his host's hand. "Congratulations, Isaac. You've given all of us a lasting memory, and one for the ages." He turned to the youthful gentleman. "Is this the painter? Mr. Copley, what talents you possess. If only our Creator kept us in such perpetual trim and finery." He extended his hand. "Josiah Quincy."

The artist pressed his full lips together as he somewhat grudgingly accepted the compliment. "You are far more well-known in this company than I, sir," Copley said.

"May I present Gaylord and Submit Chauncey," said Quincy. The men shook hands and Submit curtsied.

"And Mrs. Abram White. Sarah Singleton Nicolls White."

Sarah's curtsy was deeper, and she rose much more slowly from it than her cousin.

Copley's eyes caught—snagged—on Sarah. Even as he spoke to Josiah, he scanned her. "You have brought forward my best critics, I'm sure. What a distinguished company you make up."

Submit had seen Sarah have a similar effect on others. But there was something about the way he looked at Sarah, about the way his eyes worked over her, that made Submit feel that Sarah was no longer there. That Copley was performing a piece of sorcery by which he could make Sarah disappear.

Copley did not look like an intellectual, Submit thought; more like a vigorous, handsome farmer, with a low brow and those searching eyes, accented by the crook at the end of each eyebrow. Somewhat slight of figure, his arms and legs were muscular, as if his business involved labor. His nervousness expressed itself in his full lips and toothy mouth, which snapped at the air and tasted his own words and others' remarks.

Submit saw that Sarah had stepped over to Mrs. Smith's portrait to escape Copley's scrutiny. "How do you arrive at the conception of your portraits, Mr. Copley?" Submit asked. "Do you honor their wishes or your own?"

This pulled him back from his intention, to judge by the hand he was reaching out to Sarah's elbow. "I hope I honor my subjects," Copley said. "I hope I honor them. In what I see of what makes them who they are, and how I present what I see. The truth is the greatest honor and serves us all so much better than flattery, wouldn't you say?"

"That fellow up there is a shrewd-eyed merchant," said Isaac Smith, "and so, I like to think, am I. If that be the truth, then I am very much satisfied."

Sarah turned round from Mrs. Smith's portrait. "These grapes," she said.

"A sign or symbol," Copley said, as if a woman might need this hint.

"Perhaps too obvious a sign," Sarah said. "The obvious makes for vulgarity, and our Mrs. Smith is reticence and decorum itself. Though it's a detail, of course."

"She has raised a magnificent family," Copley said, quickly defending himself. "The wine that comes from these grapes has the richest subtlety."

"In its truth, her family," Sarah said. "That is a subtle vintage indeed." She turned away from him to the picture. "But these are grapes. Though it's a detail, of course, and the picture very fine as a whole."

"I suppose an artist has no defense against those with literal minds," he said to his clients, covering his embarrassment.

"We all see our Mrs. Smith as a woman who invites us into both the comfort of her home and the goodness of God's created order," said Gaylord. "That is the truth about Mrs. Smith and this exceedingly fine picture."

Both the Smiths and the artist looked gratified and consoled by this.

Sarah turned back to them and opened her long, graceful arms, gesturing to both portraits at once. "Exactly so, Gaylord. You must forgive the tangent. I should have stated my principal impression first."

"Which is?" Copley asked.

"That these are truly the most artful portraits in Boston. Mr. Copley's finest."

"I will say these are my finest portraits to date," Copley said, "but I will not say they are the finest in Boston. I will say that if Mrs. White were to let me paint her portrait, I would be inspired to paint a picture that would earn the Royal Academy's praise, and perhaps the world's. For all the world should know such beauty."

"What say you to that?" Josiah asked.

Sarah was looking at the floor, her nails clutching the piping that separated her dress's bodice from its skirts. "I say that Mr. Copley would mislay his ambitions through such attention to me. Though with his gifts and another subject, he should accept nothing less than such triumphs. And I say that the Smiths have indulged our own appetite for these fine pictures long enough and we should make way for others."

"If Mr. and Mrs. Chauncey, and Mrs. White, would like to come to my studio, you would be welcomed," Copley said, even as the party reassembled two by two and began to move away.

"I'll see they come round," Quincy said, "if you'll have me, too."

———

On Monday morning, Submit and Sarah went shopping in the Charles Street neighborhood. They carried their parasols and wore light, gray linen dresses with matching shell jackets. They walked, for the exercise and to be free to dawdle. Boston was coming alive after its bundling winter; the air had a dewy freshness, and the city's great houses had window boxes filled with pansies. Last night's rain had washed the cobblestone streets, and the people around them moved with a languid, early-morning ease.

At Sunday services the day before, the Reverend Edward Holyoke had taken up the subject of the lilies of the field, with much one-handed massaging of his powdered jowls. While her pastor had been considering the lilies, Submit thought of Mr. Copley and his fascination with Sarah. The men in their society often flirted with her, but as Josiah Quincy did, with an avuncular air. Young men looked—hard—then turned their attentions to likely catches. Mr. Copley was neither young nor old, and he was no one's uncle.

Their steps slid a little as they tracked over the wet cobblestones, and Submit found herself using her parasol as a walking cane. The weight she had gained with the pregnancy already made her less steady.

"Have you been thinking of the Smith gala?" she asked. " 'Ecod, Mr. Copley's remarks were extraordinary." They walked on a few paces. "You did twit him about those grapes, of course."

"Imagine that old spaniel with grapes in her lap. What a fancy he must have."

"A terrible fancy. Of course, he may well be devoting it to you this morning. Your sea captain will have to sail up the Charles and fetch you home."

Submit looked to see how Sarah would respond to this. Her cousin kept looking straight ahead, but her pace quickened.

Submit took the extra step to catch up. "Sarah?"

"I see no need for retreat."

"Retreat? You have an object here?"

"I found the grapes ridiculous, but I was glad to be introduced to Mr. Copley. I was taught to draw as a girl—my father's worship of classical education, you know—and I have always liked pattern books and anything that would show a home, a figure, or a scene. Does not this work in oils impress you as a marvel? The effects that can be achieved?"

Submit remembered the first few times she had seen oil portraits that had been carried over from England. She remembered almost turning to talk with their lifelike subjects. "They are powerful illusions. Truly. It's hard to associate them with a mere man's hand, and that must be part of the wonder of Mr. Copley—that they should come from him."

"From him?"

"From anyone."

"He has great gifts. And from such beginnings. His mother had a tobacco shop on the Long Wharf."

"His mother?" Submit asked.

"I read a narrative of his life in *The New England Letter*."

"He's not an English Singleton. Ours?"

"County Clare. No possible relation for a hundred years or more."

"I wonder at the Lord's ways in this. That He should give such gifts to someone so unprepared by his upbringing to receive them."

"You found him rude?"

"I think the vulgarity of the grapes shows a certain striving. Flattery comes from need, does it not?"

"He wants only the truth of his subjects."

"Are you defending him?"

"I can't help but be glad that the Lord has given us a man who knows something other than shipping tea and molasses and writing sermons."

Submit thought a moment. "I am sorry, then, for what I said about his social . . . eagerness. However indifferent to social pleasures I have found Captain White in the past, I have never thought him eager for false glory. Those things you both take pleasure in are so different, but his character certainly matches his gifts."

The bouncing clatter of a carriage rolled by. Submit reached out and put her hand on Sarah's forearm as they waited for the noise to die.

"If Abram's character matches his gifts . . . well, I suppose, it does. They do. Mr. Copley's gifts are of a different order. What kind of character should a man have who creates miracles underneath his fingertips?"

"That of a great saint," said Submit, rather seriously.

"Or none at all," said Sarah, and smiled broadly, cocking her head. Her indulgent expression said that their conversation had traveled far beyond what she had told Submit of her thinking. "Come with me now." Sarah took her cousin by the arm and they crossed the street to Wendell's, the best dress shop in Boston.

Inside, a good-looking, blond-haired young man with apple red cheeks appeared, and Sarah asked for the bolts of *peau de soie*, the finest embroidered Spanish lace, display boxes of gold embroidering thread, and Copperfield's pattern book.

Submit saw the designs Sarah had turned to. "You are thinking of another ball gown?" she asked.

"I want something that no one will see me in—until the world does."

"You are thinking of having your portrait painted?"

"Tell me if you like this?" Sarah asked, showing Submit a gown with a bow at the waist and a vinelike embroidered pattern through the bodice. "Mr. Copley invited me to his studio. And I may commission him as well as anyone."

"I would want to speak with Gaylord about such a thing."

"You are able to speak with your dear husband about many things that Abram and I have long since ceased discussing. I will let him put it over the mantel, and he can reflect on the woman he continues to drive away."

"Then the world will not see it?" Submit asked. "But only your husband in Newburyport?"

"The world is blind," Sarah said.

"God sees."

"This is a portrait, cousin," Sarah said, exasperated. "Now which of these designs takes your eye?"

CHAPTER 7

—

Life Studies

John Singleton Copley rented the third and fourth floors of a brick commercial building down by the harbor. Submit and Sarah found the tall, narrow building within the same week of their visit to the dress shop. The ground floor was taken by a tobacconist shop, the second floor by a solicitor, and the stairway that led past them echoed with their steps.

Copley's factotum, a dark-haired man in a full-length smock with the arm muscles of a dock loader, announced them. The way he said, "Mrs. Gaylord Chauncey, a Mrs. White," made it clear that he considered these niceties no part of his proper job.

The studio felt immense. The third-floor ceiling had been removed so that the roof's rafters towered overhead and light poured down onto the wood floors from the gabled windows above, as well as from the tall windows of the studio itself. These dimensions and the flood of light suggested a grand enterprise.

On closer examination, however, the studio's paraphernalia and

scattered arrangement took this notion away. Four headless manne-
quins in isolated locations kept watch; two were draped with cotton
sheets and the others' beaded joints stuck out or were crooked into
odd angles. A table supported a series of plaster-of-paris statues,
many of them broken, with a mallet resting beside them. The artist's
easel and canvas stood at a side angle away from view. His palette
appeared to be a marble-topped table, where the masses of color
could be dumped and blended into one another to create new shades.
By the far left outside window an upholstered chair, in a rich crimson
chintz with gold studs outlining the back and arms, sat amid a white,
painted, three-step wooden platform. The platform curved around
the chair like an amphitheater.

Copley had been looking at the chair, as if someone were sitting
in it, when they came in. Submit wondered how beauty could be created out of such rag ends.

The artist took a last look at his canvas, a slow, lingering one.
Then he turned around toward them, and his public face gradually
appeared as he focused on who they might be. By the time he came
over to them, he had emerged from his trance.

"What a delight! I've been worrying over an ancient lady's worry
lines. The family and she want frankness, I'm sure, but not an artist's
exacting definition of the same. Well. Be that as it may." He clasped
his hands. "These worrying concerns and then here you are. Beauty,
serenity, and poise, together and doubled! I am so glad you accepted
my invitation."

His eyes flicked at Submit once or twice as he gave them these
compliments, but he returned almost at once to Sarah.

"Beauty, serenity, and poise, together and doubled, Mr. Copley?"
Submit said. "Your pencil must be guided in another way than your
tongue, else you'd paint monsters. I might as well be this lady's lap-
dog."

Copley started to put out his hand, then said, "If you will give me
leave," and with that he ran his fingers along Submit's jawline and
slanted her face one way and another with his index finger and thumb
at her chin. "In fact, your face has lovely modeling," he said, and
looked at Sarah. "You see how high these cheekbones are and the
lovely little shadowed valleys beneath? The premature silver of the
hair, the black brows and lashes, the chestnut eyes with tawny and
jade lights, and the pattering of that same chestnut in the freckles. If
you look in your glass for fashion's image, Mrs. Chauncey, you may
be disappointed, but no one who sees you truly can be."

Submit could feel the prickly rush of her face turning red. For once, she could think of nothing to say.

"Whose portrait are you working on?" Sarah asked and went to look.

Copley stepped in front of her, so quickly and forcefully that they almost collided, and Sarah took a step back to catch her balance.

"I would show you the work," Copley said, "if it were nearer the mark. But I am half-decided to paint it out and begin again. This happens, although it is not something we painters like to admit."

"I am sure it is very fine," Sarah said.

"No, in truth it is not," Copley said, and he looked down and away and grimaced.

"Creating such portraits must be a very great struggle at times," Sarah said, kindly. "All the world knows your talent, and rightly gives you credit, but only you can know your labors."

Copley looked up at her. "I have heard that Mr. West—Benjamin—can do a complete head in under an hour. This is always spoken in tones that imply the quicker artist must surely be superior."

He put his head down and thought a moment. When he began again, he gestured like a hectoring preacher. "There are depths, though, ranges of feeling and knowledge, that only come with time. To strike off a likeness is one thing. To see the soul another. Mr. West may give his subjects a kind of permanent looking glass. I am trying to give them and posterity a reflection on the *life* that God has endowed them with. Do you see? That is quite different. I'm not sure I'm putting it well."

"No, no, no," Sarah said in a cooing voice, as if comforting a distraught child. "This is the true marvel of your work. That we see such a revelation of the soul in paint."

"I thought you disliked my estimation of Mrs. Smith's soul," Copley said, his voice suddenly hard and flat.

"I suppose you want to create something lasting," Submit said, "but does that warrant exaggerating Mrs. Smith's motherhood into a divine force?"

"Is not motherhood, any woman's motherhood, a part of the Creator's universal plan?"

"But to express this, the figure must be equal to it," Submit said. "You must have questioned the wisdom of tying the two together through the mere ornament of the grapes? Did she suggest this? You've used the symbol before."

"These things were suggested," the artist said, "in contact with one another, as Mrs. Smith's hands were with the grapes themselves. They were not yoked like oxen. I have to think your reactions peculiar and overly sensitive. No one else took this for the artist's imposition of meaning." The bands in Copley's neck were standing out.

"Submit," Sarah said, "these were my first thoughts, and I'm afraid I've led you to make them your cause. Give this up. I was wrong. I do see the justice of your argument, Mr. Copley. The contact, not the joining, of the particular with the universal. The suggestion, not the identity."

"Yes, yes, exactly so. I will admit, of course, that Mrs. Chauncey or you, Mrs. White, would be a far more fitting representative of such an idea. You have families?"

"The Lord has not chosen to bless me as He has Mrs. Smith."

"I'm so sorry. I cannot think why He would not choose to bless you in this way—as yet, that is, except that He means for you to remain an image of youth and beauty. Surely He has only bequeathed you a second youth so that He may satisfy himself with gazing on your loveliness."

"Mr. Copley, what sacrilege this is! The Lord is not some youth with fire in His loins."

"Submit," Sarah said, reproachfully.

Submit thought she might start speaking very directly indeed, and she went over to the window to look out at the cool spring day, wishing she could touch her cheek to the cooling glass.

"Which is why," Submit heard Sarah say, "I have come to ask you to undertake my portrait."

"You have?" Copley said, as if he doubted it.

"I'm convinced that you know the soul. You are able to capture it. At times, it would almost seem, to recreate it. So would you, then?"

"To hear you say this gratifies me no end, madame. I hate to think how forward I was in requesting this pleasure on our first meeting."

"If you have the time. Do you?"

Sarah sounded like a girl in a nursery, and Submit almost hated her for it.

"What an honor!" Copley cried. "What a portrait this will be! Hardly a portrait. A masterpiece—if I can but capture a tincture of the life and soul our Creator has blessed you with. Oh, magnificent lady, wonder to this society and soon to every race of men, what we shall create together! I pray this alone, that my gifts will enable me to teach the future the glory we know today."

CHAPTER 8

Submit's Magnificat

Submit awoke one morning in her feather bed, thinking that Gaylord must be kneeing her in the back. When her mind cleared, she found herself on her side, holding on to a pillow, arching her cramping lower back. It felt as if her spine had become a long burning fuse. She pulled her knees to her chest. This eased her back, but the cramping continued.

She tore the bedclothes off with her right hand and rocked up into a seated, fetal position. Her thighs and chest cradled her honeydew melon-shaped stomach—her unseen, growing child. It was much too small, the time too soon. Then she saw in horror the bloody stain.

"Gaylord!" she screamed. "Oh, no, no, please. Gaylord!"

Her husband came immediately to her side, and soon brought the doctor, who gave her laudanum, ordered the sheets changed, and put her back to bed. The opium and alcohol mixture quickly carried her into a nauseous limbo.

In two days, she had not yet miscarried, but the doctor advised that she remain in bed for a good while longer, meaning, she suspected, the four months remaining to her term.

Submit could not stand inactivity. She went to sleep quickly, within moments of lying down at night, and she usually rose as quickly in the morning, ready to talk the moment she awoke. To be confined to bed made her feverish.

For two days she prayed to be released from this bondage, her petitions eventually taking a peevish and then a frankly nasty turn.

"O Lord," she prayed, "thou hast not made me to be a lie-abed, a sluggard, a take-to-her-ease Sally. I'm a whirlwind in a dress. It's no use telling me, as thou told Job, that I could not have made the alligator. I *am* one. Now thou wouldst pop me under the covers like Hezekiah's blackbirds?

"If thou take this baby, I'll no more serve thee, but tell the world thou art untrue to thy promises. Zion has been abandoned; and its days of desolation shall never come to an end. I will blacken thy name with every bit of our six feet of earth. Thou art dealing with a *very* bad woman!

"Stand against this evil and deliver me, or explain thyself. Not pity, not mercy, I want a reason!"

At the end of this mental prayer, Submit found that the back of her throat felt raw in the way it did after she'd been screaming at Gaylord. Then she felt ridiculous, and as frightened as she had been from the moment she saw the blood.

She took her next dose of laudanum and continued the theological quarrel in a semiconscious rage. Once she became angry, the emotion moved in like unwanted guests who would not go away.

After some days of this, Submit decided that since she could not be physically active, she would compensate through a burst of mental and spiritual activity. First she asked the Lord to forgive her. Then she told Him her plans and asked for the grace to outlast the tedium of the days with a methodical devotion, an attribute they both knew her character had always conspicuously lacked.

She needed an object for her intentions, though, and this should be, she decided, something other than her own welfare and that of her child's. The Lord knew of their needs—she had already informed Him at length.

Her worries about Sarah came back to her. Her days in bed gave her time to consider why Sarah's troubles almost panicked her. The truth was, she felt guilty.

In the first year or two of her own marriage she had discovered that Gaylord was not the kind of companion she had imagined. He turned out to be much smarter, more capable, and loving. She had thought he would be a nitwit, but one that would stay by her side; he turned out to be a highly intelligent and increasingly handsome man, who had his own thoughts and courses of action. He refrained on principle from talking about his position in the government and spoke only when deeply convicted that silence constituted betrayal.

At first discovery, she resented this. She resented both his unexpected abilities and his refusal to exhibit them more. And it was during this period that Sarah first came to stay with them. She remembered telling Sarah, "Our men are just alike, splendid figures to the world in the finery of their positions, but very noughts when naked." Part of which was based on the trouble that Gaylord and she, like Abram and Sarah, had experienced conceiving.

In the years since, she had learned to value Gaylord for what belonged to him, rather than resenting him for what did not. Even as she did so, however, she had continued in the old banter about husbands.

"Abram's building another one of his pirate ships," Sarah would say.

"Gaylord's off buckling the governor's shoes," she'd reply.

This had continued long after she'd come to admire the way Gaylord used his position as Special Secretary. She remembered the time when a woman in such rags that she looked like an animated duster had approached her near Boston Common. The crone kissed Submit's hands, as she thanked her for her husband's benevolence. Yet she had never been able to elicit from Gaylord what he had done.

"My endeavor is to serve," he would say. "Rule is an obligation, not a prerogative."

One time she pressed him for details past his patience, and his voice actually took on a sharp tone. "I do not intend to *dramatize* my life," he told her. "If I had done these things gratuitously, I might repeat their circumstances, but as I did them as a matter of duty and obligation, they should not be made much over."

He said this as if he assumed it his place to correct her, and that's when she disliked him the most. That's when she would go off with Sarah and they would fry their husbands to a crisp.

But it was precisely in that moment, and others like it, that Gaylord communicated to her what made him admirable. On many social occasions other men filled her ears with their concerns and private fascinations, and she would remember how Gaylord pulled the berries from a juniper tree and crushed them so that the two of them could delight in their scent; she remembered how he would pause in their strolls together to praise the solid presence and lines of the new Georgian houses. He loved the world, its created order and its extensions through human ingenuity. He took pleasure in *knowing*.

It had taken Submit years to understand the consummate virtue of this and rue her attempts to spoil it by trying to make Gaylord over into a prig.

In the eight years of their friendship, Sarah and she had changed in opposite ways, while keeping ever closer company. Now her worries about Sarah's restlessness had been intensified greatly by her cousin's flirtation with Mr. Copley. Submit decided to dedicate herself to praying for Sarah and Abram, for their reconciliation and a late-flowering of their marriage as glorious as Sarah's own mature beauty.

————

Sarah visited her room not long after Submit had taken to her bed and resolved on her new spiritual intention. Sarah was wearing the fabric they had examined in the shop on Charles Street, made up into an elegant satin and lace gown. Its deep neckline made Submit swallow; she did not like to think of its effect on men.

"Eve must have done a better job covering herself with animal skins," Submit said.

"Oh, Submit, this is right from Mr. Copperfield's pattern book. I'm sure that the entire French court goes further."

"We can always be assured of that."

Sarah went over to Submit's vanity table and swung her wide satiny skirts to see them move, then smoothed them back down again.

"My first appointment is tomorrow," she said. "I wish you were accompanying me. Lily Fayerweather can be tiresome. I'm imagining sitting there under her barrage of talk long after Mr. Copley and I have exhausted our energies."

"Just so Mr. Copley's energies go into his pencil."

Sarah stopped testing the movements of her gown. "I know you are ill and confined, but I do not like being chided. This has been the direction of your talk ever since we visited Charles Street, and I do not like it."

Submit suddenly wanted to rip off the bedclothes and go shake the woman. "Did you not see how Mr. Copley looked at you?"

"Did you not see it?" Sarah asked with surprising quickness.

"His eyes devoured you."

"His eyes saw the way my face takes the light, the flatter plane of my right cheek, the pad of my chin. He looked at me as an artist looks at his subject."

"You were not his subject."

"If there was an attraction, then this was its cause. You cannot blame him for wanting a subject with a more naturally pleasing countenance than Mrs. Smith." Sarah laughed to herself.

"There may have been an objectivity in his regard," Submit said, "but you were provocative from the start in your reaction to his painting."

"How is that?"

"Mr. Copley must have the sense to know that agitation does not always indicate repulsion—rather its opposite."

"He seemed vain enough to take my meaning in a simple way."

"A vanity which you have now commenced to flattering."

"Submit, please. I will have the portrait painted and remember the hours in the man's studio with fondness. Surely this is the most innocent of things, even if tinged with flirtation. I have no one else to pay me this manner of attention. I am starved for the want of a morsel or two."

"You have a husband."

"Such a husband as you know."

"I begin to think you do not know him."

Sarah looked at Submit as if she had become incoherent. "Submit, I cannot believe the direction of this conversation. Have you had some private revelation lying in this bed?"

"Perhaps."

"I think you are grown pregnant with conceit. Or is this only maternal satisfaction? We may have less in common now."

"We may."

Sarah stepped back from the bed. She looked as if she had bumped her nose in public.

CHAPTER 9

Girl Talk

The following day Submit heard Sarah come in after her sitting, and she told her maid, Ida, to ask her cousin to come up and take tea with her. She wondered that Mr. Copley could start his portrait within the month of their first visit to his studio.

Sarah soon came in, her manner light and brisk, as if she had been out for a walk in the country.

"So what do you have to say for yourself?" Submit asked. "How did this dallying with your artist go on?"

Sarah took out the ornamental hair clasp with its spray of tiny porcelain flowers and stretched her neck from side to side. "It is harder work than you would expect. He becomes a bullying schoolmaster when you move 'out of form,' as he calls it. 'Stay in form, stay in form, now,' he says."

"Did you enjoy it, though?"

"I did enjoy the talk that preceded the sitting. I wanted to get away afterwards."

"How so?"

"You realize what men are with their ambitions, Submit. And Mr. Copley is the same, in most respects. Except that he does seem to be dealing on the plane to which ambition should aspire. He wants to create works of art in 'little Boston' that the whole world will know."

"Perhaps he only speaks of the world because, unlike a merchant, only the 'whole world's' opinion matters in art. We didn't value Mr. Copley here until his success in England. While—the world knows—Mr. Storer's good opinion is enough to shore up Mr. Perkin's illusions."

Sarah turned the clasp in her hands. "It's more than that. He *loves* the world. I mean, he loves what makes each thing individual—one face and not another, the unique person. He was not trying so much to copy my image onto the canvas, as he was trying to do what God did in making me out of flesh and bone—only with paint."

Submit thought to castigate this as pretension, but then she had a deeper thought. "Gaylord loves the world like that," she said. "He finds the small things about it wonderful."

"Yes, he does." Sarah paused and bounced her closed hands in her lap, just before she said, "You should see how Mr. Copley concentrates as he sketches. He had me positioned somewhat in profile to him, and his canvas covered his face when he moved to my left. But I would see him duck out to look at me and while he labored on the near side of the picture. He drew such definite and rapid lines. He worked so fast, so decisively. He seemed unaware of the canvas before him. He might have been a sculptor with the air as his medium. I asked him a question or two as this went on, and he made no reply."

"I recall his concentration that day we visited. He couldn't bring himself to greet us when we first came in," Submit said.

"At first this made me angry. But to be in love with the world like that and then to be able to express it. Not just in words, or even in an object, but physically, through this dance he performed. He seemed to be hearing the music of time itself."

"It sounds as if you had been to the theater," Submit said, trying to sound witty, hating herself.

"Well, no doubt it was the novelty of it all. I'm sure my next sittings will become humdrum." She said this looking away—from a lie, the truth?

"And Lily Fayerweather? What did she make of Mr. Copley's dance?"

Sarah seemed to return from her thoughts and looked straight at Submit. "Lily chattered, as she will. Mr. Copley was moved to present her with a book at one point, a volume about painting that kept her engrossed for a good long breath or two. Lily may force that trip to Europe Mr. Copley has been long threatening."

"He has?"

"He wants to see that world whose opinion he so highly values. He is, of course, rather taken with what he has achieved in 'little Boston.' He talks as if he had never seen another portrait besides his own."

"Do artists ever see anything but themselves or their own work?"

"We were only now talking of his extraordinary love of the world around him."

"It serves artists, though, doesn't it? Their love is compromised."

"While Gaylord is the true pure spirit."

"I sometimes think so now."

"You seem to have fallen in love with your husband. What happened to the Submit who would not? The Submit who spoke of her Gaylord as a dolt?"

"I hope I have not done so in a long time."

"I think the child that's coming must have stolen the better part of your heart and mind. There seems little enough left for me."

"I have been ill."

"You know what I'm speaking of."

"I have been lying here, trying to appreciate the world as it is. This room affords me a better view of what's closest to hand."

"I always thought you had the keenest sight of any woman I ever knew."

"I always thought so too." They both laughed. "Which is why I have come to doubt such keenness. I have been sharp; I have dueled with those I should embrace."

"You have been parrying these moments with me."

"So . . . to the issue, Sarah. Beware of Mr. Copley. Or beware of your own loneliness. You think no harm can come of this. What harm comes otherwise?"

"Whatever harm there shall be in it," Sarah said decisively, "shall come only to me. What could this mean to you?"

"*You* mean much to me," Submit said.

"I am in no danger," Sarah said, growing exasperated. "We will all love the picture when it is finished, I'm sure. I will give you no cause to stop loving me."

"I cannot think of how you could ever do that."

CHAPTER 10

Be Sure Your Sins

Submit invited Sarah in for a talk after the next sitting and the ones that followed, and their friendship prevailed, but in a new mode: Submit became Sarah's witty antagonist.

Sarah would say, "Mr. Copley's emphasis on reputation is only realism. He does not want his hopes of artistic achievement to produce illusions grander than his paintings."

To which Submit replied, "Is there anything in reputation but illusion?"

She could not counter her cousin for long, though, for Sarah began to sing the same paean to the man, over and over.

"As to worldly matters," Sarah would say, "Mr. Copley's background as the son of a widowed tobacconist on the Long Wharf matches Abram's in lowliness. Over the years Abram has reconsidered his flight from Ireland and decided what he hated must have been good, right, and holy. There his mother sits, the living idol of his lost childhood. Mr. Copley does not regret his rise, and he is still winging higher. Does this not distinguish their spirits? The one looks to the past, the other to the future."

"Where are you looking?" Submit asked.

"I want to aid Mr. Copley in his purpose in any way I can."

"In any way?" Submit asked, barely slowing the speaker.

"So much will have to be denied to us. Perchance this very denial will make our friendship a greater source of strength. More truly spiritual. For he needs comfort."

"You know his needs?"

"His gifts are also burdens. He works almost alone, with his patrons not truly seeing or understanding half of what he has given to them. They are satisfied with so little, really, and would not know the difference if they were in the hands of an itinerant sketcher."

"You feel as if you are in his hands?"

"They have been given someone whose work touches the divine in creation, and they stand about debating the appropriateness of one or another object in the picture itself. The fees they pay Mr. Copley can never recompense him truly. Only the most sincere and heartfelt gratitude can even make a start."

Submit found herself constrained, when Sarah's attitude turned worshipful, by her own strangling anger. She could not say what came to mind and forgive herself afterward, and this spared Sarah from hearing it.

The day after one such encounter, Submit was having her tea in bed, with the light of the early summer day outside her window and some of the brightness in her room as well. The linens and bedclothes had been changed that afternoon, and she was enjoying an unexpected freshet of energy, rather than the dreariness she usually felt at teatime.

She turned the pages of *The New England Weekly Journal* with interest. She spent a good deal of time reading about the controversy over the Townshend duties on lead, paint, glass, paper, and tea. The taxes themselves were going largely uncollected, although the commentary they inspired had already made for large, bound volumes. When she got to the back pages of the weekly, among the advertisements, the running almanac, and the shipping notices, she found this item:

Mr. and Mrs. Fayerweather's recent gala was enjoyed by all. The hosts and their daughter Lily lavished their guests with every possible attention, and Mr. and Mrs. Storer, Mr. and Mrs. Bredforet, the Honorable Peter Duxbury and Mrs. Duxbury, and Deputy Council Fortune and Mrs. Fortune, looked on the occasion as a happy one indeed. Our leading artist, Mr. Copley, was in attendance. As was Mrs. Abram White, that celestial beauty. Mr. Copley and Mrs. White entertained the party with witty anecdotes from Mrs. White's portrait sittings. Miss Charity Pierce, who has served as Mrs. White's chaperone on these occasions, scolded the pair for their witty contrivances.

Miss Charity Pierce? Charity cared for nothing but her own reputation, and Sarah would never even have suggested her as a chaperone. Lily Fayerweather was supposed to be Sarah's companion. The tattling journalist must have been guilty of his own contrivance, as a way of working in another name. Submit felt sure this must be the case.

Still, she felt spurred to write Lily Fayerweather. Sarah and Mr. Copley should not be sharing any of their sentiments in public. Even after their many talks, Submit found Sarah's lack of caution in this surprising. Which gave rise to a further concern: Submit had wondered at the number of appointments the portrait demanded; she now wondered whether both parties were finding reasons for more than was needed.

> Dear Miss Fayerweather,
> My former regrets doubled when I read today of your splendid party. I was so glad that my cousin Mrs. White could be in attendance. As usual, the press has introduced a note of confusion by citing Miss Pierce as my cousin's chaperone at her portrait sittings. I continue to be thankful that you are doing her this service while I am confined to this bed.
> I fault the Lord for His ironic sense in confining so outward a soul. This must be His preparation for childbirth—the herbs of woman's curse to pain and sorrow. Yet, I live in good hope of enjoying motherhood's estate.
> And I am so glad you enjoyed such a splendid evening, as I remain,
> > Yours in gratitude and expectancy,
> > Submit Singleton Chauncey

The next day, Submit received a reply from Lily Fayerweather.

> Dear Mrs. Chauncey,
> *The New England Weekly* reporter has spread the news of our little gathering farther and wider than one could ever imagine. I have had notes from the northernmost Massachusetts territories—from Bangor and those environs.

I am afraid the confusion is yours, though, in regard to the chaperoning duties. Miss Pierce did claim those duties, or at least I lay no claim to them. Your cousin never asked this favor of me, I assure you, and Miss Pierce seemed to know as much as she should, when asked. I am sure that Mrs. White will clarify this matter for you when you are well enough to receive her again in your chamber. My whole family joins me in prayers for your safe delivery and that of your child. I remain,

> Yours in friendship and service,
> Lily Fayerweather

Submit knew her duty, and she did not relish it. She would say what she must, though. So after a three-day delay, during which she considered her approach, Submit raised the matter when Sarah came in after her sitting, still wearing the satin gown.

Before Sarah could sweep one hand under her skirts and sit down in the velvet-covered chair in the corner, Submit said, "Be sure your sins will find you out."

"And good day to you, Mrs. Chauncey."

"They will. Make no mistake."

"Acquaint me with the subject, please."

"Your chaperone. Miss Fayerweather. Or Miss Pierce?"

"You saw the item after all," Sarah said evenly.

"Like the Ethiopian eunuch," Submit said, "I am in need of an interpreter."

"A strained comparison, I think." Sarah tried to act as if Submit were a child in need of playful scolding.

"Miss Fayerweather has written to say that she has done you no service as a chaperone. I do not guess you asked Miss Pierce."

"You guess well."

"You have been going to these sittings alone?"

"Mr. Copley has been there," Sarah said and laughed.

"*Sarah.* You know what this is, and it is not a cause for laughter."

"Mr. Copley has been, and is, a gentleman."

"He has been forced to be by your own lack of proper behavior."

Sarah cleared a loose strand of hair off her face and pulled it back behind her ear. "Submit, we have kept up the pretense of my 'visiting' you for several years now. The truth is, as you know and cooperate in, that I live here for good portions of the year. I have chosen to live without someone always by my arm."

"You lied to me. You know your behavior to be provocative."

"I know what my behavior has been. There is nothing in it that accuses me."

Submit was taken aback by Sarah's boldness. "Think of your conversations with this man, Sarah. Would you have spoken the same if you had been accompanied?"

Sarah looked away, and the hopeful and sad dreaminess that came over her when she spoke of Mr. Copley visited once more. "I would that I had said so much more. I have not spoken what I feel. Nor has he."

"You believe your feelings are reciprocated by the gentleman?"

"I think he must love me."

"*Sarah, no.* You have painted an illusion for yourself with the same care and genius that Mr. Copley has expended on this accursed portrait."

"How can you know this?"

"Our discussions have been of little else these past weeks."

Sarah sucked in her cheeks at this and waited.

"Your first thought, which was to indulge a flirtatious manner, has resulted in a feeling so deep that you cannot speak of it in civil society—or even to the one for whom you harbor this illicit affection. How can this be?"

"As yet, these are only private sentiments."

"Sentiments always intend more. They plead for actions. You can satisfy those pleadings only at the cost of alienating yourself from society. You will be more confined for the rest of your life than I have been these past months. And Mr. Copley must either indulge his lusts for a season and then discredit you or give up everything he aspires to. No such fox will be wanted in anyone's drawing rooms."

Sarah stood up. "I cannot keep you company. I cannot feel otherwise than I do."

"You have talked yourself into these delusory feelings!" Submit said.

"I have found the best in this life."

"For which you would sacrifice the next?"

"I have sacrificed nothing yet; I have not been invited to. I suppose I shall not be. But it seems I have already sacrificed your affection. My feelings have gone beyond what your morality can understand."

"Love's character does not change. Its expression must, though, if your behavior takes away the Sarah whom I do love and who is worthy of just such a love as I can give with all of my heart."

Sarah angled one knee inward and put a hand to her cocked hip. "We are speaking of nothing. There is no choice to be made."

"We were speaking of your going to Mr. Copley without a chaperone. That must end. It must."

"He may not need to see me again. He is going to write me about the matter."

"My babe will be coming soon. Help me with the child and put all of your feeling into doing so. Your regret at the absence of Mr. Copley from your society will lose its strength."

Sarah looked straight at Submit, her eyes full of fire. "Help you with your child? God himself has decided He needs no help from me with children."

"God has not judged you."

"Indeed He has. I have been faithful to God in this for nearly twenty years, and He has seen fit to abandon me. To mock me."

"Mock you?"

Sarah stretched out her hands and clenched her fists in helpless anger. "He has given a child to the only one who understood my frustration."

"If there is a God who has blessed me, then He cannot have forgotten you."

"Then there is no God."

"This is God, Sarah. You are only unhappy at not being God."

"Did you think the same when you almost lost your child?"

"We have said enough."

"Tell me the same if your baby dies."

"How can you say that in my bedroom?"

"You both may die and then we shall all be alone."

"You must not say these things!"

"I am going to live as I wish, and I will go to hell, if I must, cursing God's judgment."

CHAPTER 11

Watching

Submit and Gaylord lay in bed together, spooned up with Submit's back against her husband's chest. Her term was coming to an end, and she always went to sleep now on her side, the child's weight resting, it seemed, beside her. She could almost imagine them lying side by side, his eyes and hands closed tight, starred with wrinkles. She could almost smell the child's milky flesh.

Gaylord said, "I know your confinement has been hard. I am grateful to you."

"Grateful?"

"For taking such care of our child."

Submit had thought of the months she had spent in this room as imprisonment, not service. "I never forgot the blood."

"It was more than fear that kept you here."

Submit turned her head back toward Gaylord. "If I die, what will you do?"

"The doctor says your condition should not affect the birth."

"Many women die even after carrying their children easily."

Gaylord paused before answering, such a long pause that Submit almost spoke again before he said, "I want to think about you and the child being here with me."

"Do you?"

"I think about what a happy change it will bring."

"Yes?"

"I think about the child changing from day to day. I think about my young Bledsoe nieces and nephews. How different they are each time we see them. The lightness of children. The depth and power of life itself—that ocean. And then these little harbor buoys, bobbing and clanging, bobbing and clanging. The ones that become adults never sink. It's . . . unexpected, almost preposterous given the chances."

"So what will you do if I die?"

"I'll use such language as would make even Submit Chauncey blush. You'll repent of any such notion. The air will be so blue it will bring you out of the grave itself."

"I wish you would not evade me."

Gaylord propped himself up on an elbow. "What will *you* do then, mistress, if you die?"

It was the same question Sarah had asked. "Before my confinement, I would have given the Lord a good talking to before entering His heaven. Now heaven is too close."

"It is said we are already citizens there by faith," Gaylord hummed out. "One of the harder truths to believe, ain't it?"

Submit poked him with her elbow. She waited through his "oomph" and his returning pinch. "Stop. Think with me about the baby again."

"What about it?"

"I hope this first shall be a boy. Are you hoping for a son? Please say. You never will."

"I have no concern with posterity," said Gaylord.

"You had *better*."

"I mean, I don't feel compelled to carry on the family name. My brothers have done well enough by it."

"I feel as if I'm about to accomplish a very great thing."

"You are," he said.

"It's not an individual thing, though, is it? Not peculiar to Submit Chauncey."

"Therein lies its greatness."

"I understand cousin Sarah's plight now more than ever, and yet agree with her much less."

"You cannot agree with a lie," he said. " 'Tis enough, I fear, that we have encouraged her unwisely. She seemed so unhappy when she first visited. Now I think we are making her equally unhappy."

"I might have been much the same if I had been unable to conceive. I have not enjoyed waiting these eight years."

"But Sarah cannot make her peace by staying with us. Or find it in diversion."

Submit pulled a little away from Gaylord's encircling arm and rolled over to face him. "I have been meaning to speak to you of this. I think she has become enamored of Mr. Copley."

"Mr. Copley?"

"Her portrait painter."

"Yes, I know. But I did not know this."

"He has not sent for her for some days now. But she went to her sittings alone, since I was unavailable."

"That's . . . no . . . what could she be thinking of? You were wrong not to tell me about this."

"I did not know until the past day or so."

"How did you learn of it?"

"The manner of my discovery is unimportant. The point is that she has been indiscreet, and this has led her to conceive improper affections."

"Did he use her badly?" Gaylord asked, alarmed.

"For the portrait, certainly, but for what other purpose I cannot tell. I do not think he has made advances toward her—at least not physically."

"She must return to her own home. As quickly as we can arrange it."

"It would be much better if Abram would come here and fetch her. I will write to him."

"Tomorrow."

"*Gaylord*," Submit said, annoyed at being ordered.

"I feel a responsibility in this. A great responsibility—and more than a little fault."

"I do as well. I will write to him."

They grew quiet, and Submit rolled back onto her left side. She listened but did not hear Gaylord shifting into comfort. He lay too still. But then he drew near her again and kissed her back. He turned once more, and she heard the patting and low woofing sounds of him thumping his pillow.

As soon as Gaylord's breathing became deep and heavy, Submit rose from bed and went to the chair in the corner. Right where Sarah had sat as Submit reviewed the lie with her, Submit now kept watch. She prayed for her cousin, remembering all that Sarah had once told her about her visit with Jonathan and Sarah Edwards, about the prophecy the divine's wife had uttered.

Submit waited, and she watched, and she began to feel Sarah's heartbreak at her barrenness—her great sorrow. The Lord's goodness to one and not the other did appear cruel—her child an affront. She did not understand His ways, and she felt foolish for having felt compelled to speak for Him. "You made the crocodile," she said. "You made leviathan."

Later that night, as she still watched, Submit's baby woke, too. It kicked and kicked, as if to remind her that it had an opinion of its own about being an affront.

Yes, Submit thought, *we know not, but are known.* A rest began to come to her that did not send her to sleep but cleared her mind and kept her alert and listening.

PART III

—

Pagan Campaigns

CHAPTER 12

The Letter

*I*n the dark, having rattled open the balky middle drawer of his desk, Abram patted after his flint and lit the oil lamp. The dusty boards of his shipyard shanty beat with the flickering light as he took the letter from inside his greatcoat and unfolded its two crisp leaves once more. How he wished these pages would crumble in his fingertips.

He smelled the charred logs in the new Franklin stove and the river bottom scent that the pools of rainwater under the sills brought out. Earlier, as he lay in his bed, he had heard the drenching rain stop suddenly about four o'clock. That had released him from his tossing vigil, and he had walked down to the shipyard in the early morning dark. The low clouds were moving swiftly; the coming morning would dawn clear.

Breathing out a long breath in the cool shanty, he hoped again for the next moment to bring another release—as unexpected as the rain stopping—hoped that somehow this news that had stolen away his sleep would disappear.

It did not. The letter was still there in his hand, and he felt un-willingly compelled to read it once more. How many times had he read it already, those familiar loops and flourishes that crossed the pages?

May 1, 1769
Dear Abram,

You may well accuse me of playing a double part in the fol-lowing. My long practice of hospitality to my cousin, your wife, has kept her from you more than you wished, I know, and has no doubt played a role in what I must relate. At the beginning let me accuse myself of whatever wrongs you may advance and more. My husband Gaylord is distraught at what he takes to be his own complicity. And yet, we do truly desire your good and know, as you cannot, what danger threatens your house.

At the beginning of this social season, our Sarah elicited the good will, the praise, the admiration, and I do not hesitate to say, the envy of all Boston. As you can best appreciate, the fullness of her beauty as a woman has come to her just now. At the same time, she moves in society with the poise and ease of a great lady, with a nobility that even this democratic town cannot help but court.

She has drawn, in the course of this, the attentions of one gentleman in particular, a man of great celebrity if not equal char-acter, who has been seen with her overmuch. This has caused some wagging of uncivil tongues, which, if nothing else, should provide sufficient reason for you to see to the matter.

Alas, more particularly, I am in the increasingly discomfiting position of knowing that this gentleman's attentions may be somewhat reciprocated, if only by a quickly passing sentiment. For I detect a much greater unhappiness in my cousin, an evil that even you may not suspect; her mastery of Boston's *beau monde* does not amuse or hold her attention as it has in seasons past. This frightens her, and makes her desperate to find some satisfaction in this world.

Your liberal policy towards her freedom in society might well be reconsidered; for though you have acted out of kindness in honoring her wishes, that same kindness must now add fortitude and wisdom in its healing tenderness for the condition it thought to mend. Do not doubt me. The weakness of reason that Sarah has experienced in the past may revisit her. In this state she could succumb to wiles and practices that are the devil's work, as well as one man's lustful intemperance.

I am known for saying at times much more than is needed,

and yet I beg you not to think that I exaggerate this matter. What I have written comes as close to plain speaking as my own sense of courtesy allows.

Thus, I remain, your abashed and humbled cousin,
Submit Singleton Chauncey

Abram stood up from his desk, folded the letter once more, replaced it in its envelope, and tucked it back in his coat.

Who was the celebrated gentleman? A Tory politician or one of the gentry who reminded Sarah of her father? No doubt some wit or wag with a quick tongue and an attentive eye. Someone young and fair perhaps, as he had once been to her.

Abram thought of the day soon after their marriage when Sarah and he had sailed along the Hudson River's Palisades and spent the night at Mrs. Young's inn. That huge feather bed, its expanse of pleasures. He reached out, even now, to smooth her long dark hair and thread it behind her ear, but his heart rebuked him as his memory touched the sandy texture of reddish strands.

He went out into the yard. The sky in the east was now light at the horizon. His men had made a good start on a big schooner, the ramps and scaffolding all in place around the not-yet-closed-in hull with its whale-sized ribbing. The aftermast had been raised. It loomed over him like an upraised hand of judgment. As a boy, he had gone to sea mainly for the chance of climbing up into the rigging and flying high amid the topsails. Now, apart from judging the line, he hardly looked up anymore.

Not since Allen Farmington had fallen. His crew had tossed off the timber on the cart and trundled him away, his shoulder unsocketed as he seemed still to be reaching for a last handhold. Abram had ordered the carpenters aloft on a cold, icy day, and had thought nothing about it until the open hull Allen had fallen in boomed with his death so hard Abram thought the loading cart had struck the side of the shanty.

Abram had to pick his way, stepping over the logs lying about, down to his own longboat tied up at the wharf. He put it out now into the estuary and rowed toward the open sea. He thought of raising the collapsible mast and its sail, but he enjoyed pulling at the oars, feeling the strain and eventual loosening in his upper back.

The cold inrushing tide filtered in white slips over his oars. He felt strong enough, after the first stiffness left him, to row out of the channel and on and on into the North Atlantic. Did he want to go home to Ireland? Or simply stay afloat on the sea, which in his former life as a merchant captain had become his true country? He felt crowded in by the world. For a few moments, as the longboat headed through the light spring wind, as it bumped across the surface waves running counter to the tide—for a few more moments, while the rowing warmed him and the catch and creaking ring of the oar handles kept the rhythm of his progress, he thought of nothing, enjoyed his solitude, escaped.

The Joppa Flats, a clamming area, came up on his left. He stopped rowing, leaned over the gunwale, and scooped some water up in his right hand, let it fall, rubbed his hands together, and patted his cheeks. The astringent salt water tightened his already cold, rubbery skin. He sat another moment. He remembered running away from Ireland as a boy, and he realized that at fifty-one he had outlived the possibility of escape. The net of his past choices, his livelihood, his public commitments—such as they seemed to be and such as they were—these things held him, and delivered him from the sea of possibilities to market. His life as a boyhood poacher had finally made a meal of him.

In defiance, he shifted his course toward the open sea, pivoting around with one deep sloshing stroke of his left oar, stroked again with both oars, digging hard, angling for the deeper water on the northern side of the channel.

On the sixth stroke he looked up, and that looming shadow, the threat he felt in his cousin's letter, all these judgments suddenly gathered ferocity and cuffed his face, then dug at his eyes. Letting go of the oars, he turned to the side and lifted a forearm against the blazing gate with its radiant beams rising at the mouth of the harbor. Daybreak.

CHAPTER 13

The News

*A*bram carried the letter from Submit in the inside pocket of his dark blue swallow-tailed greatcoat for two days. He knew his duty. At least, he knew his duty toward his wife; he knew the reconciliation he should once more attempt. His questions concerned his obligation toward Anne.

For the past five months they had spent almost every evening together. His mother joked about his visits to *"Le Petit Trianon,"* a suspicious reference to the house King Louis XV had built for his mistress, Madame Du Barry.

The day Abram received the letter, he missed his evening visit, sending Jezreel out to Anne with a message that he had a meeting of the Overseers.

He walked out to the cottage the next evening, the letter still in his pocket. The summer solstice was drawing nearer, and the late evenings almost had the qualities of a second morning: endless skies filled with pellucid light. Every new leaf on the copper beech and oak trees stood out. A cool wind stirred the air as the swallows swung in loops that ended where they began, under the eaves. He could smell the turned earth of the vegetable garden. He turned his head, cracking the tension out of his neck, and his stride loosened as he walked down toward the cottage. Even the burden he carried could not prevail against the calming effect of these visits.

When he bent his head and stepped through the door, Anne curtsied low, almost knelt, and kissed his hand. Her fingers secretly worked into his palm and her lips touched his skin more than once. The first time Anne had knelt before him like this, he thought she had committed some great sin or wanted an extraordinary favor, until he realized that she had contrived this as a way of greeting him before the child without an embrace.

Theo performed his own little bow and then rushed against Abram's legs.

"Good evening to this house," Abram said to them.

His elaborate greeting brought a lingering and questioning look from Anne.

"The Overseers meeting supplied some news for us to talk about," he said to Anne, then turned his attention to Theo. "Have you had your supper?"

"Momma duff," Theo said.

"She made you a nice molasses duff?" Abram asked.

"With a topping of beach plum sauce," Anne said. "I have some for you."

"I want!" Theo said.

"Little piggy boy, you have had enough for two grown men," said his mother.

Theo smiled in satisfaction.

"What if I read to you and sing you a song while you put your head down on your pallet," said Abram.

"No, the day," Theo said.

"What?"

"The day. The day."

"He does not want to go to bed so early now that it's still light outside," Anne explained.

"You won't have to sleep, then," Abram said. "But let me read to you. I want to see what happens in that story about the water troll."

Theo turned and ran toward his pallet. As Abram stepped after him, Anne reached out and put her arm around his waist, giving him a quick, one-armed squeeze. It didn't take more than that for Abram to anticipate what might follow.

He read Theo his story sitting cross-legged at the edge of the pallet as the child made a pillow of his right thigh. Theo took his hand and put it to his forehead, wanting Abram to stroke his strawberry wave of hair, as he often would while reading.

Abram enjoyed being generous with his affection toward Theo, thought well of himself, in fact, for it. His news would not only hurt Anne. He almost understood Sarah's desperation at being barren, for nothing so confirmed his life as this simple pleasure of ferrying a child off to sleep on the tide of the story's sweet dream. Yet his every kind gesture pilfered the child's trust.

He smoothed the child's brow one last time. Theo's eyes still struggled to stay open, but Abram could tell that only his attentions caused the child's tipped-white lashes to flicker. The boy would be sound asleep within moments of being left to himself. So Abram took him by the shoulders and gently laid him back on his pallet.

The child sat back up and gave Abram's neck a hug and then, satisfied, curled on his side as he gathered the light sheet into his hands and hugged it to his chest. What a little urchin! Fifty-one years and he had never been able to help bring about such a miracle. How different things would have been with Sarah if he had.

Anne had prepared a savory fish chowder, sweet scallops in a creamy broth with potatoes and freshly cut chives. He could not keep her from cooking for him, even though he had usually eaten a light supper with his mother before he came out to the cottage. As he ate at Anne's trestle table, Abram watched her dash for the freshly baked bread, another ladle of soup, that plum molasses duff she had made. After she put these before him, she sat across the table, her hands folded, ignoring her own food, watching him.

Her solicitude reminded him uncomfortably of a servant, and he said, "You are going to let your supper go cold again."

She began to spoon up the chowder, carefully, dutifully, her eyes down.

He did not like that much either. "This is very good," he said. "You can do more with a scallop or a clam than any cook on five continents."

Her broad smile lit her face. "I was going to make it yesterday, when I cut the chives. Thank you for sending Jezreel down with the message about the Overseers."

Abram did not say anything, only nodded, and ate more of his chowder. He turned his head quickly and took a look at Theo, who was scrunched so close into the corner that he must be asleep.

"You have something—something to say?" Anne asked, carefully.

Abram had spooned up a large scallop, and with the flaking, hot, gelatinous morsel in his mouth, shrugged off the inquiry.

"I worried that you did not come until Jezreel brought your message."

"The Overseers like to talk. One might almost think the funds their own, they are so particular about their disbursements."

"These matters to be assayed . . ." and here Anne's voice dropped into an Overseer's jowly baritone, "are of the gravest importance."

Abram laughed and ate the rest of his supper and his helping of plum molasses duff. He almost spoke, but then Anne got up from the table, cleared the bowls and simple dishes, and took the oak bucket outside to the pump.

This was the start of their ritual. At the end of these humid days, Abram's silk shirts clung to him. So every night she washed his face and hands with a cold cloth. If he kissed her, she took off his shirt and continued bathing him. She treated his body as if it were as precious as her own, with a care that brought on the same desire he had felt the first time—one that blanked out the world. No one had ever treated him with such care, such good humor, such simplicity. He felt strongly Anne's essential innocence in these matters. But they had only a private likeness of a true marriage. He had better say as much before she touched him again, when their own world would seem complete once more.

She came back in, bent with the heaviness of the sloshing bucket, walking straddle-footed, ungainly.

He stood up from the table and picked up his snail-shaped hat.

"You are going?" she asked.

He put his hat back down. "No. Not this moment. I don't know why I picked up my hat. I would tell you something."

"Sit down then and tell me," she said and returned to her place at the table.

He put his hand to his mouth and massaged his whiskering cheek.

"What is troubling you?" Anne asked, looking straight at him, her eyes suddenly locked. "I can feel you wanting to get away. I sensed something was wrong when you sent Jezreel."

He started to speak.

She stopped him. "You must not deny what we are to each other— this love, though we have never called it that. You cannot deny it now. For what we have been to each other has brought a change. You are a father." She leaned back in her chair and ducked her chin, looking at him, frightened, suspicious, hopeful.

Abram's heart picked up. He realized that he should have expected as much, and yet, perhaps because Sarah had never conceived, he had not.

"This cannot be," he said. His fear made him say, "You are only thinking to keep me. But I have other duties now."

"You do have a child. He is already much more than a duty. The Lord knows us from the womb." She put a cradling hand to her stomach.

"You are certain?"

She nodded. "You have made Theo your own. This one is truly ours."

"I have made—" All that he had done came upon him, and the ground underneath his chair seemed to swing and tip. He got to his feet. His heart was plunging on. He felt he might be sick, and his one thought and purpose became to get out of the cottage.

He took gulping breaths, answered Anne's "Are you well?" with nods and hand signals. And then, his legs moving like stilts, he went out blindly, knocking over a chair as he went.

When Abram reached the air, he took what felt like a saving breath. He groaned out a despairing prayer. The night was dark overhead now.

CHAPTER 14

A Bug on the Wall

More ghost than man, Abram wandered toward Wolfe's Tavern late on a gray afternoon, the air humid with a cindery, gunpowder scent. For two days he had lived in what felt like the nightmare of his bout with smallpox. Time became a sluggish element—a drowning sea. He tried, again and again, to look at the situation coolly. What did he expect, after all? And what were his options? His thoughts soon made his scalp prickle and sweat.

Inside Wolfe's, Tristram Dalton, the young overseer, and the lawyer Theophilus Parsons were holding an impromptu meeting, along with a leading shipper, a short, thick-boned Irishman, a plain but shrewd man, Patrick Tracy. Abram joined them at a plank pinewood table, taking a place on one of the pewlike benches that lined the brick wall, and ordered tea.

"Our missionary," Theophilus said. "What holy pursuits have you come from today?"

Abram tried to smile. Theophilus, a shrewd but jovial man with a froggy double chin, always meant his ironies in the most complimentary way.

"You look as if your angels were in rebellion," Tracy said.

"This early humidity," Abram said. "It always takes my appetite. I would add a notch on my belt every time we went through the Indies."

"We were just speaking of your business—the need for more ships and shipping," said Dalton.

"To carry trade beyond British boundaries," Tracy said with a wink. The old Irishman looked ready to face the redcoat enemy anytime.

"There are no more privateers," Theophilus said, "only patriots."

"So we are at war?" Abram asked, trying to coax Theophilus back from his extreme position.

"We should be plucking what sails we can now," said Theophilus, "for when war comes, all our traders will be ships in a bottle. You'll see them bobbing in the harbor, I tell you, with nothing to go out to but doom."

"If you see it that way, you might commission your own fleet," Abram said to Theophilus.

"*I* may," Tracy said in a quiet, calm voice. "Your ships have a reputation for speed. Would you build that kind of ship—fast, ready for a fight, with only enough storage to make such 'encounters' worthwhile?"

"We've seen too many hostile cruisers astern, Patrick, don't you think?"

"We are talking about ships that carry the duties that buy our chains, Abram," young Dalton said. "They may carry foodstuffs and tea, but they are slavers just the same."

"This is a comforting sight: the guardians of the poor taking counsel with politics. God making friends of Mammon?" said a new voice.

Abram looked up to see Beniah Lynch standing by Patrick Tracy's elbow. A dwarfish hogshead of a man, Beniah had a barrel chest and short legs that seemed too insubstantial to bear his frame. His flat head of burrlike curls topped a forehead that had a bump at the left temple as if he had been hit by a rock. He had small, round puppet eyes, a hobgoblin's nose, and an irritable complexion that flashed red and textured up with hives in an instant.

Lynch was always gesturing, swinging his little arms and hands up and down, plucking his one pointed ear, the left one, and scratching his flat head. He grinned and leered as he spoke, sometimes from behind the cover of his circling hands, as if privy to the dirty joke of the world, and he ended many of his statements with a bad orator's forced laugh, *he-he*.

"I'm sure all of those in Five Points and beyond who would have no bread and butter tonight but for your ministrations are blessing your wisdom and foresight. Especially this, our own missionary, a most uncommon man who finds the common so attractive."

Theophilus turned halfway round, threw his shoulders back, and extended his chins. The lower chin puffed and rippled as he said, "Mr. Lynch, we would ask you to sit to tea with us, but you have made too great a friend of your rum bottle this day. So good day to you."

Lynch turned to speak to Tracy as if Theophilus's statement had been directed at them both. "But I want to put this question of ethics and good policy to our advocate: whether it is in the best interest of the people for public associations to be converted into private gain and commercial advantage. As in the discussion of shipbuilding, the ordering of a certain number of ships, between our public servants."

"Discretion would have you lower your simpering voice, sir," Theophilus said.

"We are not having a public meeting, Mr. Lynch," Tracy said. "Nor are we contemplating disbursements from the public treasury. So go back to your spirits. You are producing a devilish one here."

Beniah stroked his outsized forehead and half covered his right eye with his hand, as he said, "What need can there be of ships, when you are soliciting the town to agree to nonimportation? If we no longer buy from England, they will surely have no traffic with us. The orders that come in then could only be from privateers, smugglers, or a government pretending to represent the Colonies themselves. Our business then would be nothing but sedition and treason." He grinned as if, all things being equal, the notions of sedition and treason could suit a person very well. "For those to whom this business proved forthcoming." At this, he put his two little hands on the table and leaned in toward Abram.

Tracy said, "The town's refusal to import from the British may discomfort you, it's true, but the Townshend Acts would make your labor slavery. You would be no man's slave, would you?"

"I am any man's slave who would hire me, sir, and set my yard to work. I can make no distinction between what a free man finds himself compelled to do by the necessity of earning his bread and what a slave must under the threat of the lash. Methinks hunger quite as effective in its striping. To be a man of independent means is the only freedom, which accounts for its popularity in the common dream of happiness."

"I believe you have been asked to withdraw, sir," said Theophilus Parsons.

"When we are being so effectively philosophical, sir?" asked Lynch. "I will not trouble you further, then, if you will answer me the question."

"You will have your answer out of doors in a moment, drumstick," Dalton said.

"Drumstick?" Lynch asked. "Very good," he said, and *he-he*'d. "This threat reveals you even more. To set me out of your dwelling and thrash me—that you would accomplish whether I go or do not go. For if you cut off trade with our only partner, take all the business into your smuggling hands, and then deal out such orders as there be for ships to a fellow public servant—our renowned missionary, a man under no compulsion to work, as I be—then I shall be out of all doors, even the ones that keep me housed." Beniah was frantically pulling on his coat lapels, rousing himself out of his drunkenness into an explosive state.

Tristram Dalton stood up and with a long backward sweep of his arm and a loud, cracking follow-through cuffed Beniah across the cheek. Theophilus and Abram jumped up. Abram angled himself between Dalton and Lynch, with his hands out toward their chests, holding them off.

"Philosophy has very little to do with tavern brawling," Abram said. "Apologize, Mr. Dalton, and let Mr. Lynch go home and dream away the rum."

"Struck and put out!" Lynch shouted. "Struck and put out!" His voice went shrill and wheedling. "This is to be my fate! I'll not go. No indeed."

"Mr. Dalton," Abram said, "you'd better say a word."

"I shall not," Dalton said. "Not to this tool and would-be slave. A willing puppet of the Crown and a vile one. He is even more dwarf in his soul than in his frame."

At the word "dwarf," Lynch tried to jump around Abram's right side and fling himself at Dalton. Abram blocked his way. Both men circled, with Abram between them as an axis. Beniah backed up, as if he might back down, but then he took a run at Dalton, throwing himself into the air. Abram went to block his path again. The little man's leap put him well into the air, and Abram, in one of those expanded moments, time slowing down, caught Lynch under his rib cage. Abram felt himself about to topple backward, and, resisting, he put his right foot back, caught Beniah so that he could feel himself control the little man's weight, and tried to throw him forward. Not strong enough to propel him backward, Abram ended pressing Lynch upward until he pinned him against the low ceiling.

The little man kicked Abram and bloodied his lip. That angered Abram, and he pushed him even harder into the ceiling. What might have been only an extraordinary moment of rough and tumble kept extending. Abram clutched and grabbed the windmilling Beniah closer to his waist so that the man's kicks could no longer reach him. He kept Beniah jammed against the ceiling, lifting up and strangling his gut.

"What ho!" Dalton said. "Look at the spider on the ceiling!"

Lynch was raving in a continuous whistling scream. His little arms and legs windmilled and he spat out his curses at Abram.

"You may crush that insect at your leisure," Theophilus said, and the tavern broke into applause and hurrahs.

Abram felt his strength failing, and before he could think better of it, he let go and ducked out of the way, so that Beniah dropped, spread-eagle, from the ceiling to the pine floor. Abram saw him bounce, as did the rest of the tavern.

"Kill the dwarf!" someone screamed.

And then everyone was standing around them, watching to see if Beniah would get up, what he would say, whether Abram would close on him once more.

Abram found himself with his arms open, ready to take the man on again if he should rise.

When he lifted his face, Beniah's forking, purpling veins stood out, and his hives were so much in evidence that it looked as if he had been thrashed with a leafy switch.

"Kill him! Crush his bloody big skull! Do it!" several taverners yelled.

"Enough," Abram said. "Enough."

He reached down to help Beniah up, but the little man dragged himself backward. He looked up and half rose, his hands on his bracing knees. Abram had never seen such hatred in a face.

"You have made a mistake, sir," Lynch said, and started choking.

The crowd started to jeer, and then they saw Beniah crouching on the floor and retching up his own blood. That quieted everyone. Somehow Beniah got to his feet, and with his hands cupped over his mouth, still choking, he stumbled out of the tavern.

Abram remembered his friend Cain Smith beating a man senseless outside Fraunces Tavern in New York, the blood lapping from that man's mouth. He had thought that a mistake. He knew this incident was. Beniah Lynch had always been jealous of Abram's success and would use his indiscretions against him cheerfully. The laws against adultery were still occasionally enforced.

The truth had become less of an option—at least for a while.

CHAPTER 15

——

Breaking

A bram waited a week before he appeared again at the cottage. Anne opened the door, her eyes on him, waiting, silent. She reached out and caught his wrist, turned, and led him inside as if he were a tethered pony. It was later than he usually came, and Theo was asleep on his pallet, his hands clutched together at his chin, a thumb in his mouth, navigating his dreams.

Anne hurried around the room, cleaning up the remains of the evening meal, from the table to the washtub. When she finished, she wiped her hands with a cloth with such attention that it was as if she wanted to polish them. Then she came, dutifully, and sat in the chair opposite his by the hearth, where the supper fire had left a few charred, bone-shaped logs.

"We have not seen you this week," she said.

"You are well?" he asked.

"*We* are well," she said, her eyes penetrating.

He turned his face half-away and looked down. The sides of his neck and his shoulder toward her felt as if they wanted to twist up into a spastic hump. "I wish no ill to come to you," he said, a sudden note of protest entering his voice.

"How could you at this time?"

He continued looking at the floor. "I will support your family. I will do what I can—all that I can."

He heard the drag of her chair moving back and its creak as she rose from it. Before he could rise, she was kneeling before him, seemingly composed, her hands resting on his thighs. She moved closer to him, as her hands traveled to his waist. He concentrated on her gauzy white bonnet.

She looked up at him, and her eyes were so intent that he could not refuse their inquiry. "You and I share in the flesh of this child," she said. "Say what you will, imagine what you like, in this world and that to come our families have been joined."

He took her hands from his waist and clasped them in his own. She pulled her hands back violently. She reached and grabbed his waist, embracing him once more, nestling her head against him. "It's true, it's true," she said. "It's true."

"It may be so," he said.

"*It is!*" she cried.

"It is and yet—" he stood up and finished, "it must not be." She grasped him tightly around his neck, and he became aware of the skin along the inside of his arms that would touch her if he put his arms around her waist. His fingertips knew the tension of the muscles in her back. The memories of so many pleasures lived in his hands and arms, and that knowing intended to counter his thoughts.

He tried to put her away from him, and she let him go, finally. She stood once again as she had at the news of her husband's death, her face in her hands, her body shaking.

He crossed behind his spindle-backed chair and held on to the back of it. "This is what we shall do," he said. "You must have a new life and one that is truly your own, not a mockery of a union with me. I have written to my brother Zack, who serves as an immigration agent for me in Ireland. He will be offering lands and a family to a suitable young man. I have instructed him to search out someone worthy of such a gift."

Anne started to cry out, "No, no, no!"

Theo woke up and called, "Momma?"

Abram had to finish with it now. "We will say as much as can possibly be said. The nearer we come to the truth, the less that can be questioned. So we will say that you were taken advantage of while visiting in the Points and that you can bear this town and its evils no longer. You will have your new start this way and not be blamed."

"No, no!" Anne screamed.

Theo ran over to her and clasped her leg. "Momma," he said. "Momma."

"This must be agreed between us," Abram said.

Anne looked up at him, her face raw with her tears, her neck muscles stretched with anger. "I will never betray this child's father!" she screamed.

"I will let it be known, then, that you have played the harlot. You will be taken away and given no provision. None at all."

She reached down and took Theo into her arms. She held him and shushed him as she looked upward, and great tears rolled down her cheeks. "This is so unworthy of you. You have been truly loved for the first time, and yet you choose this. You will think better of it. This is not you. You will come to hate yourself for it."

"I have thought . . ." Abram said, and found his own emotions welling up.

"If there are to be new lives," Anne said, pain twisting in her words, "let your wife have what she desires. She wants nothing from you. Let her go her way."

"I cannot put myself apart from society."

"You have the means," she said. "You do."

He said nothing.

"How can you put me apart from your society?"

To that, also, he could say nothing.

"Why?"

He covered his face with his hand. "I am married. What we have, it's true, is what I want. But with Sarah."

"She has nothing to give you. I have already given you everything . . . and will."

"Sarah alone can truly supply this happiness. If she cannot, then it is not mine to have."

Anne finally looked at him with the hatred he knew he must deserve, and he left the cottage.

CHAPTER 16

Maman

That next Sunday, two days after telling Anne, Abram was sitting in the front drawing room having tea with his mother. She held an embroidery loop, working on a flower pattern—tulips and day lilies—for a bolster. He could tell by her quick industry that she had something on her mind. The way she attacked the pattern stung Abram, as if a wasp were dropping down and down again on its victim. She hummed under her breath as she worked, which intensified the effect, and her head and shoulders bobbed as if suspended by wings.

He thumbed through a book of sermons and counted the moments until he could excuse himself.

"Abram," *Maman* said without looking up, "I have heard that you are to send Mrs. Farmington away."

So the time he dreaded had come. He had already told his mother the story of the attack, and he knew what he planned to say now, but would this fleet old wasp find his armor's weakness?

"I have always said that as a young mother she needs a family of her own. Now her condition demands that we take measures."

"In what way?" his mother asked.

"I have written to Zack. On my behalf he is offering one of our young immigrants favorable terms if he will take on a family. I told Zack to be choosy—whoever comes to us can hardly be disappointed in such a beautiful young woman."

Maman put a few more stinging stitches in. "Should not such a beautiful young woman choose for herself?"

"She agrees this is best."

"Does she? Jezreel says she is most unhappy. He says she does not wish to leave us."

Abram felt a quick, intense throbbing start behind his right eye. "He does not understand the situation. She cannot speak plainly to the other servants."

"No, no," *Maman* said. "I know her to be unhappy to be leaving, and I want to know why."

"I have told you. She has been taken advantage of. Is this not reason enough?"

"Abram," his mother said, her voice as sharp as in the days of his childhood when she reached out to slap him. "I ask you again. Why is she unhappy at being sent away? You must not condescend to your *Maman*. That makes me think you untruthful."

"She is unhappy at being sent away because," Abram said slowly, "she does not know what her new home is like, though we have described it to her many times. Still, such changes disturb."

Maman picked up her embroidery ring from her lap and put it back down again. She did not lift her eyes as she said, "Jezreel says that he thinks she has improper thoughts. That she is in love with you."

Abram went to the window, where he stood massaging his temples. "Her affections are of no account. We must concern ourselves with her circumstances."

"Abram," *Maman* said, as if rebuking a pet dog, "I know she loves you. I knew this when she came here. I knew this and more when she moved into *Le Petit Trianon*. Are you at fault in this? What have you done?"

Abram went back to the couch and sat down once more. He crossed his legs, pulled at his lapels, and whisked a smudge of dirt off his knee. "This is why I did not want her to participate in the work in Five Points," he said. "This is why I avoided contact with her for many months. When she began assisting, I went out to the cottage occasionally, as you know, to talk about these charitable enterprises. We became more friendly—you began to care for her as well. Now that she finds herself in difficulties, she naturally turns to me. Which is why she must be sent away."

"And this is all?" *Maman* asked.

Abram looked at her blankly.

"You have no greater fault?"

"*Maman*," Abram said, and paused. "If I was more in the wrong," he said, his voice growing threatening, "if I had made a serious mistake that could not be unmade, would you want to know this?"

Maman continued to glare at him. After a long moment, she blew out her lips, slanted her head to one side, let her own eyes drift to the window, and said, "Send her away, then. We will speak no more of it."

———

On the day Anne and Theo were taken away by the cart and driver Abram hired, he sat out the long hours in his shanty office. He kept hearing—or thought he was hearing—coach wheels on Water Street's cobblestone pavement.

Later, at the usual time of day, after supper, he went to the cottage. He noticed that Anne had taken the few chairs and the table that belonged to the quarters. He hardly begrudged her this, but the cottage was suddenly nothing more than four walls and an ash-strewn fireplace. He paced over the wide plank floors, remembering where Anne's washing stand had been, her cupboard, the crude armoire in which she hung her garments, the old chest in which she kept Theo's things. He looked again at the fireplace to see if its hook remained and perhaps a hanging teapot or pan. Everything was gone.

He looked along the windowsills, where Anne sometimes balanced small treasures, and over the walls, where not even the cleaner outline of a picture remained.

He had one more idea, and he went to Theo's corner, the place where the child's sleeping pallet had lain, and examined the floorboards. There he found the child's thumbnail carvings—stick figures of a woman and a child and a man. The man was very tall and wore a snail-shaped hat.

He slumped down and sat where he had read the child his bedtime stories. However wrong it had been, that did not keep him from loving her. Or Theo. His love had proved their greatest betrayal.

CHAPTER 17

—

Debacle

*A*bram had been carrying Submit's letter for two weeks now. He could feel its outline against his chest as it rested like a small packet of gunpowder in his coat pocket.

He had received word of Anne's arrival in Ulster County, New York. Sarah was due to return from her Boston sojourn in another three weeks. Would she come back of her own accord, and would she stay? How determinedly had her affections turned? Her cousin's letter should have impelled him toward Boston, even if he ended uselessly, socketed into the walls of a distant inn, alone. He should do something.

Strangely, the envelope in his pocket seemed to demand changes in the fashion of his dress. He gave up his captain's snail-shaped hat for a three-cornered model, deep velvet, with gray piping along the triangulating brim. His virtual uniform of the past years—his blue coats and breeches—stayed in his armoire. He wore lighter-weight coats as the spring season matured into summer, grays and sometimes even browns, which he had never thought suited him before. He began to grow a beard. It came out patchy and shockingly white in places, but he let it grow. In his new clothes he blended in more with his neighbors.

Up until a week before Sarah was due to return for the summer, Abram kept debating whether to take the coach into Boston. Simply by accompanying her back he might make some sign of his enduring concern.

On a Wednesday morning, two weeks before Sarah was due to arrive, as he walked down to the shipyard, he detoured over to State Street, which would take him by Wolfe's Tavern. He intended to reserve a place on the coach the next day.

Abram looked into Wolfe's and saw Beniah Lynch seated at one of the round tables in the middle of the room, having an early morning mug of tea. Sitting there, his chin low above the tabletop, he looked like the troll under the bridge.

The tavern's owner, William Davenport, was alone behind the bar, washing up his mugs and tankards. A tall crane of a man with a thatch of gray hair, he had a long face and prominent features; a heavy brow shaded his gray eyes, hollow cheeks paralleled his long nose, and his chin buckled all this up with a fleshy pad at the cleft.

"Davenport, good morning," Abram said.

The tavern keeper only nodded at him, as if reluctant to awake fully enough for a conversation.

"Beniah," Abram said in greeting. He had seen the man several times in the street since the incident and had apologized to him twice. He now thought to act as if he had received the forgiveness Lynch had never granted.

Beniah raised his mug of tea and looked aslant across its rim, suspicious, cross, but said nothing.

"Would the coach to Boston have a place tomorrow?" Abram asked Davenport.

"I've rarely seen it without one," the man said. "You want a passage?"

"I was thinking of going in," Abram said.

"Why would that be?" Beniah asked, suddenly interested, with all the inquisitorial frankness to which he obviously felt his injury still entitled him.

Abram hesitated, tried to find just the right words. "I thought to surprise Sarah. Give her some company on her return from her cousin's."

"Are you anxious about her?" Beniah asked.

"No, not at all," Abram said. "That's why I was making the inquiry. I'm not sure I'll be making the journey."

Lynch looked at him as if this plainly did not make sense.

Abram turned his attention back to Davenport. "There's always room, then, in the coach?"

"Yes," Davenport said. "If I know you are coming, I can send a boy and a cart around for your baggage."

Abram had wanted to buy the ticket as a way of reassuring himself. Now he was less and less sure. "I wanted to make the inquiry," Abram said. "I'm not settled in my own mind about going. We have a ship that's nearing her launch."

"I've seen her," Beniah said. "What I wouldn't give for customers who care for speed. Mine want as much packet as won't sink."

"I'll take a turn back by this afternoon," Abram said. "Let you know for sure. I won't have more than a light bag. No need for the cart."

"A short trip to rescue the wandering missus?" Beniah asked.

"I enjoy the *pleasure* of her company, Beniah," Abram said, and then wished he had said nothing.

"Very well," Davenport said, and stood with his hands out to either side on the bar. Was the taverner's sudden ease a way of assuring Abram that they understood each other?

Abram turned and walked out. As he made his way down State Street, he thought returning that afternoon to reserve a place seemed impossible. At this realization, he folded his arms, put his head down, huddled, and kept walking in the bright sunshine.

CHAPTER 18

The Pagan Campaign

During the carriage ride to Newburyport Sarah felt herself crossing over into another country. Here, in late June, the rhododendron bushes flowered everywhere along the way, their delicate and huge blooms a sweet pink touched with blue. The woods were filled with thronelike stone outcroppings. The carriage went for miles at a trot, racketing over the hills, past the many ponds and the stone-fenced farms on their shores. Sarah thought, much, of Mr. Copley. He had not asked her to come again to his studio, but had sent jonquils and a note, promising the completion of the portrait in the fall. "I am with your image every day," he wrote, "and so with you, which keeps me happy."

During her sittings they had spoken of the tour of the Continent he planned, of Genoa and Turin and the paintings by Caravaggio. "What it would be to see these things together," he had said, and watched how she took this. She had not made light of the matter; she had said nothing, but had weighed his words. They went on to have a long talk about standing together on the balcony of a palazzo as a dying sun burnished the churches of Ravenna.

Alone in the coach, apart from Mr. Copley, apart from Submit and Gaylord, and leagues yet from Abram, she realized this was possible—and much more. She had the earnings from her family's estate, Elysia: her share of the rents and earnings from the tenant farmers accrued and gathered in her name.

Before this, she had not seen so clearly how she could use her destiny to her own advantage. Quickly she thought of Lady Pemberton, the actress Nell Gwynne, Madame Du Barry, the women Madame De LaFayette wrote about. She had less reason to be confined to "little Boston" than Mr. Copley. They could be traveling companions and carry on their affair as they liked. Everyone among the aristocracy understood these things, and she certainly need not fear embarrassing herself with a child. Such a life would suit her, she decided, for her life was already unnatural, wasn't it?

Sarah became more and more excited by the idea, alert, alive. She had everything she needed, except for the wardrobe, and she knew exactly the new gowns she would have made up, the jackets, the hats, the furs.

Still, the notion remained a little disturbing. Did she fear God's judgment or her own isolation, she wondered? As to God, He had judged her already, and she would only be showing the world His cruelty. If she decided she wanted to live this way, she would. She felt almost as if she had undergone a religious conversion—her own Awakening.

Finally, the coach rolled past the marshlands and hit the brick road that began by the cemetery. The Bartlett Mall and its pond came into view, with glimpses through the trees of the granite stone of St. Paul's Church. Then they weaved onto State Street and pulled up at the coach stop at Wolfe's Tavern.

The driver's companion put the wooden steps into place and a bearded Abram took her hand to help her down. How much he had changed. Not only his beard, with its white patches. The skin around his eyes looked puffy in a bloated, sickly way. She had seen people with heart trouble look like that. He was wearing a tan suit the color of buckskin, which added to the diseased look. She liked the white soft-brimmed hat, but not on him.

Abram drew her toward him, and she pressed her head against his shoulder. He took her hand as they walked away from Wolfe's, up toward High Street and Copper Beech House.

"Did the journey seem long?" he asked.

"It's a long way. We had nice enough weather, I suppose."

"The last two weeks have been so humid I thought I would see shad swimming in the air."

He always made this joke. "Boston saw a run of cod over the Common," she said.

"Bad there, too?"

"Yes."

She was wondering what it would be like to be alone with him, now that her thoughts had turned in other directions. They were only across the threshold of the house, though, when he stepped back and left her standing side by side with *Maman*, flanked by Jezreel and Lucinda.

"I have to go back down to the yard," he said. "We are using the light of these long days for the finishing of a schooner. The yard will go slack if I'm not there."

"What kind of homecoming is this?" *Maman* said, looking cross.

Sarah felt relieved. "No part of a thing seems so long as its finish," she said. "The boy will be here with the cart in a trice, and I'll be wanting Anne to look over my things, to see what needs refurbishing. Abram will be back before we're finished."

"I will help you with your things," *Maman* said.

Sarah saw Abram glance at his mother.

"I'll let the men go when the light begins to fail," Abram said. "A general celebration in honor of your return."

He was out the door and gone before *Maman* clasped her elbow and virtually pushed her into the front drawing room.

"*Maman*," she said, protesting.

"Sit, sit. *Assieds-toi*. It's necessary that we speak of Anne."

She took her place on the settee while *Maman* slowly shuffled around, letting her cane drop, putting her hands back as she felt for the armrests. Finally, *Maman* let her weight fall back into the rocker.

"What is it, *Maman*?" Sarah asked.

"Anne is gone to Ulster," *Maman* said. She wiped her mouth with her clawlike hand.

"Has Abram sent her there on some service?"

Maman pulled at her right leg with both hands so that both her feet were closer together. "She is to be married."

"Why was I not told before this? She is my maid."

"This has been a very bad time. Anne was helping with the acts of mercy in Five Points, and someone mistreated her."

"She was attacked?"

"Yes. *Ainsi*, she is to have a child. Abram has written to his brother

– 125 –

to send a young husband for her. This is a sad thing, but some good can come of it now."

"Did they catch the man?"

Maman shook her head. "No, no. Anne does not even know who it was. As I said, this happened in the Points, down by the harbor. Probably a sailor who is—" *Maman* waved her hand.

"A sailor?"

"We do not know."

"I think I could find him."

"That is not possible."

"*Maman*, you know what we spoke of concerning Abram and Anne. Did this not happen?"

"No, no. Abram hardly spoke to her."

"Did he visit her in the cottage?"

"A few times. To talk about the acts of mercy."

"Acts of mercy? I think the topic might more properly be called 'favors.' "

"You must not make such insinuations. No. Abram has waited these long months for your return. Year after year, you come and go— you hardly live in your own home. No, no, you must not speak in this way."

"Not speak what we both know is the truth?"

"Abram kept away from Anne. You are changing what I say." *Maman*'s head was quavering so violently that Sarah became afraid for her.

"*Maman*, I understand what you mean. I will speak to Abram of this."

Maman stamped her slippered feet. She was twisting in her chair. "You talk of Madame Du Barry. You say that Mrs. Bredforet approves of her help doing such services. Now you see that you do not care for such things. Be glad that Abram kept away from Anne. He may not always. You must be staying home now."

"She's not having a child because he kept away from her."

"Anne was attacked. I saw her. I talked with her. She was attacked."

"I am certain she was, *Maman*. I will leave you to rest. I want to see to my things with Lucinda."

Sarah was at the door when *Maman* called after her. "You understand what I am saying. You must not make any more trouble."

———

Abram arrived back at the house well after suppertime. Sarah heard the door and then his steps, coming straight up to their room.

"I'm sorry to be so late," he said. He took her hands and gave her a short kiss.

As he changed into a light summer sleeping gown, he asked whether she had spoken with *Maman*. He opened a window, which she had not thought to do, and the cooling night air started to pull out the blanketing stuffiness of the room.

They had still not said more than hello, hardly that, and the silence started to fall on them.

"I will miss Anne," she said.

"Yes," Abram said.

"Was she badly beaten?"

"What?" Abram asked.

"When she was attacked."

"No."

"No?"

"Not that I could see. But then I wouldn't."

"Yes, yes."

She went to her armoire for her own nightclothes, but she suddenly felt embarrassed about undressing in front of Abram. She pulled her nightdress over her head and went to her dressing table to let her hair down. The combs and pins came out, and her scalp bristled and prickled and started to breathe again. She began brushing the thick strands.

"*Maman* said you made arrangements for Anne to be married."

"I wrote to Zack. I expect he will find someone."

"She does not even know the father. Or did she?"

Abram waited until she had almost turned back to him to prompt his answer. "She told me little about the incident. She did not want to accuse anyone."

"If you saw no signs of an attack and know nothing of the circumstances, how can you be sure that she was unwilling?"

"I thought of that, but I did not see it making any particular difference."

"You sent this woman to be your sister's neighbor. I imagine you are providing her a home. You have arranged for a marriage. Her character is not a matter of concern to you?"

"I think I know her."

Now Sarah did turn back to look at Abram as he lay on his side of the bed. "The father might want to be the father."

"He did not come forward."

"*Maman* said Anne began to help you with your charitable endeavors. If she did so for the sake of an affair, she was deceiving you and you do not know her."

"People do many things with one intention while courting another. But I believed her about the assault. Her spirit showed the violence."

Sarah was stopped, thinking about actions courting other intentions. "I suppose her sharing in the work did give you a chance to know her. When she appeared at our door that day, her waif in tow, I suspected she came to be near to you. She was much taken with you."

"I barely spoke to her. You insisted we should take her on."

"And yet you sent her away without consulting me."

"You were in Boston," he said and snorted out a breath. She had turned back toward her glass, but she knew he was lying with his arms and probably his ankles crossed. Sometimes he folded his hands as if inviting her to slip a Bible into his clasp and send him into the ground. "I wanted her away from the town before her condition declared itself to the eye. Why do you always insist on arguing? You are hardly home."

"Why should you have been so embarrassed?"

"I will not argue with you. You have declared that you want very little more than to be kept by me. Perhaps we should take separate rooms if the illusion of intimacy has become uncomfortable."

"Is my notion that you are the father of Anne's child an illusion?"

"I will not answer such a question. It is unworthy of you."

"The action would have been most unworthy of you."

"What difference would it have made to you?"

The way he looked at her, she thought suddenly that he might know something about Copley. His question continued burrowing under her own deceptions to something deeper that she had not expected: she could still be jealous.

"I think we might be more comfortable in separate rooms," she said.

"Tomorrow we will have it arranged."

She continued to sit at her dressing table. "I am sure I will not be able to sleep this way tonight."

He got up from the bed and, without taking off his nightshirt, stuffed his legs through the new tan breeches that looked so ludicrous on him. He did not hurry, but moved at a pace that told Sarah she was not running him off; he was agreeing with her in what they disliked.

With the bedroom door open, he said, "No more about Anne—I

will not hear it. You have the room. I will set up another."

He finally stopped talking into that open doorway and left. Abram and his mother kept saying no, didn't they? They would soon hear hers.

CHAPTER 19

Snooping on Yourself

Sarah hated Abram's hypocrisy. His self-righteousness. She could understand his giving way to temptation; but then to keep parading around the town as The Missionary made her want to take her cues from the Senecas, who carved open an enemy's chest and let him watch his own false heart pump out his life—before they roasted and ate him.

There was the slimmest chance, of course, that Anne actually had been attacked. She was pregnant after all, and Sarah's barrenness might not be exclusively her own fault. Abram's obvious guilt told her something had happened between them, but perhaps this mysterious sailor had intervened before Abram's desires were satisfied. She was maddened by the way others had children so easily, unavoidably, almost accidentally. Perhaps Abram had suffered his own procreative embarrassment and was then repelled by the woman. Or worse, perhaps he had fallen in love with her and this happiness brought them a child. Or worst of all, perhaps he had fallen in love with her, not touched her, but lost her to the attacker. He might still be yearning for her.

Much to her surprise, Sarah found she could not rest until she knew.

As she had once taken the keys to Abram's rooms in New York and examined every wardrobe and lock box, finding, ultimately, his diary and answers to her questions about his feelings for her, so now she went through his wardrobe and desk and even paid a surreptitious visit to his office shanty. Nothing.

She went out to the servants' quarters to see if Anne had left any revealing remnant. She found the place shockingly bare and was angered by a wholesale move that included what she considered theft.

Sarah thought of writing directly to Anne, but another correspondent came to mind and a way past her defenses.

My dear sister Dorsey,

I do hope this comes to hand with Hugh and the children and that precious grandchild of yours flourishing in your new highlands.

Abram proposes that he finish a new schooner at the yard and let life go on without him until he does so. He asks me to write, though, in regard to Anne Farmington's welfare. I certainly needed little prompting to this task, for her drastic change in circumstance and its horrifying cause have preoccupied my attention ever since my return to Newburyport.

Dear sister, how is she faring? I find it much more difficult than Abram to believe that Anne looks forward to a new home without a few fears or misgivings. (Men have no such feelings, as do women, toward their particular place.) Surely you live in some of the most commodious country this land affords, but does it suit her? Her experience has been in the town. She has lived with her neighbors at her elbows. Has she taken to her pastoral existence with equanimity?

You see that Abram's concerns may be formal and mechanic, while mine declare themselves in affectionate ways. If you would write to both orders of inquiry, we would both be much appeased.

Maman continues to gain in strength in this place, and I sincerely believe that whatever little infirmity remains must be sheerly the product of age. She instructs me in all things, and I gain vastly by her wisdom, although, as I'm sure you can appreciate, a woman's home must remain her dominion. *Maman* has had a great hand in Abram's charity work in this town, and, indeed, the whole village celebrates them both.

     With tenderest affection, I am,
     your sister,
     Sarah

Sarah waited for more than five weeks, through the most suffocating days of summer, for a reply. When it came, it was addressed only to Abram, but Sarah recognized Dorsey's writing on the envelope.

Dear Brother,

Sarah has written with inquiries about Anne Farmington's comportment, and I wish to satisfy her, but thought to do so through whatever you choose to relate of the following.

I cannot say that Anne is happy to be in this place. We have done what we can for her, and she abided by our advice while Hugh and the boys built her cabin and set her up with the necessities. Her house is at the far end of a lovely meadow, backing into the forest, with a stream running from behind along the right border of the property, and a view down the slope that leaps into the air and alights on the next range. It's a spot that many might envy. Zack's young man, who we hear is making his passage, should be delighted with it. Indeed, if Anne looked forward to his arrival, he could not expect better prospects: a very handsome family and the means to make their place in this world.

Anne has begun to say, though, that she will have nothing to do with any such young man, and that we must find another place for him when he arrives. She is adamant. She proposes to make her living by her needle, which cannot be done in this sparsely populated place. We can feed her, of course. Hugh and the boys will put in her garden next spring, and we have enough, I'm happy to admit, to see several families through any winter. Yet her refusal causes me distress, not only on the young man's account, but for what it portends with Anne. Is she waiting on the father of this child?

To date we have ascribed this willfulness to the shock of her transplantation and the uncertainty of what she may face in a man who will be her husband before becoming her suitor.

To me, though, she does not seem undone by what has befallen her. Her ways are quiet and purposeful. However fantastic they may be to the public imagination, the woman's purposes seem truly her own, albeit unrealistic in this country.

How would you have me instruct Anne? Can you think of what counsel Hugh and I might give that would help her see her best advantage?

I leave it to you to satisfy Sarah's own particular and what she terms "affectionate" inquiries from this.

And please, if you would, send your fretful sister some word

as to how we should carry on.
As ever,
with the fullest devotion,
Dorsey

For the briefest instant Sarah regretted the guise in which she had written to Dorsey. But then her fury at what Abram might have done—to her, to Anne, even to his own sisters and brothers—flooded this barrier and pumped blood and murder until her head was swimming with it.

She put the open envelope with the letter inside on Abram's desk in the downstairs study with his other mail and waited for him to speak of it.

A week went by, and Abram said nothing. He made every effort to avoid her, though. He used their separate bedrooms and the work at the yard as a shield against her. The only time they saw each other became the dinners and suppers they took with *Maman*. The old woman, with her singsong Huguenot accent, rambled on about charitable cases in Five Points until Sarah thought she would burn those shanties down and rejoice in every charred body.

They had finished supper one evening, a light meal of smoked ham, the first of the new corn, and a molasses-laced bread topped with a vanilla custard, when Sarah decided she must use her only opportunity. Abram and his mother were at either ends and Sarah on her husband's right around the oblong cherry table. The candles of the chandelier were lit, although the late evening light pouring through the window blued the heart of each flame. Jezreel stood back behind Abram's shoulder. The room did not feel exactly warm, but as if too full of the heavy air. She waited for *Maman* to end her recitative on the plight of their adopted poor.

"I was thinking of Anne Farmington the other day," Sarah said. "How is she faring in Ulster County, Abram?"

"She must be well," Abram said. "I would have heard to the contrary."

"I saw a post in Dorsey's hand. Did she speak of Anne?" Sarah saw *Maman* turn and look at her; she could feel that look along the edge of her ear.

"She did write. She said little of Anne." Abram looked away from Sarah toward his mother, as if he would drag her eyes in that direction, pointing out the reason for his reticence.

"I must confess, *Maman*, that I happened to read this letter to

Abram, and it was much more forthcoming than he represents," said Sarah, looked directly at *Maman*. "I had written to Dorsey and thought her posting the letter to Abram merely an economy of writing—that she meant the letter for us both. But I am very glad of knowing what this letter contains, and I think we should all consider its meaning together."

Abram's puffy eyes expanded. "I might read it out so that we could all be privy to what should have remained private," he said, exasperated.

"We are a family," Sarah said. "We respect your position as its head, but you may put us in a position where we cannot trust you."

"*Maman*," Abram said, appealing. "This is not something I wish to discuss."

"Not something you wish to discuss with your wife?" Sarah asked. "Your tone seems to promise you will discuss it later with *Maman*. You shan't use her to fend me off, Abram. How can that be right?"

"What did Dorsey say?" *Maman* asked.

Sarah settled back in her chair.

Abram asked Jezreel to clear the table, quickly. Every footfall of the servant's three little marches between the table and the serving tray kept an ever-slowing time, before he finally went to the kitchen.

"What Dorsey says, *Maman*, as Sarah already knows, is that Anne finds her new circumstances difficult. She has always lived in a town, I believe, and the change is a great one."

"To be expected," *Maman* said.

"She is refusing to marry," Sarah said. "Why do you use these circumlocutions with *Maman*, Abram, as if she might think poorly of you on account of Anne's actions? You are doing—this family is doing—more than a little for this woman, and she refuses to fulfill what must have been an explicit agreement. You did ask her about the marriage, Abram? She did agree to this?"

"I thought she agreed."

"Thought?" Sarah asked. "How could you have sent her away without being sure."

"She could hardly think, wife. You know what she had been through."

"Do I?"

"What do you mean by that?" *Maman* asked sternly.

"Anne's leave-taking has become mysterious to me. She has not agreed to what we believed she had. She does not behave, Dorsey says, as one would expect. This was done so quickly. She was my handmaid and Abram never wrote me about this matter. I am beginning to suspect he has his part in this mystery."

"You are always suspecting," *Maman* said.

"Abram, you must be ashamed to involve your mother in this," Sarah said.

Abram slammed the table with his fist. "In what?"

"Your 'role,' " Sarah said, much calmer now that she had moved her husband nearly to violence.

"What are you accusing me of, then?"

"Anne does not act like a woman who is beginning a new life. Even Dorsey says she acts as if she were waiting for the father to appear."

"Dorsey says she does not understand her actions."

"Well, we do, don't we?"

"I understand nothing of this." Abram pulled back from the table so quickly that he had to catch his chair from toppling over. "You should not speak against Anne. Anne . . . ." and with that he left the table.

Maman refolded her serviette slowly and tucked it back through its ring, and Sarah followed her lead.

CHAPTER 20

Descent to the Points

*H*er suspicions seized Sarah like a demonic force. She reminded herself of her age, the price she had paid for maturity. If Abram had committed adultery, she herself was planning on spending her life in the same practice. Yet she could not keep her feverish speculations at bay.

She was reminded of her past extravagances: her first meeting with Abram and how she had chased him out into the hunting fields of her father's estate disguised as a lad, how she had bitten him on the cheek on the way to their marriage, so unsure of her prize once she had it. She had schooled herself against her own enthusiasms, and if she had lost contact with the young woman who believed in her own communion with God's presence, she thought herself far better for it. *When I was a child . . .* she thought. That applied. What did she know in the realm of the spirit but nails and thorns and a rending spear?

Had she not become preposterously concerned with a marriage

that had long ago atrophied into friendship merely because she was living in this barnacle town? She would find out what there was to know and be done with it.

Sarah demanded that Abram let her carry the daily charity basket to Five Points. He objected repeatedly but finally gave in, saying, "You're not likely to be thanked for it. That is not to say by me. I mean . . ." and with an ugly grimace he turned away.

As Lucinda handed over the basket, she said, "There's so much trouble there—a world of trouble. You might as well be walking down into Hades. You sure you want to go?"

Sarah had walked through the area for years, albeit more cautiously than in other parts of the town. She had her purpose and would not be dissuaded. She wanted to see the house that Anne Farmington once occupied. The people who lived there now might at least have been curious enough about their predecessor to listen to the local gossip.

As she entered the Points, Anne saw a tall woman with a girth like a man's sweeping the steps in front of her shanty. She wore no cap but had her hair wound and piled up into a coppery lump. Her lips protruded so much and her mouth was so large that they dominated her face, like a fish. Her eyes, too widely spaced, emphasized this fishy-headedness.

"Hello," Sarah called. "Where would Anne Farmington's old house be?"

The woman looked back at her as if she had not heard.

"I have this basket for the people who live there," Sarah called, and her voice rose involuntarily through the sentence so that she sounded doubtful and unsure of herself.

The woman gave the steps one more punishing spank and looked up at her. "You would be Mrs. White."

"Oh yes," Sarah said.

"The Missionary is finishing his ship."

"That's right. He asked me to bring the basket today."

"When did you come back from Boston?"

Did she want to answer this? She walked a few steps closer to the woman. "I'm here to bring the basket."

"I asked when you came back from Boston. That town's no bigger than ours, I hear."

Sarah came up to where she could have a conversation, regretting she had ever glanced at the woman. "Almost a month now. We haven't been introduced."

- 137 -

"People like me aren't introduced. We are sometimes shouted at standing on our steps."

"You're right. Forgive me."

The woman looked off down the street and to the left. She pointed. "It's among those roofs holding each other up like staggering tipplers. The second one—the smallest in the heap."

"Thank you. I really am very much in your debt."

As Sarah turned to go, the woman stepped down from where she swept so that Sarah turned once again to her.

"Why does your husband come here?"

"He claims it's charity."

"He's famous in these streets." The woman gave her steps a spank. "You're off a lot, ain't you?" she asked pointedly.

"Is it our business to speak so?" Sarah asked, not harshly but with a kind of apology that she could not follow the woman's lead.

"He may be a great man."

"I'll just be taking the basket, then."

"I'm not drunk. It's ten o'clock in the morning. I want to know what you think of your husband."

"What I think of my husband?"

"We'll not be sitting to tea together, I think. And you being gone so much, you won't be yelling at me at the sweeping neither. So I want to know. Is you going to be rude and not answer?"

Suddenly, Sarah thought that she might have to be. But she found herself saying, "I loved him very much when we married. I am a disappointment to him."

"You? You're like an angel's jewels."

Sarah found herself moved—her anger abating. "You remember Anne Farmington?"

"We knew her. She was the queen of this place, and we was glad she come back to us when she was helping the Missionary."

Sarah thought of all her questions, but she couldn't ask them. She raised her hand in farewell and hoped to find her voice. "I'm to go where she lived. Goodbye then."

"Another moment, if you please."

Sarah could hardly bear to turn back around.

"It's the Baskins there now. Crude people. I'd leave the basket and fare thee well. The woman's a talker."

This caused a roiling dread. A talker? What had this woman been, then?

She walked the half-block to the Baskins and called out, seeing that the slant-hung door was half-open. "Mrs. Baskins?"

The woman who appeared, a girl at one hip and a toddler at the opposite knee, was short and dark-haired with wide hips that her skirts hung from like a circular tablecloth. Baby-faced, fair-complected, dimpled when she smiled, she seemed cheery enough.

"I have brought a basket," Sarah said.

"The Missionary has come to us! Children," she said and patted her knees, "the Missionary has come to us. Please come inside." She reached forward with her short, ham-hock arms, took Sarah by the shoulders, and pulled her in.

The one-room house looked neglected and even battered, with piles of rags, a stack of dirty bowls about to topple, two small rugs skidded out of place and curling at their edges, and all the chairs but one knocked over. The air was thick with dust. Two more children were chasing the clingers now, and the effect of so much hurly-burly was like being surrounded by scampering mice grown to the size of elephants—rogues creating a dust storm.

"Children!" Mrs. Baskins said and laughed an embarrassed laugh. "Children!" She looked around her quickly, as if targeting one of them might help her regain control. "Children! I'll make porridge of you!"

"Mmmmm, mmmmmm," went up a chorus.

"Stop! Stop now! I'll give you to the pirates. Stop now. I will."

The three boys, for three of them were boys, including the toddler, slung out imaginary cutlasses and started slashing viciously at each other, while their sister put her feet and hands together as if she were waiting to be flogged.

Sarah clapped her hands together three times, and the boys slowed in their attacks on one another. "My name is Mrs. White," Sarah said. "You must all go outside now while I talk to your mother."

Sarah had captured the little tow-headed boy's attention, but not his darker-haired brother, and the dark one took the opportunity to push the other child flat. He was raising his face up in triumphant satisfaction when Sarah grabbed him by the hair and slung him through the door. The others looked at her, then at each other. Spontaneously they formed a single-file line and marched out to play.

"It is so much better out of doors," Mrs. Baskins said as they went. But she gave Sarah such a look of vindictiveness and resentment that it seemed she had turned into one of her evil children.

Then her cheery expression returned before she asked, "Why did you come? Of course you have brought us the basket. But why you? The Missionary or those that do for him usually distribute his kindness." All the twittering and feather-ruffling could not conceal her prying intent.

"To bring the basket," Sarah said. "Simply to bring it."

"Oh, you are kindness itself. Charity and kindness and good fellowship together. The most giving of women, and you such a great one. We will have to be treating you with the greatest of courtesies— all dignity and respect."

This last sounded like a question, or certainly a statement that required a response; the woman seemed in some obscure way to wish Sarah would be afraid of her. Sarah decided to speak plainly and outwit this circuitous talker. "Is it no more than any Christian should do for his neighbor? Do unto others."

"Some has the means, though, so blessed by the good Lord, and some of us don't," the woman said, "which brings us to a difficulty."

"I see no difficulty," Sarah said. "The obligation must be measured according to the means."

"You see, and then you have the words to say such fine things. Such words and such thoughts as are beyond our poor understanding. But it's for you to know the scales in such a measure, not for us, no, not for us. And that's very right and proper, isn't it?"

"I wanted to know," Sarah said, deciding to push her way through, "if this was the house Anne Farmington occupied. During her married life, that is. Do you know?"

"Oh yes, I believe it is, and afterward too, I mean after her husband was killed at your man's shipyards. I mean, the accident, after the accident. She lived here for two or three seasons. No one lives here long, they say, although my brood and me may outlive the house itself, or knock it down. The children be such brigands and grow like weeds in bricks."

How this creature smiled after every long-winded statement, a smile that defied Sarah to address what the woman had actually said.

Sarah was still thinking how to pursue the matter when the woman spoke again.

"Anne Farmington almost matched the Missionary himself in fame in these streets. You would have thought an angel had come down and lived in this place. We was over on Lime, not such a good street as this but a palace of a shanty. We wouldn't have given it up except for our late financial difficulties, which I could tell you about, yes, I could—how this world swings around on the likes of us. But to tell you about Anne and avoid such a common tale of woe, a tale of lost chances and the fickleness of menfolks, something you happily know nothing of with your Missionary—that is, to tell you about Anne: the people here would have spread rose petals before her wherever she went.

"After her husband was killed at the shipyards, after he fell and broke his neck and died, every man in the Points came by this shanty, and many from the surrounding area and even further where the news traveled of this queen of a woman in need of a husband."

"One of those men she rejected," Sarah asked, "do you think he came back and did this thing?"

The woman seemed not to hear her, absorbed in her own muttering. "Nothing but dogs, mongrels, curs, half-breeds, mutts. She had already married one and would have none of that."

"She's living a new life now," Sarah said.

"The Missionary, the Missionary and you took her away, didn't ye? She loved that cottage you leant her, we heard. Talked about living in a lord's park."

"She's in much wilder country now," Sarah said. "The forest must be two steps from her vegetable garden."

"We heard that too, and how the Missionary is making a whole new life for her. She's to be married, some unknown fellow from Ireland, when she wouldn't have anyone she could take a look at."

"She needs a husband," Sarah said, knowing that if Mrs. Baskins had any comment to make, it would be forthcoming.

"I didn't know if you would speak to that," Mrs. Baskins said. "She has one child already, and the second's not near the shock, although my Edward caused me a good deal more distress as to the birth. The Irish lad may be a good father."

"So you heard about the crime."

"We did. The fellow must have been as quiet as he was cruel, for no one talked of it until the Missionary came and let us know about Anne—only in his questions, you understand. But then a word in these streets and everyone hears. And then Mrs. Flaherty and Joe, they remembered hearing a struggle in their shed but thought it must have been cats. The Missionary didn't know if it happened in the shed, but thought it might have."

"No one else knew about this?" Sarah asked. "No one talked of the crime before my husband explained Anne's decision?"

"Some tongues were wagging after it happened, I'm sure. When the Missionary came and told a few, I suppose the ones who knew thought it all right to speak of the matter. Even in the Points such an act is not common. A most terrible act."

Sarah almost said "horrible" in reply, but her voice suddenly caught and the first syllable, "hor," came out like an accusation.

"She weren't," Mrs. Baskins said, taking a breath.

"I meant *horrible*," Sarah said. "What happened to Anne is simply too horrible. It must move anyone of sensibility."

"Oh yes," Mrs. Baskins said, but gave Sarah another of her pinched and hateful looks as if she had been caught out too clearly in her lack of genuine warmth.

"I must be going, then," Sarah said.

"The children must be wanting back in," Mrs. Baskins countered, giving a final dig at Sarah's presumption in dismissing them.

"As their mother, I would keep them outside for as long as nature allows," Sarah said. Then she turned with every bit of grandeur that Mrs. Baskins had thought to impute to her, and with a slow nod and a regal closed-eye smile gave Mrs. Baskins her parting blessing.

The woman looked at her with a triumphant contempt.

"Goodbye," Sarah said. "Enjoy the basket and let us know of your needs." She turned toward the door.

"Arnold, the oldest boy, he's already started to work, 'prenticing at the new saltpeter works. He could use more schooling. . . ."

"Let us know," Sarah called back, pulled the door closed behind her, and found herself, much relieved, back in the wasted street.

She was surprised to find that the weather had changed completely. The sun had been blocked out by gathering clouds, the earth darkened with the angry gloom of a thunderstorm. She could taste the sea as the rounding wind swept over the open ocean, came up the estuary, and invaded the town. She half staggered as a squalling gust blew her toward the shanties close on her left. She ought to go home, get out of the storm, away from these streets.

Even as she thought this, the rain came on, those first big splattering drops, and then its frequency increased. She would soon be swimming in her long wet skirts. People were dodging into their shanties. She leaned back against the wall of a home built flush with the street and listened to the thunder boom at her—felt it roll up under her feet and catch at her heart. The lightning flash to her right must have hit Plum Island. The next would strike the town.

She was still close to Water Street and the two distilleries at the district's base points. She knew they served customers, and she felt wet enough to seek any place she could sit down for a moment or two. She went into the house distillery of the Spaniard, Cornejo, and sat down at one of the two tables on the side of the long house where he accommodated his unofficial customers.

Tall, stout, with a wide, flat face, his complexion unnaturally pale from the New England weather, Cornejo saw her but said nothing.

"Innkeeper," she said, not knowing what else to call him, "would you bring something to warm me? Some tea?"

"*Qué?*"

"Tea?" she asked again. She knew no Spanish, but tea must be tea in any language.

The man nodded his head, but his expression retained a stiff worrisomeness about it. "*Té?*"

"*Por favor,*" she said.

He went into the distillery's residence and in good time brought her a teapot, a tin mug, and a small bottle of rum. To please him, she poured a finger or two of the clear liquid and took a clutching drink that ignited in a fireball over the back of her throat. She poured out the tea and quickly soothed her throat, nodding her thanks all the while as her sinuses filled with the tears she had suppressed.

She heard the door. Turning round, she saw Beniah Lynch come in, strut up to the makeshift counter, and actually pound on it with his fist. Cornejo took one look at the little man and went back into the other side of the house. Lynch turned and looked out over the room, wearing a baleful and contemptuous expression. When he focused on her, she returned his gaze, daring his recognition.

"Mrs. White," he said.

Cornejo came back and put a few coppers on the makeshift bar and started counting out the money. The stumpy figure swept the coins up into his palm, put them in the side pocket of his long coat, and waved Cornejo off to show he considered the account settled. Sarah gathered that Lynch must be the Spaniard's landlord.

Then he turned back to Sarah again and grinned. "Mrs. White," he said, this time with a welcoming inflection.

"Mr. Lynch," she said and nodded slowly.

"You must have been caught by the storm."

"Yes," she said. "I was just delivering a basket in the Points when the clouds burst. Mr. Cornejo offered me tea and a thimble of something stronger while I waited."

"A literal fulfillment of 'the just and the unjust,' " said Beniah, "but you'd think the Lord would make an exception for His dispensers of Christian charity." He gave his forced laugh, *he-he.*

Without being asked, he sat at the table with her.

"Señor Cornejo," he called sharply.

The Spaniard glanced into the room and hurriedly brought a large bottle and tin mug.

Beniah tried to lace her tea, which she refused, then held his mug out to her. "To this unexpected celebration," he said, "this chance meeting with a woman I have often wanted to converse with. Too infrequently, much too seldom, have I seen you through the years at our neighbors' homes or about the town, and I have thought on the excellent destiny that brought the good Captain White such a lady. Your health and good fortune," he said.

She did not know how to reply to this unwelcome toast.

"I'll run get you a carriage myself in a moment," he said. "You must be wanting out of the wet. It shan't stop for the rest of the day, I think. For this one moment, though, I would like to know how you found the Points. You see, I own some of these properties, and, like your husband, I labor to see that my friends are well satisfied— though of course our relationship is much more in the fiduciary realm. Nevertheless, I like to think myself no less anxious that they should find their circumstances comfortable, however small the rent." He grinned that horrible self-satisfied grin again.

Sarah found the man so hateful that she refused to lie to him. "Mr. Lynch," she said, "I had my own purposes for coming here, as you have yours." She took another sip of her tea.

"And these be?" he asked.

She looked at him as if he were a bug. Then she answered. "I came to find Anne Farmington."

"Anne Farmington? The one sent away to Abram's lands in New York? She is not here."

"Not her person."

"Then what did you come to discover?"

"What she found in charity."

"She grew very close to your husband in this work, I believe," Beniah said.

"She was our servant," Sarah said, insulted. "She was my maid."

"You are away so much. Yet she never went with you?" Beniah questioned.

"She did the mending here for me at home."

"Yet she worked much with the Missionary here."

"As you say, Mr. Lynch."

"Someone has taken advantage of her, it's said."

"That's a polite expression for it," Sarah said.

"Indeed, that's so. It's a wonder no more was heard, the Points being so small. When such a thing happens, even between one of our salty visitors and a lass whose resistance might be questioned, the man's usually found easily enough. Most are brazen enough about it."

Perhaps this toad knew something. "I have been wondering about the attacker not being found," she said. She looked at him and dared him to guess her thoughts.

"A woman may call the same man an attacker whom she wants

her babe to know as his father," Beniah said.

"So you see," Sarah said, "I had to come to the Points to understand the ways of these people. This is not how 'we' conduct ourselves."

"Those that rise a long ways may fall as steep," Beniah said.

She looked at him as if she did not understand what he said, although she knew he was angling toward Abram. After another moment, she said, "There are those naturally great of character, and those naturally small."

"Betimes," Beniah said, "the greatest can have an unsuspected weakness, so that like a great barrier with a breach, a drop and then a flood comes through." He raised his mug to her. "I'll go fetch that carriage," he said.

———

Two days later, after a good night's sleep, Sarah awoke to a cool August morning. The light that came in when she folded back the shutters of her windows stretched out with the end of summer. On the lawn below her bedroom she could see a few small yellow leaves: not yet the fall's chill, but the summer's exhaustion. The cuff of the sea that could be glimpsed from the house looked deeper and heavier, no longer bleached white as it was in the height of the summer sun.

She thought of her preoccupation with Abram's attachment to Anne as part of the season's excess, its volatile heat and humidity, its too-rapid growth and subsequent breakdown. Her encounters with Mrs. Baskins and Beniah Lynch made her wonder again why she should care. She took in slow, deep breaths of the cooling air and felt as if she were breathing again. Her own life as she had determined to live it seemed to be possible.

She thought of returning to Boston. She thought of Mr. Copley. He might have already finished the picture. She had been so preoccupied with the shabby dwellings and doings of Five Points that she had not written him the several polite and amiable missives she had intended. Her writing would give him permission to disclose his thoughts to her in return. She would also write to Submit. She had not heard as yet about the birth of her child, as last's week letter only brought word of her cousin's improving health and ruptured patience.

She would also write to Josiah Quincy. As she could not rely on Dorsey's candor or even her willingness to communicate, she must have her own reports, and she believed that Josiah, that old rake, would understand the need for intelligence in matters of the heart.

August 22, 1769

Dear Mr. Quincy,

I am writing concerning a most delicate matter. Upon my return to this town, I found that my handmaid had been sent away to my husband's lands in Ulster County, New York. It seems the woman, a young widow, has been cruelly treated and is to bear an illegitimate child.

My husband, I'm afraid, has been less than forthcoming about the circumstances surrounding this unfortunate event—no doubt in deference to my sensibilities. I find, though, that I cannot dismiss the woman's welfare from my mind and would have some independent report as to her situation. We could do so much more for her, I feel, if she would divulge the identity of the child's father. Such reports as we possess tell of a landed seaman. These reports appear more indistinct than the face of such a scoundrel could ever be to his victim.

Perhaps now that some time has passed, this young widow, Anne Farmington, might be persuaded to give a more fulsome account. My husband felt that to press her too closely on the matter would be to deal her a second injury, and this may have had the unintended effect of making her feel as if she had some complicity in the act. With Abram's influence withdrawn, she may be able to speak of matters he encouraged her not to, however unintentionally.

I know you will find the right sort of man for this work and that he will make the best use possible of our purse. I have always been able to trust your perspicacity and discretion, Josiah, as I do now in entrusting this most urgent and sensitive matter to your care. I am fully prepared to hear whatever may be reported, howsoever close the news brings this matter to my own home. And I remain, confident in my confidant,

Your most solicitous friend,
Sarah Singleton Nicolls White

August 22, 1769

Dear Mr. Copley,

I had meant to write earlier, many times. You have been so much in my thoughts, so many letters composed themselves in my imagination—as indeed did several that were committed to paper without seeing the post—that I have some difficulty discerning whether I have written or no.

At these times of mental composition, I have found myself turning my chin, positioning my elbow, taking a breath and focusing once more, all to be "in form." I know you are painting a picture, but I seem at times almost to be the clay you are molding. Away from your influence, the boredom of life as I live it now seems, at times, almost crushing. I would be that woman I felt myself becoming in your presence. Is this too bold? But then I am only speaking of the spiritual experience of participating in your art.

Yet, at times, it seemed, I caused more than the agitation of your pencil. Am I wrong? When we spoke of all that we would like to see on the Continent, in England, France, and Italy, did we not truly visit those places together? I thought the day we spoke of what Genoa and Turin must be like, and how you would copy the Caravaggios, and then evenings on the balcony of some great palazzo—I thought we must be standing on that balcony together. We seemed to be, if only in our imaginations, but where else would an artist and a woman who wishes to be with him meet?

My cousin Submit should bear her child soon, and I will be returning to Boston to care for them and make the most discreet of inquiries as to the portrait—if I have not heard from you before then. I am sure if I am ever known to posterity at all, it shall be by your accomplished hand.

I remain, in form, your obedient model,
Sarah S.N. White

————

Soon after she had posted this letter and written a simple request to Gaylord for news of Submit, Sarah received a reply from Mr. Copley.

August 29, 1769

My dear Psyche,
I have been much concerned with you. I have never known a lady whose society I would more readily keep. Indeed, our sessions come back to me almost as a *tableau vivant,* a living picture at which I gaze, fascinated and grateful. In you, art requited me for a lifetime of toil. You were so good as to come in and sit for me, and what happened in the next hours I can hardly recall, for they passed without any sense of effort, only delight. The record of my sketches and the picture itself witness to the tremendous

spiritual power you imparted to me.

I have thought of little these past weeks but the magnificent hollows of your eyes, the way your bottom lip curls out in its fullness, the delicate whites of your cheeks. Yes, I am speaking of the portrait, but the portrait as consolation, since I feel almost as if you are with me. I do miss how we talked of all that we would both know and see.

I shall make a confession to you if you will not share it with the world. My manservant must think me fit for Bedlam since I sometimes address the image before me (I plead, I beg, I murmur), and I feel as if I should wish you good-night at the end of each day.

However bold this may be on my part, I feel we shall always be together and cannot be separated by circumstance, though we must not let what has passed between us be seen as yet by the world. Even as I say this, I realize that I would obscure the power of this attraction even from my own mind, for how else can it be possible for us to live apart? Do we though? In my mind, we live already in that Genoa and Turin you spoke of and soon shall forever. Those who have eyes to see may read this in bold terms when the time is accomplished. Until then, I remain,

> Your Cupid,
> J.S.C.

At first, this letter displeased Sarah. She understood how its surface flattery and intimacy constantly referred, in its secondary and greater meaning, to the artist himself and his work. As she read it again—and then again—and as she thought about the matter over the next days, she thought it must have a third order of meaning as well, half intended and half leaking from the artist's egotism. Something was coming to maturity greater than his powers of manipulation and self-control. He wanted to believe that the portrait contained his feelings—the "spiritual power" she had imparted to him—but his need to communicate with her was tearing that fabric. He might wish her to remain his secluded and unknown Psyche, but would he not feel, in the end, that any humiliation was worth the miracle of a life together?

Another letter soon came from Gaylord informing Sarah that a daughter, Mercy, was born and that mother and babe were healthy and vigorous. This was followed in surprisingly short order by a note from the lady herself.

September 5, 1769

Dear Sarah,

I am glad to say that I am well and have my babe in my arms, but I do not recommend childbirth to anyone who does not believe strongly in the Resurrection of the body. Those of us women who don't die must wish that we had, and I believe that in my worst extremity I used Gaylord's name like a dish towel with which to tidy up hell. When, after Eve's sin, the Lord Almighty cursed women with bringing forth children in sorrow, he squeezed that bitter fruit dry. Even the new watering is agony— my breasts burn at the slightest touch. I know that you much regret not enjoying these pleasures, but I counsel you to think again.

Even hangings are celebrated in some towns like Thanksgiving and the Old Election Day, and we will be having people in this next month to view the infant, and I am sure that Mercy will oblige us all by spitting up on her mother. This is her one talent. Otherwise she is as peaceful as Gaylord (obviously not her mother's daughter) and wears an unearthly wise look.

In order to provide a more fitting attraction for this occasion than Mercy's feat of regurgitation, we wondered whether we might also offer the unveiling of Mr. Copley's portrait. Shall it be completed? May I write to him about this?

I long to see you. Until you return to town and bring me your saving fancy, I remain,

    Eve's Daughter,
    Submit

Sarah liked this. The proposed occasion would ally her once more with Submit and allow her to test Mr. Copley. Would he be able to resist claiming her, through private words, or even a public act, in such a setting? When all the world saw his love manifested in the bold terms of the portrait, could he pass this off as mere artifice or fail to acknowledge his own oath?

And she? Did she love him? Would she pursue that life on the Continent? She knew only that she wanted to be away—wherever that led.

CHAPTER 21

A Fishing Expedition

"We've caught these fish, you see, too many for ourselves, and we thought the owner of this land might like 'em for his smokehouse."

From the look in the eye of this blunt-nosed gentleman who stood on her porch, Anne expected him to wink at her. He would have been handsome in his day, and his look held both a saucy appreciation and dead calm calculation. He wore a rough dun outer coat, but she could see the satiny sheen of a much finer waistcoat beneath. He held up a string of brook trout that pooled at his feet, a hundred or more.

"The fish are easy to catch," she said.

"Yes," he said. "We started out casting for our supper, and then my man's enjoyment kept him at it over long." He turned back toward a fair-haired youth who stood up straight, even as his face flushed red.

"He's your son," she said, noting the same thin lips and a similar tightening about the eyes that accompanied their pursed smiles.

The old gentleman rocked back. "You have your eyes about you, you do. Yes, my son, my son." He waved his hand in the air as if he were in the habit of wafting away trouble.

"I'm fond of fishing," the youth said, almost as if the remark were a pained question.

"Never understood the attraction apart from the eating," the older gentleman said.

"My neighbors guard their waters," she said.

"That's what took us by surprise," the gentleman said. "We have been coming down from Canada, on governmental business"—he pulled on his coat and cocked his head as if he really were about to give her that wink—"and we thought ourselves still quite far from any settlements. Then we saw your house and thought again about the fish, the quantity we had taken, and thought we might be on someone's land."

"What do you want?" she asked.

"Your forgiveness, lady," he said, relieved to be at the point. "And we would offer your husband some payment for this bounty."

"You can give it to me," she said.

He pulled out his purse and counted out six shillings. She could put in next year's garden for that, and besides, the stream was thronged with trout.

"Good day to you, then, and we thank you for your honesty." She started to shut the door.

"Madame," he said.

She held back, waited.

"I like to know I am in a man's good graces. Where would your husband be?"

"No husband," she said and again started to close the door.

"Madame, madame!" he called.

She cracked opened the door again, a bit afraid now.

"Madame," he said, "is there any assistance we could offer you? I'm astounded. You, a woman of such beauty, alone in this wilderness. Have the Indian savages done you any violence?"

"The savages I've known have been like yourselves, sir." As soon as the words were out, she regretted them. His head was cocked again; he had a way of standing partly sideways, leaning in and cocking that head, as if he needed to draw closer to speak above the din of a party, and for a moment she imagined him at a ball. He seemed to carry dancing music with him, and then she remembered the way he had been rocking back and forth, his step exact and sprightly like a dancer's. His manner made her feel that all his insinuations would result in light remark, a joke under his breath.

"It's a savage thing that beats in a man's heart," he said, "a thing that must be civilized by our ladies. So it becomes incumbent upon us, who have been so blessed, to aid such a benign and persuasive influence wherever we may. Let us do you another service, then. My son and I shall camp here, not close you understand, but hereabouts. And we shall pay you for the privilege. Then my heart shall rest easy and sleep come as a balm."

He was such an old poseur. "I have no husband, but I have a house, and you are welcome to supper within and to use the porch for the night." She opened the door wide, then stepped back in front of him. "I do not run an inn, though, and you need not pay for my hospitality."

"Madame, you are too kind." The man turned back toward his son. "Samuel?"

They came in, and Anne remembered again the weight of a man's steps as theirs sounded on her wood floors. She introduced them to Theo, who went to show them the wood-carved family of dolls that Dorsey's husband, Hugh, had whittled. Without having to be invited, the gentlemen took the two rocking chairs at the hooked rug that served within the one great room of the house as her parlor. They wagged their heads in long strokes up and down, approving of Theo's fine toys, showing they knew how to treat a child.

They had left the cleaned fish in a heap on the porch—they must be gentlemen indeed—and she kicked the gathering flies away and took up the string and went around the house to the shed. She knew nothing about smoking fish, but had been told that she could do so in this tall closet of a building. Pausing for a moment in the cramped quarters, she breathed in the resinous scent of the pine boards, still so newly cut, and the watery, oily smell of all those fish, and then she did not know what she could have been thinking—to have been so misled by her desire to be alone and think for a moment—for she had still not gotten over the nausea and her stomach was lurching into her throat. She managed to slam the door on the offending fish and stumble the few yards to the brook, where most of what came up ended.

She sat down on the ground, recovered her breath, and then gave in to a comforting cry. There would be enough fish scent on the wind that night to bring down raccoons and opossum. She could only hope for this, because if they didn't come that meant wild dogs or a black bear. She hated this country. She felt so unprepared for its quiet and how it tuned her hearing to every threat. And she would be having two men sleeping on her porch!

She sniffed back her running emotions and tried to open her puffing eyes, clearing the last tears from their underlashes with her fingers. As she stood up, she brushed the sandy dirt, leaves, and pine needles from the back of her skirt and told herself that she should be glad that two people from beyond these forests, however unexpected, had come to be her guests. They had treated her with kindness thus far. The older man said they were on government business. She thought he was lying, but didn't quite know why or why he should. They might have been meeting somewhere with the Five Nations, but that business had been settled, everyone thought, and without an escort they would have to be spies. Smuggling? More likely, but what could they carry in the packs of the two horses they had loosed to graze in the field before the house?

She took full breaths of the cool night air and started back, stopping twice to think how she was going to get through this. What would she serve for their supper? Her stomach was still too squeamish to clean and cook the fish.

She went into the root cellar for more vegetables and dried beef and threw these and a liberal hand of salt into the kettle on the hook in the fireplace when she came back into the house. She had bread and butter. And then she remembered the blackberries and the cream at the top of her milk jug, which Hugh had brought by. She distributed the berries in four bowls and went to pour the cream.

"I'll help you," the young one said, getting up.

"There's no need to help," she said and finished the business. "But you can move your chairs to the table."

She set out the bread and butter and served them their stew in rough wooden bowls. She had three pewter spoons but no plate, so she left them to the wooden spoons and their fingers, for weren't they pretending to be rustic men? Theo was playing intently with his carved figures by his pallet, and she saw that their head-wagging good humor had put him off his supper. She thought he would join the table sooner if she did not call him there, so she sat down.

The old gentleman took up his spoon as soon as she did so, but the younger stayed his hand with a look. "We should be thankful for this," he said.

"What are your names?" she asked.

"Our names? Forgive me. I am Josiah Quincy," the older gentleman said and quickly bowed to her.

"Samuel. Samuel Quincy," said the younger.

"Mrs. Anne Farmington," she said. "Anne." She looked over to her son. "And Theo, Theodore."

"Yes, you called his name," Samuel said agreeably.

"He seems to have his work before him," she said, apologizing. "You gentlemen eat your suppers."

Josiah took several quick and appreciative spoonfuls, picked out a piece of dried beef with thumb and forefinger and twisted off a bite. His son followed suit.

"This government business?" Anne asked. "What might it be?"

Josiah looked up, and Anne saw how the dead calm in his eyes provided the background—and what a sprawling territory—to everything else.

"We have a report to make," he said, "on the inhabitants along the frontier of New York. The Indian issue may be settled, but this imposes on the Crown a terrible sentry duty. The taxes that so many protest against are for the welfare of people like yourselves, living in such unguarded conditions. We must know where we need to be strongest."

"You are taking a survey of the frontier and yet you are so easily lost?"

"We were only lost in our fishing," Josiah said, gestured his spoon at Samuel, and then he did wink at her.

"We need to know the circumstances of the inhabitants," Samuel said, so quickly that he seemed to be running out of breath. "The numbers of children, how they came to these places."

Josiah looked at him and seemed to be warning him off. "If you will consent to tell us."

"I was living in the Commonwealth of Massachusetts, Newburyport, at the mouth of the Merrimack River. My husband worked in a shipyard and died in an accident. The owner took me in and then thought I might have a life for myself, here. This shipyard owner also owns these lands." She began to eat her own bowl of stew.

"Life is so often tragic," Josiah said.

"Coming here seems to double the hardship," Samuel said.

"This must have been recent," Josiah said. "You are expecting a child, aren't you?"

He was the first one to have commented upon the signs. Until now, strangers had merely presumed her heaviness her natural state.

"I noticed how the food makes you color," he said. "The child is your dead husband's? I only ask because your neighbor spoke of some violence being done, and if you have suffered some attack, I must know these things for my report."

"Violence takes many forms," she said.

"Did it form the child?" He had his shoulders back now and wore a suddenly judicial expression.

"God formed this child. That's what it shall know, gentlemen."

Josiah leaned forward and gestured, as if wrapping his knuckles on the table but without making a sound. "Your neighbor says your husband has been dead long since. The report will make no mention of your name. I know this is a difficult matter, madame. Speak frankly. We will finish our suppers and disturb you no more."

Anne stood up, took her bowl to the kettle, ladled out another spoonful, and went to Theo. She bent down to him on her knees, and she could see that her look was scaring him. He half opened his mouth and she pantomimed feeding him. Neither of them could swallow, she was sure.

Then, suddenly, she was angry. It felt as if all her blood suddenly rushed to her head, and in the force of that rising, desperate fury, she turned and screamed, "What have you to do with me?"

Josiah stood up and leaned on his hands over her frail table. "Madame, we want to know a simple thing. You need not be afraid of this. If some cruelty has been done, no fault attaches itself to you. I can understand you wanting the child to enjoy the protection of the marriage state you once enjoyed. And I will own it for the gospel, if, in confidence, you help me with my task."

"You cannot be from the Crown," she said.

"We have come on behalf of Sarah White."

She forced herself to stand and go back to the table and sit down. She could not think of what she could do or say to her advantage, though she had already spent many days thinking to that end. "Mrs. White wants to know why she lost her maid?"

"Yes," Josiah said. "That's all this matter is."

"A matter for gentlemen taking a survey?"

"We thought you might speak more freely under those circumstances," Josiah said.

"More economically?"

"Mrs. White knows of the difficulty of this place. She instructed us to provide whatever you were wanting."

"Mrs. White must have heard of the violence I suffered. What more would she know?"

"The truth."

Samuel suddenly backed his chair from the table. "I enjoyed the ramble, Father," he said. "I am not enjoying this. We might leave this woman our purse and also her dignity." He walked over and stood by the fire, keeping his back to them.

Anne thought again of advantage. "Tell Mrs. White that we share too much and too little," she said.

"I take your meaning, I believe," Josiah said. "Her child might be the brother of this you carry?"

Anne put her head down and thought that she had nodded.

"If I give you five crowns, you will have agreed to this statement?" Josiah asked.

She looked up at him and put out her hand.

PART IV

—

Cold Eternities

CHAPTER 22

———

The Unveiling

Sarah could not seem to get into her dress. She could hear the musicians, a string quartet, running through the opening bars of fugues, quadrilles, even a light tavern melody. The long, low buzz of the cello came up through the wooden floorboards into her stockinged feet.

Her whole room smelled of unguents and powders, and she could taste the tang—the oily sizzle—of her French scent as she stood there in her corset, chemise, and petticoats, looking into the mirror at her dressing table. She adjusted the string of small pearls at the gathered side of her hair, smoothed the tones of the pink coral rouge and the flour white powder.

She did feel like the artist's accomplice, or perhaps his rival, for what would she have their guests think—that Mr. Copley had improved on nature?

The stomacher gown with its vine-embroidered bodice lay waiting on the bed, an invitation and supreme challenge. She was terrified and yet absurdly happy. She knew the image in the glass, and what the portrait would reveal, belonged to a mature woman, and that these emotions did not. But what she realized, then, was that such feelings are always young. She was in love again.

Submit walked in carrying her infant daughter. She had her silver hair done up with wild roses and baby's breath. Her gown had satiny skirts and a soft velvet bodice—a material used almost exclusively in men's clothing. A velvet as dark as a forest at nightfall, with the same almost imperceptible glow of green. She was carrying Mercy up against her shoulder, and the child turned its head instantly to look at Sarah.

"Are you wearing white tonight?" Submit asked with a smile, nodding at Sarah's petticoats. "So late in the season?"

The child, in its own white nightdress, seemed to stare at Sarah whenever they were in the same room together. Mercy had big dark eyes, a small snail nose with definite crimps at the wings, lips with flaring edges emphasizing their outlines, and exquisitely formed ears like seashells. Her head, with its dome and exact chin, looked the perfect miniature of an adult's. She was one of those infants who do not look like they are on their way to becoming anything; they look only as if they have traveled from God to earth.

Babies usually made Sarah uncomfortable, but Mercy actually unnerved her. The child's stare seemed to carry a secret opinion, which involved the reason she had made her journey into the world.

"Sarah?" Submit asked.

Sarah leaned across the space between them and kissed Mercy on the cheek. "How Mercy looks at me. Have you noticed?"

Submit put her thumb in the palm of the child's upraised left hand and shook it. She would not be diverted from staring at Sarah, though. "You are nearly the most beautiful thing she has ever seen. She keeps remembering the angels. Don't you, Merry Mercy?"

"Your momma is your angel," Sarah said and patted the child's tummy—then thought quickly about how Abram always did that to babies.

"You must finish dressing now," Submit said. "The first guests have arrived."

"They have? I was listening to the quartet rehearse."

"It's only Gaylord's parents so far, and his brother. But the man's at the door greeting others." Submit shifted the baby to her other shoulder. "We'll go down. Mercy's spirits won't last, I'm sure, and then the nurse will take her." She hugged the baby. "Except they may," she added, pleased. "Who would have known I would give birth to such a peaceful child? If she's not hungry, she just *looks*. My mother said I had a habit of pounding my tiny fists at her on all occasions. This is Gaylord's child, thank heavens. Now come and help your momma behave, angel."

"I've just got to put on the gown and I'll be down," Sarah said as they left.

She took a long breath and felt a jolt of nervous tingling in her fingertips. She might have a sherry once she was downstairs.

No one was on the landing at the bottom of the stairs, but she could hear music—Vivaldi—and voices in the parlor. She walked down the stairs conscious of her gown and its huge hoop skirt, the sway of it, its cloudlike illusion. She thought about the instant she would take the right turn into the parlor, how everyone would glance up, look again, and how some would keep looking. She thought the moment of entering a room the best part of being a beauty. She should not think about this and yet could not help herself. She already feared the first instance of failure. The portrait would always remind her of her too-brief glory. Would she like being reminded?

She turned into the front parlor: Gaylord and his parents looked up; Mr. Storer and his wife, Nancy; the Reverend Epes Sargent; the Quincys, her spy Josiah and his brother. Even Submit's attentions detached from Mercy when she became aware of conversations dying and heads turning. The portrait stood to the right of the mantel, still veiled.

Another cluster of guests arrived, and by now the parlor allowed barely enough room to turn from one conversation to another. Nicholas Boylston was talking at her, but Sarah could see Josiah making his way toward her, bumping shoulders with Mr. Perkins, his right arm out, carving his way.

Without any preamble, Josiah said to Mr. Boylston, "I want this lady to myself, sir, as does every fellow here, I'm sure—but you will understand if we have a private moment? Thank you."

"Josiah," she said as lightly as she could, "you are importunate." She did not fix her attention on him but continued to look around at the other guests. "You might simply have written," she said, and her tone grew abruptly harsh.

"Even so, fair lady," Josiah said and took her hand, which surprised her until she felt the smallest of envelopes in her palm. "I thought to make the delivery secure," and he smiled his pursed-lip smile.

She tucked the envelope up her three-quarter sleeve at the elbow. A mischievous light shone in Josiah's eye, but a mischievous light always shone there. "Look now," he said quickly, "our prophet has finally come among us."

She looked toward the door and saw Copley standing with the merchant Richard Clarke, the representative of the East India Tea Company, and his daughter Sukey. The crowd was turning toward them, too, with a dramatic hush. Then Copley took the young woman's arm and walked toward the portrait, with Clarke following behind. The artist stopped close to Sarah and offered her his other arm. Not knowing what else to do, she took it, and the threesome approached the draped portrait.

Submit came up to them. She looked at Sarah steadily and yet with little expression, then placed Sarah to the left of the portrait and John and Sukey Clarke to the right. Submit held Mercy in her left arm, and, predictably, the child looked up at Sarah as if she were the only one in the room.

"Dear friends," Submit said, "Gaylord and I would like to welcome you to our evening."

"Please, ma'am, let us see the child," came from the back.

"We have a series of presentations and gifts for you," Submit said, pressing on, "and the first is, yes, our Mercy." She hefted the child up and made a small circuit of steps before the audience, who oohed and aahed. One of Submit's better friends, Ellen Storer, leaned out of the crowd and gave Mercy a kiss.

"The question remains whether I will be a Mercy to her."

"Oh, Submit," Josiah said, "you are a Mercy to us all." Submit smiled at that. "Since Mercy's charms are limited these days to her unearthly gaze and several elementary functions that shan't be mentioned," she said, "we thought more entertainment might be provided through the unveiling of Mr. Copley's latest portrait. I believe he must be under the greatest of pressures tonight, for seeing his subject, my cousin Sarah White, standing before us, how should any artist other than the Lord himself do her justice?"

"My great opportunity," Mr. Copley said, "was to transmit something of the divine handiwork for the ages. How well I have done, I leave to Him and you to judge."

Gaylord stood among the crowd, but as he spoke up, his status as host came through. "Shall we have the honor of another unveiling tonight, Mr. Clarke? Or will you make us wait till next Saturday?"

"I must remain as silent as this portrait on that matter," Richard Clarke said good-humoredly.

"Perhaps Sukey will do Mr. Copley a prophetic honor by uncovering the canvas?"

Sarah saw Sukey Clarke's blush flow down her neck into the hollow at its base and out along her shoulders, and Sarah felt the fall of that color, that blood, herself, as the top of her head lightened and everyone around her seemed to take a backward step.

Sukey pulled the drapery off. Sarah looked round the gilt edges.

She saw someone recognizably herself and yet how changed. The image reminded her, somehow, of the woman she had always wished to be—there were suggestions around the nose and mouth of her mother, of a woman at once older and more alive. The next moment another thought came: how could such a delicate intuition proceed out of anything but love?

The gathering applauded. Then they applauded louder, and many shouted "bravos" and "well dones." Someone said, "The glory of the age!" and the Reverend Epes Sargent, in a more expostulatory vein, "So much of God's work in little that He is truly magnified."

Before the applause ended, Sukey Clarke turned to Sarah. "I am so proud of John," she said. "Aren't you pleased? You must come and see me this fall when we are settled. John has been so grateful to have a fitting subject."

Sarah wanted to find Submit. She did not know what she said to Sukey, or even if she spoke.

She went to Submit's side and stood there until her cousin turned away from all others and addressed her unspoken question. "You will not go mad. You have not been betrayed. I knew only what Boston has suspected for a number of weeks. Thank your Lord that this man has the sense to be cold and hard in his judgments and leaves his excess of sensibility to his canvasses." Submit eyed the glorious portrait fiercely and turned away from it as if ashamed.

Sarah felt that the world had narrowed to the ground beneath her feet.

Josiah came up. He was talking to her. He said something about immortality. "Even angels need friends, and I am always ready to be that to you," he said, and squeezed her elbow where his note remained hidden.

Hardly knowing where she was, panicked, she blurted out, "What do you mean? To seduce me?"

Josiah looked around him as if to see whether anyone had overheard how foolishly she had taken his remarks. "I mean, dear lady, that my house, with my brother and his wife and the ancient aunts we keep, is always open to you. Submit has given you a shock, I see. I think I'm actually feeling compassion for one of the few times in my life."

"Does everyone see this?"

"No. The painting has blinded them all, and they only see the treasure before them."

"What am I to do?"

"Eat your supper, good lady. Say good-night to your guests, for they are yours, still, tonight. On the morrow wake up and face the day. Sleep when the day ends. The only blessing of being an old rogue is that one becomes an expert in the healing of broken hearts. There is no remedy that I have found, other than the day after tomorrow."

At this, she started to break down, and Josiah pressed so close to her that she smelled the drink on his breath as he said, "No, no. Stop, shush, shush, stop. Take my arm and I will lead you through this dance."

He kept by her side the rest of that long night, and at its end, when she was at last in bed, she read his note and knew the fullness of his rogue's compassion.

CHAPTER 23

Love Letters

The morning after the party, Sarah sat at her secretary with her quill pens, her imported inkwells, her personal stationery, her wax and seal, and went to work like a banker on his accounts—even if she purposefully chose to wear her diaphanous ivory dressing gown and matching robe. The matters before her demanded an exacting attention, but she must be single-minded; her multicolored faculties blended into a piercing light in addressing each. So for now she set Anne Farmington and Abram aside to address the most pressing matter.

September 25, 1769

Dear Mr. Copley,

How can I thank you for the work of art you have given to the world? I do not say "to me," for I feel very strongly that I must account myself only the steward of this work. Indeed, I feel such a degree of impersonality about the matter because you used me only as a starting point for your greater purposes: to present to the world your own peculiar vision of a universal. This is recognizably Sarah White, yes, and yet so infused with your own understanding of the Masters' fascination with the Madonna that even our close friends commented very little on the likeness.

I must congratulate you as well on the open secret of your engagement to Sukey Clarke. She is such a sturdy-looking girl. And so well connected to all that proverbial tea in China. I warn you, though, that Massachusetts is not used to licensed agents and monopolies, and Mr. Clarke's pungent leaves may brew you up some trouble in the end. Of course, the woman's fortune should lessen the need for you to work so rapidly and allow for your expansion into the allegorical subjects we spoke of.

Again, thank you. Now that all the world sees your "Psyche," the light flooding in certainly has destroyed my illusions as to your identity. In this case, sir, Cupid appears to have exchanged his identity for another sort of golden shower. And still, I remain,

    Your living ideal,
    Sarah Singleton Nicolls White

His prompt reply came by the next day's post.

My dear Mrs. White,
Thank you for your kind words concerning the painting. I'm sure we shall both not forget its unveiling—the grand theater of the gala. I must thank your cousins for their munificence, which I shall do anon.

As always, I'm afraid, the lay person gives the artist too much credit—and perhaps too little as well. I was not thinking of the Masters' Madonnas, although now that you suggest this, I realize again how strict attention to the particular always makes for an intuition into the universal. No, I can truly say that what appears on that canvas came by way of prophetic intuitions. I was truly surprised by the deep truth of your soul as it communicated itself to me day by day, and indeed many things registered there escape any understanding that I might articulate. I count this a high privilege and even a divine grace, and I ask you to think of the sittings and the portrait itself within that context, not those pagan furnishings we bandied with.

Sukey is a dear girl with her own individual beauty, and we shall be happy to see you in our home after our marriage in November. I will, of course, understand if you are unable to attend the engagement dinner this Saturday. Society has its claims upon our lives—ones greater than we ever suspect in our private musings. You need not, though, pay it court in this instance, even if

I must in the larger matter. And so, in life as well as in art, I remain,

Your most attentive friend,
John Singleton Copley

She had intended to address the matter of Anne Farmington and Abram next, but one of Mr. Copley's admissions proved too hurtful a dart, as if he were still playing Cupid despite his disclaimers.

October 3, 1769

Dear Mr. Copley,
I thought not to write anymore, but find that I must address, for integrity's sake, what seems to me a manifest injustice. Not to put too fine a point on it, but your art is coming to seem a ghoulish practice.

Do your subjects truly understand what they are agreeing to—indeed, paying for—in commissioning your work? They ask for you to render their likeness. You are not content with this. No, you must peer into the soul.

I know that I virtually encouraged you in this practice, but I never realized the great hurt that can come from such exposure. You must have known and offered not one warning. You encouraged me in every possible way—through courtesies and even small gestures of affection—to believe you held me in genuine regard. In the end, you were only interested in the "prophetic intuition" of the work. Your ends certainly do not justify your means, sir.

I can well see why you are so interested in insuring your place in society, for necromancers are not generally accorded places at the best tables. You can be sure that if any ask me about your art, I will give them a more accurate accounting than its practitioner.

You think to excuse me from your engagement party? Whatever permissions or forgiveness may be granted in our relations are my prerogative. For I am,

The Offended Party,
Mrs. Sarah White

After a little delay, this brought a short reply.

October 6, 1769

Dear Madam,
Forgive my delay in response, as my engagement has preoccupied my attentions, as you can well understand.
I did want to say that your reflections—or ones like them—

often occur to subjects. Such honesty as art requires is a hard thing for everyone to bear. And yet this candor constitutes a tremendous gift—a bequest to the future.

For as long as you like, for your life's entirety if need be, keep the portrait as your own treasure. Let future ages judge of any additional uses.

As to the rest, I can only say that I hope to sit by you at many a table in the future. Indeed, this will be one of the chief pleasures of my life in Society.

I remain,
Your devotee,
John Copley

Sarah debated her response for a long while as she read the reports of Mr. Copley's engagement in the newspaper and heard of the Reverend Sargent's pleased and ostentatious manner of publishing the banns in Trinity Church. Sukey Clarke was so impossibly plain. Courting her while envisioning the image in the portrait must have required such a maddeningly divided mind. She could understand why he wished to remain friends, to see her in Society. She almost came to feel sorry for the man. Then she saw the possibility that he would not be able to speak of his true feelings, certainly not commit them to paper. She was free, however, and she considered the risk worth taking.

October 18, 1769

Dear Mr. Copley,

I realize that I have misjudged you. I am married to such a man as you are, at least in terms of his first station in life, and I should have understood immediately why you are making such a marriage. For you must have a place at those tables, mustn't you? Knowing as I do how deserving you are of your commissions, how could I have resented what may only be expedient, as nearly all marriages are?

I have to think that you are still and even more engaged by that prospect of touring the Continent and studying the Old Masters. This summer I determined such a course in life for myself, and after a little while, your marriage need not preclude you from joining me in it. Sukey will have your children to raise. As I do now, you will have more and more a life of your own to pursue. Why forego any of the possibilities that life has to offer?

I will be seeing you at those tables we have been discussing, and do not be surprised to find your elbow lightly touched. We have directions to turn in, you and I.

> Your great and good friend,
> Sarah S.N. White

No reply came to this. Mr. Copley was getting married, it was true, but could he not spare a moment? Her surprise at his delay gave way to the recognition that he must be finding the courage necessary difficult. To carry on an affair—even an epistolary one—in the midst of marrying another woman would caution most men, at least for a time. Although Josiah Quincy could have carried it off easily enough, she was sure. And Abram was able to profess love to her while getting Anne with child . . . but she shoved off this thought as soon as it entered, continuing to keep that matter to one side of her calculations. She had courage. She knew what she wanted.

November 23, 1769

Dear John,

You will have to make some reckoning with me, you know. You cannot as much as profess your love to me, as you did during our portrait sessions, and then forget the matter.

Your marriage says nothing as to your sentiments. How could you be in love with that bovine girl? Let her bear your children and her father's pockets support your artistic ambitions. Well enough. Very good. You are too great a man to be bound forever by mere convention. You must not deprive yourself of inspiration and beauty.

As for love, I have no doubt who inspires that in you. I will not let that future we envisioned together elude us. Remember how you looked at me from the first? Even a memory and fancy as powerful as yours cannot substitute for my presence.

A banquet awaits you. Do not starve yourself for long.

I will come free you soon, if you do not come to me.

> With every tenderness,
> Sarah

She thought long before sending this, knowing how ridiculous she might appear. Her need, though, of some satisfaction in the matter threatened her with a humiliation, an impoverishment, greater even than John Copley's refusal. Her appetite, her craving, her obsessional intent, made her feel almost as if she were being controlled by another's will. She found her action extraordinary, even as she handed the letter to Submit's footman for delivery.

No reply came. None. She inquired and found that Mr. and Mrs.

Copley were now in residence in the town, receiving visitors. They were to stage a grand reception that Christmas season and would be building a new home on Beacon Hill.

Still, Sarah kept writing letters. She kept sending them. She kept explaining it all to them both, and as she did, she found herself as sad as she must appear.

CHAPTER 24

No

"I want to be done with you," Sarah said.

John Singleton Copley continued to paint, holding up the butt of his paintbrush and squinting with one eye to take a rough measurement, check dimensions.

"I want to be done with this," she said. "I write and write and you do not answer. Courtesy demands more. Decency. Stop painting please! I hardly need any further demonstrations of your indifference."

In his studio once more, the brick wall opposite the windows patterned by the sun on a clear December morning, she was saying what she had come here to say. She found herself quick with an argument, even eloquent, and astounded to be saying so much.

Copley put his hands on his hips and hung his head. He wore a full-length apron over his suit of clothes. "Madame," he said, "I am trying to be kind."

"Then speak to what I am saying."

"It is not the answer you wish to hear. It should not need speaking."

"You must at least give me the satisfaction of knowing whether our conversations here, as you painted, were nothing but the ornaments of your commission. Pretty words to achieve your effect."

Mr. Copley went to the marble-topped table that served as his huge mixing palette and started sorting and cleaning his brushes. "Such speech is unworthy of you," he said at last.

"How do you estimate my worth, then? That is precisely what I am asking. I seem to have meant nothing more than the rent."

"I found you an enchanting woman and a perfect subject."

"But which meant more?"

"I am a painter," he said. "And you a married woman. I cannot distinguish the several motives that combine in every word I say . . . no one does, for that matter."

She went over to the long table with its plaster-of-paris statues and let her fingertips lightly graze its surface. "When you wrote to me, you were even then putting me off. You were pursuing this woman you married."

"I will admit that I should not have written that letter. I knew it to be unwise." He wiped his hands of the cleaning fluid.

"Then why did you?"

"Because I enjoyed the flirtation, madame—just as I believed you were only doing the same. You could not have been so stupid as not to understand our proper relationship."

"If you cannot distinguish the several motives of your every word, then I could hardly have known what prompted them. Is this stupidity?"

"I should not have said."

"You should not have said a great many things."

"Nor should you have come here alone. I see how unwise it was of me to allow you to flout convention in this way. I thought you daring."

"I thought you a gentleman."

"Your daring is something else . . ."

"Something?"

He took off his apron. "Madame, I am becoming afraid for you."

"I believe you are afraid," she said. There was a small sculptor's hammer close to her on the table, one end blunt, one spiked. She stared at it, then quickly checked for his reaction. He crossed his arms loosely but with such deliberation that she knew his wish to guard himself. She did not pick up the hammer but turned to him. "You are

- 172 -

afraid of your genuine emotions, afraid of your humble origins, afraid for your position in society, afraid to cross the waters and look at the Masters and see how little you have truly accomplished in your 'little Boston.' "

"Madame—"

"No, you would rather marry well and continue in a flattering ignorance. How she must make up for her common appearance by propping up her artist. A very easel of a woman, isn't she?"

His mouth worked over his reply before he delivered it. "You could not be more mistaken. My marriage to Sukey Clarke Copley is not one of convenience. I *am* a man who knows beauty. I know how little it takes to produce its illusion." He held up his hand, gesturing toward her. "Due proportion, fair tones—anything, really, that delights the eye." He looked back over his shoulder toward his marble-topped palette. "The mess there is nice in a place or two."

She moved to where the hammer was back within reach.

"Such beauty belongs to surfaces and is, as I say, easily produced. More illusory than real. The beauty of a mature character is much more substantial. It is, in fact, rare, as all the world knows."

"And your Sukey has this?"

He looked straight at her. "I would say she taught me its meaning."

"I have known of Sukey Clarke for years," she said. "Your testimony as to her character is very touching indeed, and how fitting for a new husband." She hesitated. "The woman is no paragon, I assure you, which a little time will reveal. Her money apart, she is a very common thing. You may yet want to venture out into a greater world."

"I may," he said. "Someday, Sukey and I may move to England. At least for a good period of years."

"Your merchant father-in-law will never let you go."

He breathed out impatiently. "Even so, madame, this is my affair."

She could have left then, easily, but at the thought, the encroaching pain-saturated days surrounded her. She could not find the way.

"It does not move you?" she asked.

"What?"

"My feeling."

"Do not speak of it."

"Why?"

"I would like to preserve some memory. A way to greet you in the street and in Society."

"You find me ridiculous?"

"Poets speak of it more often as a madness."

She waited, trying to gather her thoughts. "So I am either absurd or grotesque."

He said nothing.

"I cannot separate myself from you," she said and looked up at him. "We were together. In Genoa. In Turin. We saw the churches in Ravenna."

"We talked about such things. Here. And in one or two letters."

"We were together there. Our splendid life."

"Madame, please. Say no more."

She reached for the hammer. "This, this, is the illusion. What you are saying. You cannot know what you are saying." She looked up at him and thought to brighten their talk and find him in a better humor. "We are there, forever, for those who have eyes to see. The time has already come when this is written in bold terms. I see it. We are there."

"You have been imagining such things, madame."

"No, no," she said. "I know the truth. You must come to see it too."

He reached out and touched her shoulder and arm, perhaps to calm her, and she struck at him with a backhanded movement, the spike-end of the hammer ripping across his chest and piercing his upper arm.

He howled in pain, half crouching, guarding his wounded arm. "Mad!" he shouted. "You have gone mad!"

Her hand tightened on the hammer, and she turned away from him and began smashing the plaster-of-paris statues, sending hard flakes into her own face and eyes.

She heard his staggering steps and she struck harder each time he hesitated, smashing whatever she could reach until he had gone out.

CHAPTER 25

The Wisdom of Others

Abram could not quit looking over at the portrait, to the right of Submit's shoulder, in the far corner by the bookshelf. The light from the window overexposed much of the gown, but Sarah's visage commanded his attention—that look of self-possession and its deep and searching appeal. Uncannily, the artist had rendered the Sarah he had always known, her youth, her maturity. He had seen her as God might, from a perfected future. Sarah, the subject of this beatific rendering, had refused to come home for her usual Christmas visit, and Abram had finally found the courage—long after sending Anne away—to go reclaim his wife. Now, immediately after the first of the year, Gaylord, Submit, and he sat in their parlor, discussing the matter.

"We have made a mistake," Gaylord said, leaning over his long, crossed leg toward Submit. "We ought to have had the portrait removed." He reached for the servant's bell.

"No, no," Abram said. "I'm sorry to let myself be so distracted by it. It awakes . . . it's the reason I've come."

"She's adamant, Abram," Submit said. "We have been friends to you in this, more than you know, and sometimes, I venture to say, more careful of your interests." Submit's face was coloring. "Why did you not come last spring?"

Abram and Gaylord both looked around, their necks twisting like seals.

Abram tried to reply, but Submit barged on. "My cousin's happiness must ultimately lie with you—however unhappy the thought!"

"*Submit!*" Gaylord said.

"Why will you not give her back to me, then?" Abram asked. "She has always returned for the Christmas season. I want her home."

"How?" Submit asked, exasperated. "Are we to call the Justice of the Peace and have her bodily removed? She *refuses*."

"You have influence," Abram said, turning to Gaylord.

"If you saw her," Gaylord said, "I doubt you would insist on her return. She lives with sorrow in a way I have rarely seen, and it is my business as the governor's Special Secretary, Abram, to see such things."

Although he knew the reasons, Abram still wanted to ask why. He loved Sarah. He had always loved her, and he loved her now. He thought of rushing up the stairs to her. Why didn't he? He was sitting in a commodious parlor, being civilized, and the clash of his thoughts and actions made him feel as if none of it could be true, even his presence.

"She is my wife. I will see her," he said and stood up.

Gaylord grabbed his wife's forearm and clasped it, holding her to her chair. "We cannot prevent you," Gaylord said quickly. Then he continued on, his voice very even, if not quite calm. "We could not prevent the commissioning of the portrait. Nor the loss of Sarah's maid to a difficult life on the frontier. We can only advise you." He took a breath and swallowed, his big Adam's apple bobbing. "You desire the return of your wife's affections, as do we. But we advise you to consider the wisdom of others."

Abram sat down again, very lightly, on the edge of his chair, and he felt such a rush of emotion that it was as if his head were being swarmed by stinging bees. "You will tell her I came," he said.

"Yes," Gaylord said. "She knows. You mustn't imagine her despondency has produced another walking nightmare, as I understand it has in the past. This is not another bout of madness . . . exactly. She's fully . . . she knows what your wishes are. And I'm sure it's important to her that you visited."

"We fight not against flesh and blood," Submit said. "You have visited in darkness, Abram, and now you bear it with you. As does Sarah, I'm afraid. You must learn to walk again in the light."

Gaylord looked a little embarrassed at his wife's prophetic utterances.

The shift in the conversation left Abram wherever he might be, certainly alone.

He grabbed his old snail-shaped hat and went over to the portrait. He imagined the artist applying each brush stroke, thousands upon thousands. He thought of how he had worshiped this same body with his own hands. And yet he had never seen her as clearly. His shame drove him from the house, and by way of goodbye he could only half raise his hat out from his side to Sarah's hosts.

CHAPTER 26

A Winter of Discontent

*T*he winter of 1770 began with a series of nor'easters that brought snow and then freezing rain. The trees wore a crystal glaze. Limbs came down like daggers and one hardly dared take a quick step, even out of the way, because the snow's crust was pure ice. The sky clouded over for so many days that on the one occasion when Abram saw the shadow of a tree segmented by his neighbor's clapboards, he realized how much he missed open sky. Everything stood by itself in a numbing cold, preserved in appearance and yet hollowing out. The persistent wind blew wispy traces and vapors off the ridged snowbanks that recoiled like snakes.

Abram mostly stayed away from the shipyard, which was, in this weather, nothing more than an abandoned pier, its framework covered by black tarpaulin, showing in patches through the snowdrifts. Here and there the tarpaulin had ripped, and the coffered sides of the framework showed through like a hive that the fiery ice was melting.

He felt the cold most when he went to bed. Jezreel's warming pan beneath the coverlet only warmed his feet. His toes swelled even as the rest of him lay on what felt like an ice floe and his hands cramped and his muscles knotted. He remembered the virtual hearth of Sarah's presence. He remembered the years and the times when she had wanted children and her way of reaching out for him and drawing him into the warmth of her life.

Sarah remained with the Chaunceys in Boston. He had heard little except that her physical health remained good and she needed more time.

Maman had taken her usual winter cold. This year, though, she seemed to be using her illness to escape him, to court her feebleness.

At the end of January a rectangular packing crate that came up to Abram's chin arrived from Boston. He thought one of his clients had sent him a late Christmas present, and he ordered Jezreel to open it.

The next time Abram came into the front parlor, at midmorning after he had spent two hours sketching ships' plans, he met Sarah looking down at him from over the mantel. He heard *Maman* being escorted down from her room by Jezreel before he could order the painting removed. He felt expelled from his own home by the portrait and exasperated at having to explain why he did not care for it there. No one would listen. The servants would do as he ordered, if reluctantly, of course, but he could already hear his mother's reproving words.

He turned his face up and gazed at the portrait—as he heard Jezreel and *Maman* bump down the last few steps—with the resolution of a warrior falling on his sword. Her appearance pierced his heart; he could hardly stand to remain in the same room with her image. He knew too well what he had suffered to contemplate going after her again, even as the portrait issued its own magisterial summons.

Jezreel's arms wrapped his mother up in such a close embrace that he half carried the quilt-shrouded bundle into the parlor. He stood her up like a roll of carpet, then pulled her rocker around and back out into the center of the room where she could look up more easily. Abram stood by during all this, helpless in his preoccupation.

When she had been seated, *Maman* prepared herself for the viewing by adjusting her quilt about her shoulders, settling it over her knees.

"Look at this painting!" she exclaimed. "*C'est magnifique!*" She glanced over at Abram. "What a wife you have, my child. She really is so beautiful."

She was looking at him with the undoubted pride of a mother who knows her son has, at the least, good taste. He thought she might prefer Sarah in this form to any other.

Still, he could anticipate what would come next, and he said to the West Indian, "Thank you then, Jezreel."

"Would you have some tea, mum?" the servant asked.

Maman coughed into her handkerchief. "No thank you. Lucinda brought me a second pot with breakfast."

"And for you, Captain?"

"You have done more than was required, Jezreel."

The servant raised his chin, questioning, but Abram had no intention of letting his feelings show. The servant gave an unnecessary bow and went out.

"You like her there?" *Maman* asked.

"I cannot be sure. It is a good enough place for a healthy first viewing, I suppose."

His own word "healthy" surprised him, and he realized that even in his preoccupation, his mother's frailty, the heaviness of her cold, had communicated itself. The angles of her cheeks flattened down with the stuffiness of her nose and her mouth hung open. At every third or fourth breath her shoulders pulled up as she labored to fill her lungs. This looked maddeningly uncomfortable.

"She is so high up," *Maman* said. "Always." Her expression did not change, but Abram knew well what she meant. "You want her home and her friends think to make you this present. Is it a good one?"

"They say the painter is the finest ever produced in these colonies. Along with Mr. West."

"Does it please you?" his mother asked.

He wanted to tell her something of the truth. "He has captured something about her. I see what I had hoped for."

"You no longer hope, *mon petit*?" she asked, distressed.

"No. You see her attitude, her expression. It's as if she's come into what we hoped for."

"The painter imagined he looks down from heaven?"

"Yes."

"How high his mantel must be," she said and gave a coughing laugh. "I do see, though. He knows her. He thinks he does. Enough to predict what she will become. Who is this painter?"

"John Singleton Copley."

"He is an arrogant man, and, I think, a very gifted one. This is good for the painting, but for us, I do not know."

"Your meaning, *Maman*? For us?"

"If she were here . . . but she is away. This must be hard for you."

This was all she saw or knew, then. By itself, it was enough. "I may not keep the painting above the mantel."

"You should for a time."

"Why?"

"You owe this."

"To whom?"

"Where would the Chaunceys want to see it? Where would Sarah?"

"As you say, she is not here."

"Perhaps she comes back to us like this first. To see whether she will be welcomed."

"*Maman*."

"What did they tell you? You said we would speak of this later. Is it now later?"

"What you have said to me. Society and her birth allow her many choices."

"All foolish. *Fauve*. Wild."

"Still they are hers. She feels driven to them by the absence of children, as I have also said before."

"Nothing else drives her? To these choices? Away from you?"

"I am here. Her place is here for her."

"Could you not make another place?"

"Shall we move into Boston and hope that she chooses to join us?"

"I think, Abram, that you will not have to worry about 'us' for so much longer."

"You have your winter cold, *Maman*. You always say these things."

"I would like to see you together again and happy before I die."

"If we are together again—as I hope we soon shall be—you will see it."

"You know the span of our days?"

"Do not tire yourself any longer. Let me see you back to bed."

His mother pointed her shaking finger at the portrait. "She shall remain?"

"As you like, *Maman*."

———

Maman's condition worsened, as each slight lessening of the winter cold brought meltings that quickly refroze and were covered by new layers of snow. Her breaths came with a shudder, and her chill became a racing fever. Abram began to hear that sound of rocks tumbling in water that he had heard before when his father-in-law contracted pneumonia. Her face did not look red and boiled, as did his, though, but blue. The disease was smothering her.

On February 14, 1770, Abram received the letter he had been expecting from Dorsey, which arrived much delayed by the bad weather or through being temporarily misplaced by the post. He took it to his study, where he sat at his bulwark of a desk for a long time before opening it. When he realized he was hoping for death, he tore the letter open.

December 23, 1770

Dear Abram,

Anne is delivered of a son, whom she has called Titus—after a favorite uncle, evidently. Mother and child are well.

Perhaps we pressed the matter too closely, but we thought her confinement and the new responsibilities of this child might work toward softening her heart in regard to marriage. After a first meeting, Anne would not hear of seeing Sean Murray again (the lad Zack sent over the waters). We took him back round and he held the child as if he were his own, but we could see how displeased this made her.

We think it best now to give him other lands to cultivate in the spring. He will make a good farmer, if not a husband.

Anne is a good mother. Perhaps it is too easy for her, or she would be wanting a man more.

Hugh and I hope this finds you well and that *Maman* is having a better winter. We hold Sarah and you before the Lord.

All shall be well,
Dorsey

Post Scriptum: Greet *Maman* for us. We miss her so.

His son, Titus. Not a name he would have chosen, but in any event, his son. He wanted to feel proud. Who would he be? Who could Abram be to him? These questions would have answers, and likely not happy ones. He wanted to be kind to the boy, to love his infant son, yet he could only be generous, which would never be the same. His part sickened him.

A father after so many years, and what he felt came like a blow— a force as hard as his head hitting against the stone wall when his own father had lost his temper and thrown him. He would live all of his life in a betrayal no less violent for being silent. The worst thing he had ever known, and he had become that very thing, forever, to his own son. His blood was pumping so hard into his head it felt as if a clawed hand clenched the back of his scalp.

He stashed the letter in the left-hand drawer and stood up. Deciding not to take his coat, he slammed through his office door and went straight out the front entrance. He heard Jezreel calling after him but did not turn round.

The cold outside tightened down on his body so quickly that his rushing head began to explode with headache. He went on, though, his only thought to walk until he became absolutely numb. The glare off the icy streets connected like lightning with his headache. He drove into the wind, clawing the tears away from his eyes.

When he finally returned to the house, Jezreel had to help him in, for his hands were so cold that even using both together he could not turn the doorknob. His hair was a frozen helmet, and ice crusted his eyebrows, nose, and beard. He felt nothing until the warming pan and three extra coverlets over him brought the return of sensation and with it a feverish chill that kept him in a suspended state—a dreaming waking.

Abram recovered slowly, for he had put himself in more danger physically than he had known. Still, he wanted to live. His walking out had gestured at escape or reprieve, not suicide. Thinking of what he had done, he became frightened at the desperation that had driven him so far. Only after a week could he begin to get out of bed and read or keep up with his correspondence for short periods, sitting in a chair by his bedroom fire.

His first venture out of the room itself took him down the hall to his mother's room. Jezreel and Lucinda had said little about *Maman* during his own illness, but as his own faculties focused and sharpened, he guessed that her condition must be worsening.

The tasseled curtains around her four-poster bed were drawn, and he pulled them back with awful premonitions. She looked even worse than he had anticipated. Her face was gray and blue, the veins from her throat snarling in coils up into her cheeks, and her caramelized eyes were unnaturally dilated. She did not turn her head but blinked in recognition of his presence. Every breath she took now demanded that heaving of her shoulders.

"*Maman*," he said.

Her voice came out surprisingly strong, almost normal, except for the pauses to breathe. "What have you been doing with yourself? I hear you have been most foolish."

In all that time, he had not really thought how he would explain what he had done. "I was looking at Sarah's portrait that day," he said.

"I felt I had to leave the house, and then something kept driving me."

"Are the demons after you? Have you invited them here?"

"How do I banish them, *Maman*? If only I knew how to make things right."

"You know," she said. "We always know this."

"The still small voice," he said. "What if it quits speaking?"

"Then the demons are here."

"No," he said. "I still hear it. But tell me how you are feeling."

"You see me. I am close to the earthly side of death. It is a place I have visited before, though. The Lord seems to draw me near and then tells me to go away. I hope He invites me this time."

"No, *Maman*."

"Why not?"

"For me," he said quickly and without thinking. "Yes, for me. I need you still."

"You need to listen to that voice and act upon it."

"I will."

"Then tell me this. For I hear this voice as well. You once asked me whether if you had done something that could not be undone, would I want to know." She took in a strenuous breath. "Yes, I want to know."

He questioned whether she was too frail to hear this. "*Maman*, it is not much more than you know already. I gave Anne some cause to think my sentiments tended toward her. I did not act on this, though."

"You did not? No?"

"When I visited her in the quarters, I ate a bit of supper. I put Theo to bed. We were like a family."

"This is all?"

"It proved enough to mislead her."

"And the child?"

He began to repeat the lie about her attacker, but stopped himself. "I cannot be sure of how she had the child. She may have thought to take some vengeance on me with another when she knew I would not become more involved."

Maman raised herself up on her pillow. "You are lying. Anne is a better person than this. You are my son and you lie to me. You make yourself worse than Anne would be if she had done everything you say." She began to cough violently.

"*Maman*," he said.

"Abram. Abram, my son."

He hated making her worse.

"You are not well," he said. "I will let you rest now."

"Who is unwell?"

"Rest, *Maman*. We will speak of this tomorrow."

"We will?"

"Yes. I'll explain so that you understand."

She eased back down in her bed and turned her face a little from him.

He waited for a moment more. Should he tell her all he had done? Which was the question he considered through a long night that saw something like the dreaming wakefulness of his fight with the cold return. She knew already, so why should it be so hard to admit the truth? Twenty years at sea working to be the hero of his family, their savior, and he had made himself completely ridiculous with a handmaid. No, not ridiculous—evil. For had not his son's birth taught him that he had betrayed every sacred covenant in his life and subjected an innocent victim—his own son—to the destructive consequences of his own act? He was so much not the man he wanted to be, considered himself to be, that he could not tell his mother. For she was in so many ways everything to him, and he had made himself nothing.

He remembered how he had felt his father's spirit come near as he had walked out into the Irish night with his sister Dorsey on the eve of his family's departure to the New World. The grace of such a reconciliation had been granted him once; he dared not risk a second.

Abram rose from bed about five o'clock. His mother always awoke early, even when ill. He thought whether to visit her in his nightshirt and robe and then decided on dressing. He put on the breeches to his heavy captain's uniform, a silk shirt, a waistcoat, his buckled shoes, and a navy blue coat that went with the breeches well enough but in a less martial fashion.

Suddenly, he felt the chill return, the dreaming wakefulness, and his thoughts lost their determination and went out to a devastated landscape. He looked over his shoulder and above him, half ducking, as if he had fallen under the wing of a dark spirit. He took several breaths and his heart raced, and then he felt so much as if nothing remained to be done, could be done, that he almost sat down on his bed again. *Maman* was dead. Sarah had known hours before her mother had died, but this had just happened—as he was dressing, standing in his bedroom, ready to face her judgment.

He walked down the hall and into her bedroom, pulled back her bed-curtains and found her, as he expected, with her fingers knitted on her stomach, self-composed.

The earth was too hard frozen for a grave to be dug, and so after the brief memorial service, *Maman* was put in the Batchelder crypt, awaiting the spring.

————

In March, the *Gazette* carried the story of what was being talked of as the Boston Massacre, with troops firing into a crowd protesting the Stamp Act. Four had been killed, seven wounded. The next *Gazette* brought an engraving of the scene by Paul Revere, as taken from a similar work by John Singleton Copley's nephew, Henry Pelham, and announced that on March 23, the Newburyport selectmen voted to continue the nonimportation of goods order. Since the town was drawing together to enforce this order, this meant the end of business for Abram's shipyard and those of his competitors. The British would not be ordering new ships made in America, and the local merchant fleet would have nothing to trade for but sugar and molasses in the Indies. The British embargo that would follow on the heels of the Colonies' rebellion would soon cut that leg off the trading triangle as well, though there might yet be that boom in fitting out ships as privateers that Patrick Tracy had intimated to Abram more than a year ago.

The end of trade would also make Abram's lands in Ulster less profitable, for apart from the quit rents and the sheer capital he had in the bank as a result of his previous speculations, his land holdings would be of little use to him. No one with money for land would be emigrating during such hostilities. He never touched Sarah's income from her estate, Elysia, which had stayed under Cousin Delancey's control and produced far less than it should. Estranged as he was from her, he would not start now, although legally, he knew, he could force the issue.

He had never worried about money before—not in this way. He had been a poor seaman, who thought of accruing a fortune in order to rescue his family from poverty and then to make and insure the health of his marriage; for him, money had always meant accomplishment. So he had become rich. But to have money and then to lose it, and late in life, this made him feel afraid and small.

The week after the Massacre, Abram attended the Tuesday evening church service at South Presbyterian. Sitting alone in his front square pew, before the sermon, Abram tried to sing out the second hymn, "Come Thou Fount of Every Blessing." This had been a favorite of *Maman's*.

As the hymn ended and Rev. Parsons began to pray, Abram could not drive away thoughts of his lost son. His child that he could not hold and celebrate with the shouts of joy that turned now into despairing cries. He began to weep, not quietly to himself, but with the booming thunder of a huge frozen lake quaking as its layers of ice shifted. He found himself shaking the front of the pew, trying to hold on against it, raising embarrassing creaks and cracks. He gulped at the air. The breaking howls came again and again, and the Reverend Parsons himself was at his elbow before he could hurry away.

Abram reached out and feebly patted the clergyman on his robed shoulder, as if to deny his own need of comfort, then hurried down the aisle to a collective gasp and muttering. In the street, the cold air struck him, and he raged back against it with shouts that he kept reconsidering as he thought how they would enter his neighbors' prayers.

Then, the unexpected. The charity that quickly flowed back to Abram made him marvel, even as he found it more and more discomfiting. The Reverend Parsons came first, of course, and sat in his parlor and drank the camomile tea patriotic colonists were using now. Abram had never heard such loud teacups and teeth-jarring scrapes as their conversation proceeded from awkward pleasantries into silence.

"Your mother was indeed a saint," the clergyman said.

Abram nodded.

"How you must miss your wife at this time."

"I do," Abram said.

"Yes," said Parsons. "Your difficulty at the evening service . . ."

"I do miss my wife . . . and my mother," Abram said.

Whether because of Abram's work in Five Points or because of the immediately understandable need of a man deprived of warmth and companionship and his mother's love, Newburyport now requited every attention Abram had ever paid it. The end of March brought rain and a sodden trooping of visitors to Abram's door. Though they stopped in only for a moment with pies and cakes and tarts and duffs and dandies, the women usually insisted on embracing him in a motherly way.

He overheard one visitor saying to Lucinda, "The Missionary being so miserable, missing his wife and his dear mother, crying unto the Lord in church, we thought to do something for his house."

"Why such a one isn't being loved—and that regular—stones us. He can take some comfort in his neighbors if he can't in his bed."

Then Patrick and Nathaniel Tracy, Theophilus Parsons, and other gentlemen of the town also came by and gave him so many orders for outfitting privateers that the nonimportation order now promised huge windfall profits.

When even Beniah Lynch showed up at his door one day, Abram was almost persuaded that he had built up more credit in heaven than he had known, and he ushered the little man into his parlor for tea with a collegial remark about Bowditch—how Beniah might make use of his services, on his upcoming spring visit, if he felt the need of a designer.

Lynch could not properly settle into the high-backed chair Abram offered, and he worked his haunches, swiveling back into the chair and then to its edge again, where his feet rested on the ground only when he leaned forward. The dampness had tightened and frizzed the curls of his brown hair, and his flat head looked like a field of burrs. His small hands gripped the arms of the chair so tightly that he looked as if he were going to swing his little legs under him, Indian-style, or push off into the room.

"Beniah?" Abram asked. "What can I do for you?"

"Do for me," Beniah said. "You can—indeed you can do something for me. You can explain to me how your whimpering in church has attracted to you every piece of business in the yards." Beniah laughed, a little *he-he*, as if insults could be sport.

"There's not much business now," Abram said. "If the Colonies and the Mother Country go to war, we'll have to find other employment."

"I have no other employment as do you," Beniah said.

"Those I visit in the Points, they often talk of owing their rents to you."

"Without employment in the yards and no means of shipping fish, few enough have been paying," Lynch said, his voice rising.

Abram almost stood up and ended the interview, and yet he wanted to know why this man would be bold enough to come to his house for a shouting match.

"I have no control over these things. And remember, some of the coppers you do have may come from this house."

"Pray answer my question, please."

"I thought I perceived an insult more than a question."

"It's a wonder, don't you think? Perhaps it's these distracted times. You make a woman of yourself in church, you cause those around you to think of Bedlam, and then one of the wealthiest men in town becomes the object of the town's pity and even richer in his disgrace."

"You may not pry into my business, Beniah. You have been doing so, and you will stop."

Beniah let go of the chair's arms and folded his hands over his chest. " 'You may not!' " he said in a twiddling voice. "I may do precisely what I will."

"I see no point in this discussion," Abram said and stood up.

"We are getting to the point," Beniah said, and pointed his stubby finger at Abram below his waist.

The angle of his aim caused Abram much embarrassment and he sat down once more. Then he thought he would get up again and throw the man from the room if he had to.

"You may be missing your wife," Beniah said, "and I'm sure you are. Cooped up here and thinking of your many happy years together and now the sad division between you."

"Lynch!" Abram said, finding himself shouting now.

"She does have an unfortunate habit of telling the truth. Telling secrets. We met one afternoon at Cornejo's and she told such tales. Perhaps that's why she's gone now. Perhaps you actually sent her away. She might say too much otherwise."

"I sent no one away!"

"I'm sure you sent Mrs. Farmington away. With her child and the child to be. I imagine it's come into the world. I wonder who it looks like? Your wife had her ideas about that."

At this, Abram reached for Beniah's shoulders, thinking to hoist him out, but before he could snatch him, the little man flew out of his chair and socked Abram right across his jaw. The blow landed with the doubling force of his arm and his body's momentum.

When Abram's eyes cleared, he saw the man pointing his finger at him again, standing at an angle, his left foot out, his right back, his knees still flexing.

"You will not handle me. Never. Not again. I vowed that in Wolfe's Tavern, and I'll die before I break that vow—or kill you in return." His breath was running fast and shallow.

"I *will* see you out of my house in a moment and by my hand if I must," Abram said levelly.

"No, you will only see your way to do what I ask."

Abram waited.

"You will direct the earnings of fitting these privateers to me. Every copper."

Abram kept silent.

"If you do not, the town will know you for the adulterer you are."

Even as he considered that Beniah must be guessing, and cautioned himself not to confess by his actions, Abram felt his confusion growing, his reason eclipsed. "The town knows you, Beniah, and it would know how to value such statements from you."

"The testimony of your wife, whose absence will then find its proper reason . . . it will be my corroboration."

"A man who knows the truth can have nothing to fear."

"Which makes you the devil's own candidate for terror, I'd say."

"You have said what you have to say?"

"You have not."

Abram refused to understand.

"My contracts are standard and call for three payments, at the signing, midterm, and finish. Yours I expect are much the same. You will need the first payments to begin the work, but at the midterm you should be solvent, particularly with so many agreements in hand. As June draws to a close, I'll collect my bill of five hundred pounds. Agreed?"

"How can I say this, Beniah?" Abram asked. In the midst of the question he was moving, boxing the man's ear so that his eardrum would explode with disabling pain. Then he grabbed the handful of burrs on top of his head, meaning to lead him out. Beniah spun wildly away. Abram hit him on the temple opposite the bump, so hard the pain went from his own knuckles into his elbow, and he grabbed the devil by the neck and led him to the back stairs, past Jezreel and Lucinda in the kitchen, who listened to the little man's torrent of curses and homicidal threats with blanching faces.

Abram knew this would hardly be the end unless he inflicted his own terror, and at the top of the back stairs he threw Beniah so far into the yard, where he landed flat on his back, that he thought Beniah might be paralyzed. He waited for long moments until the little man finally rolled onto his side, and then Abram did not want to see any more of him and left him to recover as best he could.

Abram pulled his waistcoat down, adjusted the white ties of his shirt, and settled back into his coat. On his way past Jezreel again, he heard, "He be needing what you give. That be the bad man."

PART V

Evil Loves the Night

CHAPTER 27

Spitting Image

*A*nne thought she heard raccoons on the steps, although she had never known them to forage at midday. Then a knock came. She opened the door to the late March chill and recognized the creature who stood there—his great head, the size and shape of a huge smoked ham, and his gimlet eyes—but could not recall his name.

"Mrs. Farmington," he said. "Beniah Lynch from your old hometown of Newburyport. I let the house next to you there to Mrs. Ulrich?"

She opened the door wider. "Why have you come here?" she asked.

"I've been sent as a kind of emissary from the town. May I come inside, please? I've been traveling these days."

She could see his horse cropping the new grass in her field. Everyone presumed they could use her pasture. She would have to ask Hugh about putting in a hitch. She opened the door to him.

He landed in her house—that's how he conducted himself—with

his feet spread, angling his body to and fro, looking the place over. She remembered Mrs. Ulrich speaking of him now as a particularly nasty creature.

"Sit down," she said, half ordering him. He chose the rocker with its low seat. "Why would the town send an emissary to me?" she asked.

He rocked, plainly enjoying the ride. Putting out his hand to the chair opposite him, he asked her silently to join him.

"I'll fix us tea. I have tea. I don't think there can be harm in using what's already come so far from the coast."

"The harm may well be in turning the ships away. Yes, tea will be very good."

"I have no political sympathies," she said quickly, and took the kettle off its hook and went to the rude cutting table under which she kept the pot, the tea, and her three cups, among her other utensils and pots and pans.

As she let the tea brew, she heard the baby, Titus, waking from his nap with his characteristic snuffling cry, a short protest against the blanket in which his face must be burrowed. Soon he would hunch up and wail. He was rolling over onto his stomach now, but remained dead set against rolling back, despite his anger at not being able to get his breath. This made her life more difficult, and yet she would not change it. She was already nostalgic about his first helplessness, when he could not roll at all but only wave his shaking arms, as if opening up each time with a titanic shock to such a massively stimulating world. He was a good baby. She thought he had Abram's defiance, his sometimes courageous rebellion. If he had only had more, she thought.

"Mrs. Farmington? Your child is crying," Lynch said.

"I'll serve you the tea and see to him."

She gave the little man his cup, then went up to the child. Rolling him onto his back, she saw him look up at her with that full and yet clouded expression, as if he were still wondering whether there were two worlds or one, his mother and another empty place, or only, as he preferred, his mother.

"Go back to sleep," she said, and with the crook of her index finger she rubbed his cheek. That would either soothe him or remind him he was hungry. He did not turn to her finger but closed his eyes. He'd had black hair at first, like Abram, and then it had fallen out; now, as the days passed and he took on weight, his eyes were assuming the smiling set of Abram's. The new hair coming in was lighter like hers. So far.

She climbed back down the ladder and poured herself a cup and sat opposite this goblin of a stranger.

"You have an older boy?" he asked.

"He's visiting with Mr. James. What have you come about?"

"I suppose I've been appointed or deputized, in a manner. The town remains concerned about . . . your betrayal. As I have many interests, commercial and personal, in the Points, I think the selectmen believed I would have reason to investigate such a violent incident."

"The government is doing a wonderful work in seeing to its citizens these days," she said, smiled, and sipped her tea.

"Are you not resentful of being victimized?"

"That child in the loft has given me some recompense."

"One might think you would hate the fruits of such an act."

"My baby, Titus, is my baby."

"Yes, I see," Lynch said. He seemed to be searching for how to go on. "We thought . . . the town thought that now, and as you are so much reconciled, as it appears, to your life, now especially you might be willing to give a fuller account of the event."

"Being pleased with the child, why should I want to see its father punished?"

"So you can say more?"

"I say only that what you assume, as to my ability to say more, is wrong."

"Were our assumptions very wrong? I mean, this was a violent act."

"What is your concern in this? Do you have any document to present as to your mission?"

The man pulled a buckskin pouch from his coat pocket and tossed it in the air. From the sound of the coins, she guessed at least silver, if not gold—they did not ring tinny like copper.

The bribe leapt her defenses so quickly that she had to remind herself to rethink who this might be and his purposes. From the beginning she knew he had no commission, the same as the previous gentleman with his son and catch of fish. Who would be sending him, though? Mrs. White must be satisfied with what she had given the first gentleman. Or else she wanted to do her some service—and a nasty one to judge by this emissary. Yet she did like taking money from the woman, if only as a means of outwitting Abram's plans for her. She had nearly spent the last.

"Has the government become so generous?" she asked at last. "I remember the Overseers of the Poor as being more desirous of their port at meetings than their charges' small beer."

"I think you have been wronged, Mrs. Farmington, and I would like you to receive justice. You are right to doubt justice from any government. There are those who work for justice, and often in its cause unusual measures must be taken. For human affairs are far beyond human law. What's justice can betimes be against the law, I venture to say. What's right and true may even run against common opinion. Do you believe these things?"

"I know you want something from me," she said.

"True enough. Every man acts on what he wants. Sometimes in the gaining of it he violates the honor of a woman he loves or traduces her reputation. Women have so little recourse in the law. They can often be victims twice over."

"What do you want of me?"

"I prefer to think of an alliance, a partnership that unites what you may desire and what I have in mind. Would such an alliance interest you?"

"You have no knowledge of my wishes."

"I know that you love Abram White," Beniah said, looking pleased with himself. "I know that you have borne his son, and I suspect that you would prefer he make his life with you rather than his wife. He has little enough life with her, in any event, since she lives now in Boston and is estranged from him. Such an arrangement as you would have with him is little known in our colony towns, it is true, but common enough, common enough, on the Continent. And I would prophesy that one of the advantages of the frontier will be, if it is not already, the accommodation of just such arrangements. Have you seen the wedding licenses of your neighbors?"

She did know, in fact, of several common law marriages among her neighbors, and she had wondered whether they might have left former husbands and wives. What she had been thinking of, when she had moved into the Whites' household, were those longtime acquaintances between master and servant that provided the substance of marriage to so many great men on the Continent, or so it was said, when the form served them so ill. That was all she wanted and what she'd had for those months with Abram. She had loved him enough to settle for it.

Now this man wanted her to say what she wanted. He knew so much. How did he know so much?

"How is it that you think you know these things?"

"I found Mrs. White in the Points one day, probably searching after you too, if I guess rightly—the neighbors said she was asking after you, and she let me know you had not been attacked, except by the fraud who sent you away. I talked to Abram himself, and he confirmed the story, if not directly, through a number of redoubtable signs."

"You have seen Abram? You have been talking with him?"

"He is a very confused and sad man right now. He broke down in church, cried so loudly people talked of it for days. He must miss you greatly, for I cannot think he misses that cold Sarah White. She wants nothing from him now."

"He owns these lands," Anne said.

"So he does. And he might live on them. Others have shipyards in Newburyport and can serve the trade. Methinks he should be serving his child and the one woman who does love him."

As he said this, she remembered his occupation and now knew the game. "I do not want him harmed," she said.

"He bought these lands for his family, landed his ancient mother here at first, where his sister and brother and their kin still live. So rich a man would not keep them in a place he did not treasure."

"You mean to disgrace him," she said.

"I mean to persuade him to requite the love he has been shown. He is too full of disgrace. Shame sent you away. I would only restore a perspective that is higher than any mean opinion of mere men."

"His greatness consists, I think, in his refusal to be compelled. I cannot compel him to love me."

"And yet you once persuaded him to treat you as his wife. Seeing his child, will he not acknowledge what he owes to this life and the life that you might have together? When he sent you away, he did not know that his wife would want nothing more to do with him. He may not care for her opinion, but as much as we might wish differently, he once cared for her. She has made her decision now. Nothing prevents him. Nothing but mere prejudice."

"And God."

"Did you care for God when you called him to your bed?"

She had wanted Abram then and she wanted him now, and she had wished that Sarah would leave them to a full if always shadowed love. And God? That consideration might wait again.

"How much money do you have?" she asked. "Thirty pieces of gold and silver?"

"Not so much. Ten crowns."

A year's wages for a laborer—maybe more. "What do you want me to do?"

"I want you to sign letters attesting to the child's paternity. I will use them to persuade Abram."

"What letters?"

"Letters I have written."

"I should prefer to write my own."

"You are able to do this?"

"I am literate. You neglect to think of my intelligence, as did Abram. He could not have loved me else, though."

Beniah folded his hands, knitting his fingers over his stomach.

"I will seal the letter, and you may not read it. Only give it to him."

"Write two, then."

"Why?"

"I have a double purpose."

"I'm sure. But why two letters?"

"I shall not say."

"I will write exactly the same letter, then. You may use the second for your own purposes, if you have another pouch in your greatcoat." He readily pulled forth the second she had suspected must be hidden there. "And a third?" she asked.

He moved forward in his chair aggressively.

"Two for two, then."

CHAPTER 28

Taking a Walk

Sarah walked along the perimeter of the Common, watching the
white-and-black-faced sheep crop the tufts of new grass sprouting
amid the dormant turf. She pushed Mercy in her perambulator. The
child lay sleeping, enfolded in her white swaddling blankets. Only
her pink face and her hands could be seen. Her fingers, as tiny as the
forsythia buds just then in bloom, picked at each other as if num-
bering her dreams. Her long, tasseled stocking cap curled beside her
head and trailed into the box's far corner.

The violet redbud trees were out; the white crab apples would
soon follow. The wind bending them still had a scything edge to it,
though. Sarah wore a hooded wrap and walked with one gloved hand
clasping the cowl and the other pushing the carriage. It was getting
later in the afternoon, and the once clear and blue day was clouding
up with high antipodean clouds whose dark undersides shadowed
the ground.

Sarah felt almost numb, except for her feet, which stung with each step. She nodded at the other walkers, hoping she would not meet anyone she knew, or if she did that they would not engage her in conversation.

Sarah thought she would just go down to the Long Wharf and see the ships and indulge herself a while longer. Submit might worry for a moment or two; but then, Submit always worried.

She turned down Tremont Street, and then St. Charles Place, and kept walking until Mercy and she had come all the way from the town's high ground to the shore. The Long Wharf, John Copley's childhood home, stretched out into the sea.

Sarah's next thought came to her as if she were overhearing an indecent joke and brought with it an excitement that made her neck tingle. "Would you like to visit the Continent with me?" she asked Mercy. "See the Tower of London, baby girl?"

Mercy opened her eyes and looked up at her in that way she had. At the same time, she was tasting her lips, her hunger rousing. Submit always fed her about this time. But the walk had taken so long, Sarah wanted a rest.

She saw a tea shop that had a large, carved, three-dimensional teapot for a sign, with a mechanical device inside that emitted smoke from the spout. She went in and ordered tea from the proprietor, a heavyset man in an apron, whose full beard looked like his own muffler. His hard agate eyes drew attention to the knife-thin bridge of his nose. He seemed to be expecting something more than her mere order, but he went away after hearing it.

As she waited, she felt skeletal under her clothes and her teeth were actually chattering.

Mercy began to fuss as the tea was brought. She fed the child the tiniest crumbs of cake, and Mercy gummed them and quieted. Looking around at the other tables, Sarah spied no one she knew.

When the shopkeeper came back with more hot water, Sarah said, "Must be good business on such raw days."

The man looked at her a moment too long. It was plain he was asking himself why such a well-dressed woman with a fussy infant should be stopping at his tea shop alone. "No cause to complain." He waggled a finger at the perambulator. "He's yours?"

"She. Yes. All mine."

His beard ruffed around his neck as he ducked his chin. "The father, your husband, will be along? You'll need a larger pot."

"No. No thank you."

He did not go away from the table.

"My husband is the governor's Special Secretary. He often works into the evening—while I have tea."

"Mr. Chauncey?" the proprietor asked.

Sarah was surprised. "No. A second Special Secretary." She paused. "That's all we'll be needing."

When he left, she watched him until he disappeared into a storage room. Then she wheeled Mercy round and left the shop without putting any coppers down.

The cold immediately roused Mercy, who started to cry with a waking hunger that would not be stopped short of being nursed, and Sarah found herself at least half an hour's walk from the house. She took the baby up and tried to comfort her, and when she would not be, Sarah put her down and pretended not to hear.

The baby cried so hard she started gasping. Once Mercy succeeded in gathering enough air, she used her whole body as a bellows, her hands and feet reaching toward one another as she cried out.

Sarah leaned her face down into the deep box of the perambulator and shouted back, "Mercy! Stop that! We're close now."

Mercy screwed up her little face and howled again. She gave such needy, retching screams that passersby looked at Sarah in disapproval, and her own nerves soon screamed out as well from the intolerable strain.

Sarah reached down, sweeping aside the covering blanket, and suddenly pinched the child's side, hard. She squeezed, twisting her pinching fingers, until she was certain the child's hysterics matched its punishment. *Your mother can have you*, she thought.

She covered the frantic infant with its blanket, gave the perambulator a shaking bounce, and continued up the hill to the Common. As she went, Sarah kept her head down and her cowl wrapped as tightly as possible, suspecting everyone as an acquaintance.

Long before they arrived, Mercy's cries began wearing themselves out. Sarah's hands gripped the bar of the pram even more tightly, and her fists began to seem a match for the circumstances arrayed against her. The baby's exhausted protests renewed her own tingling satisfaction.

"Oh, little Mercy," she said, pretending to be exhausted herself. "We have so much farther to go."

The baby renewed its cries as if understanding.

"Yes, I'm afraid we do."

The baby screamed pitifully.

"It's a long way yet, a very long way. Will we ever get home?"

CHAPTER 29

Paying the Piper

As soon as Gaylord returned home, Sarah began hearing the creaking of the stairs, doors clicking open and banging shut, muffled words coming up from the first floor, approaches and retreats in the hallway outside her bedroom. She found herself sitting at her secretary, waiting for someone to come in, not knowing whether she preferred Gaylord or Submit.

The overheard conversation spun into the master bedroom at the opposite end of the hall. Its door struck the wall, and the hallway's oriental runner could hardly muffle the stamp of a long-legged approach. Gaylord walked in without knocking.

She could not turn to face him. She kept her hands in her lap, her shoulders hunched. She could feel him looking down on her, his gaze pouring down over her head, turning molten at his first words.

"This is no common mischief, Sarah White. I had a letter from Mr. Copley a day or two ago. Now I have Submit's report of your unconscionable treatment of our child. She has a welt where . . .

There is nothing else to do but send you back to your husband. Nothing. I can't say what he shall do with you. I should most certainly whip you if you stayed here."

His voice had kept rising as he spoke; now it swiveled around and tried to turn her. "You might say something to this? What have you to say?"

She did not know what she would do, but as she heard his denunciation, she felt unexpectedly freed. His violence made her unknown intentions rise to a higher pitch.

"You may not hide in this mad dissimulation!" he shouted. "You have turned violent and criminal and that is how you shall very soon be treated."

He was not going to call the Justice of the Peace. He had already said he would be packing her off.

"I am tempted to speak of our hospitality. You tempt me very much to it. I would just have you answer now."

No one had been hurt so much. The babe frightened. The painter winged close to where he deserved it, in his painting arm.

"Will you not answer?"

"Who have I to answer to?" she asked, rather quietly.

"No one!" Gaylord shouted. "No one at all. Your husband waits in vain. And Submit . . . how could you have done this to Submit, who has been goodness itself to you?"

Sarah did not rise but turned around on her chair. "You have your answer. You are to send me away."

Gaylord had his hands on his hips and was leaning over, stalking the room, his face engorged. His hands shook as he lifted them and he folded them across his chest, then hugged his own shoulders. His not knowing what to do with his big hands did frighten her.

"Keep to your answer," Sarah said. "In Submit's opinion, you always know what to do."

"You would be haughty with me now? You have hurt my child, woman, and only my fear of God himself keeps me from whipping you senseless."

She turned round again toward the wall. "The way she looks at me—she seems to have had insolence bred into her."

She heard a muffled bang and the wall before her yawed as the room shook with the reverberations of Gaylord's punch. She glanced his way and saw him nursing that fist in his other hand and swallowing down the pain.

He had made himself ridiculous. Fortunately, he quickly left the room.

So she was to be sent back to her husband. She sat at her secretary and waited for this judgment and all that had transpired to come to her. She broke out in a sweat, and the tears that she might have shed before him came to her now, as her feelings of regret hammered her as hard as Gaylord's punch. If she could only have found some other means of relieving the pain. Not traded for what she did not want.

Now she would go away.

CHAPTER 30

—

More Letters

*W*here Sarah actually went—when Gaylord put her on the coach
home—proved a mystery. Her relations were only given clues,
contradictory ones.

April 7, 1770

Dear Abram,

No doubt you heard from Gaylord and Submit that they
packed me off to you.

They packed me, it's true enough, but I have outgrown the
habit of letting others throw me in coaches and take me where
they will.

I mean to make this my consistent policy and travel just
where I will from this point on in my life.

You know about this, don't you? I am thinking of you as a
small lad, about to get himself kidnapped into the wide world.
Fortunately, I have the means to effect my own escape, and do

not have to pretend I am being called by God on a grand mission.

I have no mission. I do have a purpose.

The same purpose you pursued in kidnapping me into the life so eloquently described as being your wife. This means, as far as I can understand, to act as an appendage of your will—the instrument of your desire.

These years of living almost apart from one another have taught me that I have my own will, my own desires. I mean to pursue them.

This great reversal will take me back to the Continent from which you came. Perhaps, all along, you read the wrong message in circumstance, and destiny has given it to me to riddle both our tales aright.

Reconsider your opinion of Captain Hawks. He still knows more than you have credited.

In my heart, I am, no longer,
Your wife,
Sarah Nicolls

April 8, 1770

Dear Gaylord and Submit,

I do not blame you in wanting to be rid of me. Clearly, I wanted to be rid of your influence, too, else I would not have misbehaved. Your house, however commodious to yourselves, became confining to me, as might be expected. I am sorry to have pretended to be happy there long after I ceased to be.

Forgiving you for sending me off in such a fashion presents a greater difficulty, as if my destiny were actually in your hands. Even this, though, I am taking as a needed prompt.

Did you really think I would return to dreary port and the good captain whistling his hymns?

There is something you need to understand, which methinks has received too little notice from everyone. God himself has cut me off from the only vocation He thought to designate to women. This scissoring has rended whatever veil within me—be it fleshly or spiritual—houses a Holy of Holies. God is departed indeed, and the dead do not rise, the buried do not leave their graves. Hell simply annexed the world I had hoped for.

I cannot think, then, of life in your terms. The necessity presents itself, therefore, of conceiving it in my own. I must be born of what is barren.

And what can that be but ambition and pleasure? I have but one resource, my inability to be a mother, and I intend to use that talent to its utmost. Like a man, I can dwell on conquest rather than conception; on the service of my own will rather than the procreation of another's.

This is well understood on the Continent, where I intend to seek my kind and prove with them that the will can triumph over nature, art over theology. Madame Du Barry be my guide!

Mr. Copley and you have freed me to find everything possible to a woman such as I, and for that,

I thank you,
Sarah

Of course, Sarah's baffled correspondents tried to work out their own strategy in response. Letters flew back and forth in this most epistolary of ages.

April 14, 1770

Dear Gaylord and Submit,

I have had what I can only call a torturing letter from my wife Sarah. There are many things in it, but the upshot is, she says she will soon be departed for the Continent.

Do you know where she is? I have written to a number of newspapers with a posting of her absence and the offer of a re-ward for information. This is an extreme measure, surely, of the greatest embarrassment, but what else can I do? You must tell me if you have had any word from her.

I cannot help but say how unwise it was of you to offer her a second life and then go so far as to deny me the privilege of seeing her when she was in such danger. You advised me to "prefer the wisdom of others." Would you had taken your own advice in that instance.

I suppose I have not the luxury of quarreling. We must find her. However strong she believes herself to be, I know my wife, and I know she is in several sorts of danger.

Do you have any word?

Most sincerely,
Abram White

April 21, 1770

Dear Abram,

We do not blame you for being impatient or angry with us. We are distraught over Sarah's taking flight, and we join you in your efforts to find her.

The word we have had from her is much like your own. She boasts of her own will and tortures us with the same proposal for her future.

These speculations may remain altogether imaginary, though. Our letter certainly did not come to us from a landing ship. Gaylord has made such inquiries as to ascertain that bribes brought it to hand by the most circuitous of routes. He has not been able to find its true origin, though. Her money has so far proven that much proof against his authority.

Perhaps we should meet to discuss strategy?

We are so sorry and ashamed.

> Together with you,
> in this grief,
> Submit and Gaylord

And Sarah did not stop writing, either.

April 16, 1770

My dear Mr. Copley,

I was just speaking with Mr. Benjamin West today, here at the Court of St. James, and he remarked on what a pity it was that you have been unable to avail yourself of Continental models— the Old Masters and such.

This was rather good of him, as my Tour has taught me much about what you would find here.

As I went through Pisa, Turin, Genoa, Florence, Ravenna, and of course Rome, I could not help but think that the Old Masters lived in a time where the very air had depths of sentiment we no longer know. The best of our contemporaries suffer from this, although Mr. West understands that decorum and fancy and even wit are no substitute for true passion.

He asked me whether I would sit for him, and I have agreed. You do him a great disservice for mocking his facility, saying as you were wont that his quickness makes for superficiality. Judge not! You may well be right not to cross the ocean, because the revelations awaiting you could prove too much. For, I think, you are one of the most decided victims of this age's disastrous propensity—its substituting of arithmetic for art. Your marriage proved sufficiently that you can add and also, perhaps, that you shall never truly paint. Do not come see for yourself. It is better not to know many things.

Of course Mr. West is nothing but courtesy in regard to your reputation. Think no ill of him. His numerous commissions here, I'm sure, allow him the greatest latitude in his praise.

> I remain,
> Your model (and Mr. West's),
> Sarah

April 18, 1770

Dear Handmaid,

My reports tell me that you have served me not on your knees but on your back, and that this has led to the birth of your illegitimate child.

When I think of you appearing at my door that day with your first offspring in tow, how you insinuated your way into my very home, and then repaid me by taking my kindness as a sop to a bawd, I can think of no words strong enough for such treachery; or only such words as I, being a Lady—and not a Strumpet, Worm Box, Pox Hole, Slut—such words as a Lady cannot use.

Your first Judgment,
Mrs. Sarah White

And even those who knew much less joined in.

April 21, 1770

Dear Abram,

It was reported to us that you have posted notices asking for help in finding out where Sarah is.

Every time I think of this, I grow confused. For your wife to disappear seems fantastic.

Anne received a letter from Sarah the other day—Hugh handed it on from the circuit rider. We asked whether it contains any news of Sarah's whereabouts and received little reply. She would not show us the letter, although we pressed her closely.

Hugh and I are ready to force our way into her home and search it if necessary. She owes us more explanation than she has provided, on many accounts.

Would you have us do so?

Your anxious sister,
Dorsey

CHAPTER 31

No Hiding Place

"Madame? You have a visitor." The boy who ran for her, John, was at the door. She opened it.

"Madame," he said again, this time in greeting.

"Someone has asked for me?"

"Someone is asking for you downstairs, yes," John said.

"Does he wear a captain's hat? What does he look like?"

"A short man, nearly as wide as he is tall. He looks like no acquaintance of yours."

"Go and ask what he wants."

She heard John's steps on the stairs, coming back. She opened the door before he knocked.

"Yes, John," she said. His runner's posture relaxed and his chin came forward; he was glad to serve her. She wondered what she would require of him this night—whether he could fend off whoever it was. Had the visitor asked for her by name?

"He says he's come to help you. He won't give his name, but says you be neighbors in the Newburyport."

No, John would not be able to put him off. How had this person found her? "I have to see this man, John."

"Not against your own wishes," he put in quickly.

"So, you are ready to defend me? Good. Stand by the door as we talk. Don't listen too closely. But if I call out for you, be ready."

"Is he an evil man?" John asked.

"Whoever might find me here must be somewhat," she said, speculating.

"I'll tell him you have retired."

"No, bring him up and then stay near."

"Yes, madame."

She had been alone in this room over Fraunces Tavern in New York for three months, writing her letters, reading the articles about her disappearance in the *Gazette*, watching Abram's postings of a reward.

The room was lit by two candles, one beside her bed, the other at the small table where the uncleared and largely untouched remains of a pheasant supper lay.

She had come here thinking to take some small measure of vengeance and then, her true object, resume her life at Elysia. She might visit the Continent later. The coach the Chaunceys had put her on had brought her quickly to a new purpose, and she had changed at the first stop and begun following her own plan.

She realized she had already stayed at Fraunces too long. She was finding something in her letter writing, though—an attraction and power that granted a pleasure similar to smashing Mr. Copley's plaster-of-paris statuettes. She could not seem to let go of it, or it would not let go of her.

Her letter writing had come to promise her more than a trite vengeance or a merely destructive pleasure. She felt herself to be clearing the ground of the forest into which she had wandered and making a new place for herself. Isn't that what the frontiers allowed to so many?

Her new ground had its own stumps and rocks, and she found herself living in a settler's three-sided structure, an underground dugout. This worried her, and caused her to question her wisdom, her thinking, and, as the others who were thinking about her, her sanity. She no longer knew whether she was deliberating or merely waiting.

She had stayed too long; now she had been found, or more as it felt, discovered.

The knock came at her door and John showed in her visitor. A little man, a small man, his greatcoat nearly reached his pixie ankles:

he looked like a performing parrot in human costume.

"Ma'am?" the visitor said.

She thought she recognized him but wasn't sure, and she wanted to make dead sure, so she took her candle from the table, and, crossing over to him, pushed it against his chest so that its taper singed his chin.

"Ma'am!" he screamed, and shook his head away from the flame and stumbled backward.

Before he did so, though, she had seen the burrish curls, the bump at the temple, the oversized face with its eyes flush with the skin.

"Beniah Lynch!"

"The world is looking for you," he said.

"The world is not always a fit place for women," she said. "I am out of the world for the present."

"You are near to many hearts," he said.

"How did you find me?"

"I am the kind of man who knows how to do such a piece of work. The stagecoach drivers, the barge captains—I'm familiar with the people the others who are searching would never want to know."

"The boy asked me if you are an evil man. I thought only the devil himself could have found me."

"Do not say this, ma'am," he said. "I thought to do your loved ones a service, which they would not have enjoined and might have prevented, but should be, nevertheless, most grateful to receive."

"You are looking for a reward."

"I have been looking most assiduously for you, and finding you, lady, is reward enough for any man."

She pulled out lengthwise a strand of hair from her falling tresses that were growing dead from lack of brushing. "You have found me at my most elegant."

She poured him a drink from the rum bottle the innkeeper insisted on sending up with her suppers, then pushed the flagon to his chest. His little hands, with their fingers of equal length, grabbed it and kept most of it from hitting his shirt front as she had intended.

"Thank you," he said.

"*Pas de quoi,*" she said. "How do you think you can do anyone a service here?" she asked. "I'll not be brought back. I'm paying the taverner well, and he'll not see me out of this house without a struggle."

"You misunderstand me. I am at your service, lady," he said, and he swept out the hand holding the flagon and bowed deeply, one foot stepping back. The motion of his larger upper body and his diminutive legs suggested a toppling curtsy.

"No, Mr. Lynch, you are ever and always at your own service, and I have wearied of this most surprising social occasion. Excuse me, then?" She sat back down at the table.

"The world believes you to have gone mad," said Beniah, "but I know you have an object in view."

She did not turn her face back toward him.

"You are a fraud, lady, because the farther you travel from your salty man, the more you want him to come to you. He is a wise idiot and does not realize this. You are equally foolish if you do not as well."

She did turn back then. "Abram has nothing to give me."

"He has proven he can give you the child you want, with your own handmaid."

Did he know this as reliably as she? She was shocked by how much she hated hearing this spoken of. "You must not say such things without proof, Mr. Lynch. The man is my husband."

Beniah waited for several moments, glaring at her as she returned his gaze. "I have never known anyone to become angry except at the truth. Your hatred convicts you."

"What I want from Abram," she said, wondering as she began whether this would be the occasion when she would hear her own explanation, "what I want . . ."

"Is for him to do your bidding," Beniah said.

"That's . . ."

"That's what you want," he said confidently. "Now we must reason as to what you will bid and how."

"I want nothing to do with Abram," she said.

"Nothing? How can you let him pose as the Holy Ghost and make you out to be a madwoman? He's been enjoying every sensual pleasure an exceptionally beautiful woman—common as she may be—can give him. Would you have him go to her and live his life with her?"

"He would not," she said. "No, never."

"I have this present for you, then," he said, and he took Anne's letter from the inside pocket of his greatcoat and let her read it.

"He will not join her there," she said. "I know he will not."

"You see," said Beniah, "you must reckon on a world with more wills than the two of yours. There is my will in the matter. That's a will that must be reckoned on. For, besides what the comely lass wants, I wants my will as well. And what I want would have Abram and his shipyard gone from Newburyport. A simple enough matter, one that I can manage in my way, or Anne's, or perhaps yours."

"Explain yourself, then. I have been waiting for this entire accursed interview just for that inevitability."

"Abram in his lying imposture of virtue has snared what business there is in these times. The devil seems to promote him the more he is in the wrong. I want to be sure of his withdrawal as a competitor. Anne will never keep him, howsoever she tries—you are right there. I can shame him from Newburyport with Anne, but he might take himself off, and the business itself—men are such blackguards—to East Boston. I want him finished. I want him leading a wholly different life. Here our bidding may combine."

A wholly different life, and perhaps in the end the life she had always wanted. She had never reconciled herself to being forced to live in Newburyport; whatever she had said, she had not.

"I am going to extend an invitation to him," she said and looked up at Beniah's stumpy figure. This would contradict her earlier letters, she knew, but if Beniah ever did deliver it, Abram would have no time to doubt its authenticity.

"You must say that you will expose his adultery. You must write this and let me carry it to him."

"Yes."

"And this invitation will be to join you in this town."

"At a place he knows well, not far from here."

"Your family's lands?"

She nodded. "This will be festive work," she said. "Order up another bottle for yourself. I'd like some tea."

He picked up the neck of the empty bottle and hung it on his index finger. "I'll insist on something better. This had a cutting edge and false quantity."

"Please yourself," she said.

As she wrote out her letter and a copy to Abram, John came in, asked after her, and then tidied up the dinner things. He hesitated before going away, and she reached out and squeezed his arm. "This looks to bode well," she said.

"Shall I still keep by the door?" he asked.

"If you would," she said.

He left then.

Beniah reappeared with two bottles.

"Are you so thirsty?" she asked.

"You haven't been traveling, as I have. From such a distant place to this moment and time." He opened a bottle and poured out his drink.

Beniah stayed close by her table as she finished her letters, close enough for her to hear his swallowing and smacking and his increasingly raspy breath. She thought the drink might actually be making him sick, adding the thickness to his tongue and swelling his windpipe. He seemed to have to swallow a gulp down now and again before being able to pull in another breath. She tried to finish the letters quickly, else she would be driven truly mad. He watched over her shoulder, mouthing a thick-tongued commentary. "Oh yes, I see what you intend. That's good. That's good. He'll not escape your conclusion. I wouldn't say . . . but then, yes, I see that direction. You are most persuasive. I'd not want to incur your displeasure."

She handed him the letters to get his face away, but he kept one hand on her shoulder even as he put the letters in his greatcoat pocket with the other. "I am so pleased that you have joined with me in this. That our desires are one."

She stood up, and at first she thought he was pushing her back into the chair, but he was grabbing her, pulling her into an embrace. He was so small that his head would meet her chest if she let it. She threw him away. He came at her a second time, and this time she pushed him away with a strength that was a shock even to her. He proved surprisingly light and staggered back. She would call out to John if he came toward her again.

She managed to stand up straight and move to the door. "Our business is finished now," she said, realizing how hard she was breathing.

He moved from his place only to sit at the foot of her bed. "We have the rum to finish. It's my rum. I paid for it. I want to enjoy it," he said, then showed her a terrible grin. "Think about it. Many women have trouble with one man, but not another."

"What filth you are!" she said. She started moving toward him. "Give me the letters. You have made my lack of wisdom too clear."

At that, he hopped up. "So it shall remain a business matter," he said, sidestepping toward the door. "So it shall." He went out quickly, shoving John aside as the boy was rushing in.

CHAPTER 32

The Devil's Soothe

*A*bram was trying to enjoy a late afternoon glass of punch, as the world finally greened in late May and the front sitting room once more became pleasant away from the hearth. The light from the windows, with its leafy stains, suggested happier meditations should fill the cathedral of spring. Abram believed that Sarah would be found. Her letters, as mad and maddening as they were, showed her intent on revenge, yet even that evil was something to live for.

Without warning, the back door at the kitchen bumped so hard the whole house shuddered. Abram heard choked crying and muffled screams and Jezreel's voice becoming louder. He had just stood up to go see what the commotion was about, when he heard a rocking progress coming down the central hallway, with shouts and more flailing thumps.

Jezreel huddled Lucinda into the room. She had her hands to her mouth and was grimacing and throwing her head back to breathe.

Suddenly she went into a crouch, shaking and crying and giving the sharp yelps of a penned animal.

"Lucinda," Abram said. "Lucinda, what is this?"

She wailed and wailed.

"*Jezreel*," Abram demanded.

"She come into the house like this, sir. She be to the Points and then come into the house just now." He put his arm around her, this time gently, like an older brother. "Lucinda," Jezreel said. "Don't you cry now. Tell Captain what's happened."

"Here now," Abram said. "Sit in this chair. Sit there then and catch your breath. Now explain what you can."

"That creature said to tell you," Lucinda said and took a huge breath. She gave another shrill cry and shook her head, as her terror and confusion kept surfacing. "He took me . . ."

"Who, Lucinda?" Abram said.

"That shipbuilder, Lynch, that wharf rat. What a vicious little man!"

"Tell us what he has done," Abram said.

She turned her puffy, dimpled face up to him, with its shower of tears and wet red skin. "He took me, he dragged me into that shed where Anne . . . he took me there, and I thought . . . and I was screaming and he hit me, and he called me such vile things, and then he told me that this was how it was supposed to have happened to Anne." She took several more breaths and swallows. She wiped her running nose with her arm. " 'It didn't happen that way,' he said. And he wants to tell the captain how it did. He wants you to meet him at Cornejo's this night. That bottle shop. To tell you."

"I'll be going to Cornejo's," Jezreel said, "and Lynch not be coming out."

"Jezreel," Abram said. "I will see to it."

"You not the one to go there," Jezreel said.

"I will see to it," Abram said. "I must."

———

Abram left the house at nine o'clock that evening, after the decent citizenry were all in their houses and unlacing their boots. The sky in the west this late in the spring still held some light, and the streets of the Points ran with long, inky shadows. Trudging through the damp lanes down to the water's edge, Abram felt that the world wanted to blot him out; he wondered whether he did not wish it would.

He came upon the small distillery with its peaked roof and went through its banging door. The heavy smell of new molasses brewing rolled out to him and coated the inside of his mouth.

Beniah sat at the table on the right, his elbow on the chair's arm, his ankles crossed. He raised his tankard to Abram and gestured with it toward the opposite chair. He would have appeared at his ease had not his attenuated body crumpled in the ill-fitting chair.

Cornejo came out before Abram took the chair. "Señor?" he said, questioning, warning.

"How are you, then, Cornejo?" Abram said, and he could hear the raised pitch of his own voice, its false heartiness. He took a breath and searched for the bottom of his stomach. "I don't see you now that you have your business. I'll have a half bottle of your best." He looked quickly at Beniah and back to the Spaniard. "The shipyards are stewing."

Cornejo raised his eyes and jogged his head as if he wanted to believe that, yes, the shipyards must be having many difficulties, and the shipyard owners would want to meet together. When he brought the bottle, he poured out the shortest measure in a tankard. "The best in the house for the Missionary," Cornejo said. "You drink and talk, but not too long now, I think. I am having to close early tonight." He put his hand on Abram's shoulder before walking away.

"Everyone takes such care of you," Lynch said.

"The care I mean to take is to see you in jail. Lucinda might have died of pure terror."

Beniah turned his head one way, then back the other. "I see that my message reached you, then," he said.

"I am not a frequenter of this place," Abram said.

"You have, though, visited more widely and darkly than your careful neighbors know."

"What is your purpose, man?" Abram asked. "I shall not give you my business or my money or let you harm those of my household."

"I would not harm them," Beniah said. "I come to you as their protector."

Abram was about to reach across the table, and Beniah lowered his glance and held up a hand, tamping down Abram's temper. "Read these and see if you do not agree," Beniah said. From the inside of his pocket he pulled two letters, one with a red ribbon tie and seal and the other of coarser paper with blue veins.

He opened the coarser missive first.

March 12, 1770

My Dearest,

Your child has been born, and I have called him Titus. Do you like the name? It comes from an uncle, the only kind old dodge in my family. The baby looks like you. He will have your strong nose, and his chin is as square-rigged, with the White cleft.

Do not think me the dupe of my strange visitor. Betimes wonderful things come from what is not customary. I see this every day in Titus's smile, and believe that no one who causes so much joy could have been begotten through sorrow. I do not remember it that way. Your memories, I think, are the same, the ones that are true.

So I call you back to me. You have lands here and a family, your relatives, your child, a woman who desires nothing but to serve you. If this be uncustomary, then let custom have its place and yet not rule. For Nature makes greater demands. And how shall we know even God's will except by these things?

I know that you have not forgotten me, that you can never forget, nor ever will. If you think of obligation, think of your son and the chance to love him and his mother. Your other thoughts are but lonely wishes. I am here and would be where you are.

> Your eternally devoted and
> most adoring,
> Anne

Then Abram read what lay under the crimson ribbon tie and seal.

May 3, 1770

Husband,

If that is what you are, although I am more sure of other appellations and would call them, but that is not my purpose now.

This gentleman means to publish your transgressions to the world, and for this, I salute him. You are an adulterer, have fathered an illegitimate child, and conspired to hide this from the world through the story of your paramour's violation. She was doubly violated by you in this.

I cannot be surprised, being so ill-used through the course of our marriage that I have been driven to live much of what the world would call our married life in another city, housed by kind relatives.

When great injustices are done, as those you have indeed committed, sir, then such rectification as there may be must be severe. Being a dutiful, subservient, and yet dignified wife—for all your slanders and abuses—I propose such reforms as would serve the healing of your own soul and the mending of our union. Tell the tale of your lying adventures, leave Newburyport, and join me at the seat of our proper estate, Elysia. I am going there now to take its physic of mild climate, sweet air, and ample provision. The world so conspires to favor you that your remedy, save for its public humiliation, chiefly consists in the enjoyment of God's created order and the sacramental union that He has sanctioned for all eternity.

Those who may read this, as I hope many will, may understand if I sign myself,

Your much mistaken,
Sarah

Was that truly where she had gone? Abram wondered. He looked up at Beniah, whose humming breath had been billowing with an ever greater cloudiness around his thoughts as he read.

"Where did you find my wife?" Abram asked.

"I may not say."

"I will beat you senseless otherwise."

"With these witnesses against you?"

"You must have copies."

"Lodged appropriately." Beniah went on. "Dear sir, in this I am but a messenger. These so good ladies expressed their wishes to communicate with you and I have done them this small service."

"So I must do what they ask?"

"They seem to leave you so little room to respond in any other manner."

"How would you have me respond?"

"My wishes are yet again my own."

"What be they?"

"I have not determined on the *exact* measures, for you see I must take these ladies' thoughts into account, and they have a contradictory character. For me, I know the direction of what I wish, but as yet I remain in a quandary as to how to accomplish everything needful."

Abram took a quick, finishing draft of his rum. "You must say what you would have me do, though I do not suppose that I will accomplish your will entire." Would the man know he wanted more time? "Still, your remedy may be less harsh than these."

"Less harsh?" Lynch looked around him as if questioning an unseen host as to how anyone could devise less harsh solutions. "These ladies ask for simple justice. What presents me with difficulties is how their wishes might be reconciled and my own. For I do have my own wishes. I do. I have already expressed versions of these wishes to you, and I believe, as I recall, that you answered negatively. Quite negatively. It would be, as I may say, more than a small mistake to respond . . . negatively . . . to any request I might put to you from this time."

"You want?" Abram said, his voice rising.

Beniah settled back into his abbreviated lounging position. "I want you to go away now. It's getting late, Cornejo will be closing, I am tired. I would simply have you go away."

Abram understood that he could not strike the man and that he had finished his rum and could not even take a last departing swallow. He didn't have a gesture left. He stood up and, just as Beniah had asked, went.

CHAPTER 33

——

Night of the Soul

"John! *John!*" she screamed.

She heard him clambering to his feet in the hall. He opened the door and poked his head in.

"The room is darkening. I would have another lamp."

"Madame?" He looked around the room, lit, populated, by almost two dozen lamps, too many to crowd together on the table; the secretary, the top of the armoire, the bed stands, even the corners had their own encampments.

She found it harder to see the letter she was working on, though, and every time she succeeded in obtaining another lamp, her head and eyes ached a little less. The more she asked for, the more the boy would take out during the day, but then he kept them ready to hand for hauling in again. The more she asked for, the more he would find additions.

"Madame," John said, "the light is growing outside. The lamps only seem less because of the coming day."

"I did not ask to know the hour. I know the hour. Because of the hour I want the lamp." She gestured for him to come closer to her side. She stroked his upper arm. "You can do that for me."

John was at that age where his joints were gnarling with his coming manhood, and he looked all shoulders, elbows, knees, and ankles. He had brilliant flax-and-heather-colored hair, with darker underlayers that speckled it. It was cut so that his bangs nearly touched his eyebrows. His face had a foxy triangular shape, the foxiness reinforced by a long nose, but his cheeks were hollow. The hours she had been keeping him up had stamped his eyes, and he had become so perpetually tired that he stretched into every movement. He should be sleeping during the days, as was she.

"You ought to sleep now," he said.

"This is a five o'clock letter," she said.

"Is it done?" he asked.

"Nearly."

"I'll stand watch and you can finish it and then give it to me. I'll see to its sending so you can sleep."

"Will you sleep then?"

"I have slept for most of the night."

"You want me to finish it, then?" she asked.

"As you wish."

"It is a five o'clock letter," she said. "It must be finished now." She went back to concentrating on the missive.

Five O'Clock
A Five O'Clock Letter

Dear Mr. Copley,

You are going to bed with Sukey and you lie beside this woman with her thick neck and bowling-pin legs. You take her in your arms and I am there with you, in her flesh, which turns as curved and graceful as a fish. You are Jonah, in the belly of the great fish. You cannot make a sound because you are there with me. Whenever you touch her, you touch me, because I am there, consuming both of you.

Reach out to her. Hold her. Grant her every nicety. She changes at your first touch and the warmth of her body is mine.

Your spirit,
Fancy

———

Her correspondence had become infinitely more important after

Beniah found her, for she expected that she would soon be discovered by everyone else. Her time was short. She could not write during the day, and the tavern downstairs was often noisy until well past midnight. Then she had to wait at her table for the inn's guests to stop banging doors and rattling the house with their stomping boots. The hours grew shorter and shorter in which she could truly concentrate. Her thoughts were very often unclear and her head felt loggy. The following night, though, the house slipped under its covers quickly, and her mind quickened.

Down in the street, the night watchman soon called out the third hour. She saw from the window that he was questioning two men who might be breaking the curfew. They kept talking there beside the Garvey's lamp. Why did it take so long to interview them? He would not actually want to stop his pleasant stroll through the town and take them to jail. She went back to her table and another missive before she saw what happened.

Three O'Clock
A Three O'Clock Letter

Dear Theo,
You are most mistaken in your parentage. She surely did not love your father. And she was not driven into a wasteland or Egypt or Nazareth. The angel that appeared to her announced other tidings.
Tell your brother . . .
No, keep your silence.
Your nuncle,
Theology

———

She asked John every night whether anyone else had asked after her or written.

One night, he asked in return, "Why did that one man come here?"

"He is helping me," she said.

"He attacked you," John said, vehemently.

"That was useful, too."

Two O'Clock
A Two O'Clock Letter

Dear Abram,
    Find Anne in her bower. She waits for you. She is calling to you.
    Take what she offers. Take it. She has made herself nothing for us. She is nothing. Only what she gives. So take what she offers. Take her.
        Your pleasure,
        Share

————

Another night she took all the lanterns and put them in one place in the middle of the floor. The brown threads of their imperfectly trimmed wicks conjured up a brown veil, a wall, a smoky temple of onion domes in the middle of her shambles. She felt as if she were alone as a child in a room with an unattended pouch of gold coins—the kind her father had about in his study from which he paid the servants. And something more. Something like being in her mother's room, her armoire half-open, her clothing there to be tried on. Her notion seemed both farcical and tempting—the idea of using that ring of fire for her own ceremony. This sent her to her writing once more.

One O'Clock
A One O'Clock Letter

Dear Mother,
    I remember the fire of the vesper lamps, their spade-shaped singe on the church's walls. My prayers for you to come back to me.
    Did you know I saw your death before it came? The blood pouring from the hand pump by the well. Felicity told me not to be foolish; not to scare Livy. I saw these things, but seeing them was of no help to you. Is this like our prayers? The sight we gain by faith comes without power?
    To be able to do a thing in this life, to effect another's will, is not easy. Why should we then not worship what allows this? For then worship becomes a true means to our own ends. Women need such powers to hold off the Giants who are arrayed against them.
    Why did you leave your small girls? You were forced, taken by your death. Everywhere, that's the weapon holiness uses against us. "Be it unto me," the Lord's Mother said, but I do not

remember her being given a choice. Could she have refused?

Do you pray for me in heaven? Are you calling me to you? I could not bring you back, and so how shall I find you now?

Your lost,
Daughter

Five O'Clock
A Five O'Clock Letter

Dear Abram,

You found me the other day, sir, and you did what you always do; you deprived me of my will and used me most cruelly. You have become lazy, not mistreating me yourself, as you did Anne, but through your emissary.

Sauce for the goose, sauce for the gander, cauldrons for each. Now I am carrying the iron in my womb, this ferrous and feral child.

Are you thinking then of writing to Cousin Submit, telling her you have had a letter from a poor, confused woman, lost in her own imaginations?

No. I am trying to speak of something difficult: that Beniah Lynch was here and did to me what you practiced on Anne. His evil has proven more potent, and I am now with his child.

If I am in hiding then, you know the reason. And I protest that you are still the reason, as much as if you had bludgeoned me in this closet yourself.

I am now,
Lying In,
Sarah

Two O'Clock
A Two O'Clock Letter

Dear Captain Hawks,

When you had my husband in your loving grasp, twisting his throat, taking his life away, why, sir, did you not hang on another moment?

He never learned. You were so good, had so much to give him, and yet you let him escape with nothing learned. His regrettable virtue intact.

You did try to show him the way. The truth that is so hard for us to bear that it must be inflicted on us by cruelty. I know, as you did, that there alone lies human salvation.

I do understand, and for that,
I do not thank you,
Your Better

———

The steel bowl of blood still sat on the table from that morning. If the proprietor of Fraunces Tavern could insist on her being seen and bled by a doctor, she could insist on keeping her own blood. How else would she summon the dead? She took the bowl and poured it in the circle where the fire had been.

Four O'Clock
A Four O'Clock Letter

Dear Father,

Are you there with the shades, mournful as Achilles, deprived even of a glorious death? Or do you speak with these heroes of what alone can be valued in life, which you knew so well?

You gave me away and he took me and now it is for me to take what I can back. You look at me from that ashen place and you cannot speak and yet I know this is what you are saying. My poor sympathies have taken so much time to be tutored, and yet the whole world has conspired to instruct me. The only lessons in life must be learned from the dead.

Stay. I would see you no longer. I shall have to turn my face and walk steadfastly for as long as eternity.

Your daughter,
Sarah

———

Five O'Clock
A Five O'Clock Letter

Dear Beniah,

As you have been my love, be my father and Lord. Let me know nothing but your resolve and will. Speak in my every action. Declare yourself in my triumphs. Give birth to what you have wed.

I praise you,
Your own,
Child

"John!" she cried.

The boy came in immediately from the hall. "Madame?"

"My letters," she said.

"Yes, madame?"

"Where are my letters?"

"I mailed them, madame."

"*Why* . . . all of them?"

"Yes, madame."

"How long ago?"

"I mail them every day. You asked that they be promptly mailed."

"How long have I been here?"

"Weeks, madame."

"Weeks?"

"Many weeks, madame. Three months now. Too long."

"Why do you say too long?"

He went back toward the door.

"John, answer!"

"You cannot stay here too much longer, madame."

She bundled her nightgown around her. "Has the proprietor spoken of this?"

"You must be taken care of, madame."

"You do what I ask, John. You will keep doing what I ask?"

"Not much longer, madame."

"Why?"

He opened the door. She raced to him, turned him around and held him with her hands on his shoulders. "What arrangements are being made? John?"

"Nothing unhappy. Your family is coming."

"My family?"

"From the Long Island."

"Felicity, Livy, Cousin Delancey?"

"You have been writing to the dead, madame."

She let him go. "That is why, John. That is just why. I wish you had not taken all the letters. Sometimes, one needs to write . . . but you cannot send such letters." She twisted the long lace sleeves of her gown and began pacing.

"Would you like me to get you anything, madame?"

"No," she said. "No. Leave now."

He went again toward the door.

"John!" she called, her voice demanding.

"Yes."

"When are they to arrive?"

"I do not know, madame. But soon."

"Tonight?"

He looked as if he could not answer and then he went out.

The thought that her family would come made her shake with fear. The blood started to her head so suddenly that she felt bolts of it work their way into her scalp like so many fingers. She did not want to be discovered. She had been discovered by Beniah, and that had deflected her. Led to the wrong letters. Living at night. Now the family would take her away and she would be the poor, the pitiable Sarah again. Had she learned nothing? No. She had.

She thought of arranging the lamps in a circle again. They would be better distributed. She took one to each corner and then made a crossing axis and then a box of the two dozen lamps. She picked up the one left for the center point, where she now stood. Before she committed the act, she took a breath and felt the heat at the lamp's base which she held. Whirling round, she threw it against a corner, where it hit another with a pop of glass but not the whoosh she hoped for. She threw another lamp. Two more. John was calling from outside.

The room soon looked like a field, a grassland of fire. Then a lamp did explode, and she turned to see a billowing cloud of fire unscroll toward her so fast that it licked the roof of her mouth. She tried to breathe.

The next explosion came, behind her, and she was knocked almost off her feet. She could smell her own skin roasting. Another explosion.

The boy had his arm around her shoulder. "Madame!" he was screaming in her ear. "Madame!"

PART VI

—

Let There Be

CHAPTER 34

The Way Forward

*F*elicity and her husband David, Livy and her Paris, and stark-eyed Cousin Delancey came to the old house at Elysia every day at noon to have dinner with Sarah. She had been able to eat at the table now for about a week, although the stalk-shaped burns on her legs still made walking painful. The blistering of her face and the swelling of her lips demanded a turban of bandages that tied under her chin. These dinners could be horribly silent, as everyone seemed to be wondering what she would look like when the bandages came off— how terrible her disfigurement would prove.

Today, the long, round-ended dining table appeared festive, with two silver candelabra, the hunting-scene china, and a dinner of roasted pork, applesauce, squash, freshly baked bread, the new beans from the garden. This was Livy and Paris's tenth anniversary. She had become plump, as her figure always suggested she would. She still looked youthful, though, with her cornsilk blond hair, blue eyes, and her straight nose that gave her pretty face such definition.

The talk went on around Sarah, almost circled her, it seemed, and the faster it went at the beginning, the more horribly it would soon die.

"How much better you are looking," Felicity said to her.

"Yes, yes indeed," her husband said. "Your perpetual youth seems to apply to your recuperative powers." David had a way of finishing his statements and then rolling his eyes upward, as if looking for heaven to reveal what he could possibly have meant.

"Ten years, Livy," Felicity said then, turning to her other sister. "My baby sister."

Livy's husband, Paris, might have been even better looking than his wife, with his chestnut hair and his ruddy complexion. And he remained in youthful trim. He could be snappish, though. "You must stop describing my wife as such, Felicity. At this rate we are going to be wizened by the time you let her out of the nursery."

"We have Cousin Delancey as our bulwark against heaven," David said. "We may not have to consider ourselves ancients yet."

Cousin Delancey reared back, his baggy eyes growing so loose that his attention seemed hung on a slouching clothesline. "You are counting on me to hold off mortality?"

His dislike of the notion reminded everyone of how close mortality had come. Sarah saw them all turning back to their dinners with too much interest.

A moment went by. Another. She had been preparing, and before the silence reached down and squeezed her own windpipe, she determined on speaking. "The boy, John, staved off mortality for me."

They had not spoken of the boy's death openly, and she saw them drawing in their shoulders, glancing at each other uneasily.

"You need not fear me saying anything amiss. I am only thinking to clear the air."

"He must have been quite a lad," David said.

"He saw after you, didn't he?" Felicity asked.

"I thought to order my life," she said, and laughed a quiet, sad laugh. "I thought to order my life, and the only order in it came from a lad with the courage to treat a mad woman decently."

"You have suffered, Sarah," Livy said.

"Through my own doing," she said. She held up her hand, asking that she be allowed to finish. "I always thought to come back here. To take back my place."

"Is that your idea?" Cousin Delancey asked.

"No, not now, dear cousin," she said. "Now that I am back, I see how such reasoning would have made for unhappiness. You have your lives. We are no longer children together. My life is elsewhere."

"You need not think of this until you have recovered," Felicity said.

"In another week, I shall begin my journey home."

"Too soon," Paris said. "You have hardly been able to enjoy the company of your family."

"It is just the company of my family I am thinking of."

"Are you strong enough?" Felicity asked. "Forgive me, but as yet you seem so troubled. One of us should accompany you, at least."

"I shall have to depend on another's strength, I know. John taught me that. It is only in outward appearances that I will go alone."

The haze that clung to the rolling mountains turned into a greenish band before the sky deepened and brightened and swam into its depths. Then the road along the escarpment, which allowed this vista, pitched downward again. Streams with amber, rock-covered beds, sudden fern-brushed glades, and the scent of pine and grasses turned to hay brought Sarah into her husband's lands. She was riding with her brother-in-law Hugh, in his buggy, over to Anne Farmington's house, and she kept thinking of that Scripture about not planning what to say. She kept remembering her letters to the woman, fearing she might have written worse things that escaped her memory. Mad woman, incendiary, murderer. She had never confronted anyone other than her family in these new guises, and yet she meant to speak as a moral authority.

"Would you have me come in?" Hugh asked, and squinted his smiling eyes.

"If you would wait. I don't mean . . ."

"No offense taken. *None*. I'm not *that* curious." He laughed to himself.

She knew the home from Hugh's and Dorsey's descriptions when she saw it set behind its front pasture: a snug log house, a little tall and narrow for a country home, and she wondered whether Anne had taken a hand in the design, for it might have sat cheek by jowl with its neighbors in Five Points. Here it seemed to draw in its own isolation. The shed behind and the stone wall lining the pasture side of the approach accommodated their setting better.

"Let me walk in," she said.

Hugh stopped the cart at the turn from the common road, and Sarah dismounted and marched up the slight incline toward the steps. Wafts of desultory smoke blew from the chimney.

Anne opened the door to her immediately, as if she were expected.

As Sarah crossed the threshold, her eyes took a moment to adjust from the glare outside. Her blindness cleared in the almost cavelike interior, and she took in, at last, a fresh view of her handmaid. The second child had further exaggerated her gourdlike figure and had put a softer touch to her cheeks and a care-worn dry crimp in her auburn hair. She remained unexpectedly tall, and Sarah thought again about Abram with this big woman.

Anne did not welcome her but stood back with her hands together.

"Hello, Anne," Sarah said. "I came to see you in this new life. Would you talk with me awhile?"

"What has happened? You mean to talk with me? You look . . . madame, is that really you?"

"There was a fire. I will never be as I once was, but I am who I claim—right enough."

"Who brought you?"

"Hugh brought me over."

"I meant, did you come with anyone?"

"No. I came alone, and not from Newburyport. I was in New York, at my family's home on the Long Island, after the fire."

Anne kept standing in one place, her hands clasped. She smoothed back her hair and then held her hands fast again, with a twisting that whitened the knuckles.

"I have not come to harm you," Sarah said.

"Why did you come, then?"

"Could we sit?"

Anne glanced enough to the left to indicate the chairs before the hearth. Sarah sat down in the spindle-backed rocker and Anne stood by the opposite straight-back chair, now quite tall and looming.

"Would you sit?" asked Sarah.

Anne took her chair as if ordered.

"This seems a lonely life," Sarah said, trying to work some feeling into her voice, then quickly thinking better of such an opening.

"I have more visitors than you would think," Anne said. She lowered her eyes and smiled to herself.

"One would have been Beniah Lynch."

The woman looked up, as startled as a hunted animal.

"He showed me your letter. I wrote one as well—to a similar purpose."

"You know . . ."

"I have known since my return to Newburyport, just after your departure. Would you not have known if you had been in my position?"

She saw Anne thinking. The house was incredibly quiet and still.

"We would both prefer not to think of what we have shared," Sarah said. "But we do. Which is why I have come. You have a baby somewhere abouts, and his father is in Newburyport. I think it time for his father to vouch for the child's paternity."

Anne got up from her chair and took almost running steps to her kitchen sideboard. "Would you have some tea?" she asked. She put her overlapping palms on the sideboard and rocked her weight onto her stiff arms and back down onto her heels.

"Let the question of tea wait. We have my question."

"Were you asking me?"

"I meant to. Tell me. Would you have Abram acknowledge your son as his?"

"How should I understand such a question?"

"For what it promises alone. Abram and I have made a covenant, one I shall not break, nor invite him to do so. That would be tempting his own destruction. I shall ask him to have the child's paternity legally acknowledged so that you may share in our household's wealth."

"You have come to tell me that Abram is yours."

"I have no need of telling you such a thing."

"You have not acted as if you wanted him. Except in your letters."

"No, no, I haven't. I shall now, though."

"Because of our child?"

"No. And yes."

"Madame, Mrs. White, I have very little . . . I feel these things too much to be riddling. I want more than you are offering. I want Abram and a life together here. You read my letter, you say. I meant those things. Beniah Lynch, he only prompted me. I love Abram. *I want him.*"

Sarah took a moment. "You are forthright. But you are wrong, and you know you are wrong."

"What declares this?"

"Heaven and earth," Sarah said.

"I have a child that speaks another sentence."

"You are remarkable," Sarah said. "However, you are wrong."

Anne did not seem in the least chastened by this. She looked up from underneath her brows at Sarah. "I am glad you will have the child's paternity acknowledged, and I think it more fitting that we join in this than use Beniah as our emissary."

Sarah rushed in upon this point. "What has been started through Beniah must be stopped. I know what he practices, and it is not simple mischief."

"I knew him for the devil as well. You saw how my letter guarded against its misuse?"

"You tried. You cannot guard against what Beniah will do. He will do anything."

Anne had taken a few steps back toward her chair, without doing anything more about preparing tea.

"I will be leaving, then," Sarah said. "And I shall do as I have promised. As to Abram's choice, I cannot make it for him, although you must remember, Anne, that our ties are stronger than passion knows. I cannot think Abram will forsake our union if I ask him to honor it once more."

Anne turned her head away severely and folded her arms.

"Truly, Anne, I suddenly find myself so tender of your affections that I would not have them be disappointed," Sarah said. "Yet they must be."

"You will give him his choice?" she asked.

"No one, not even God himself, will take that from him."

CHAPTER 35

Beniah's Favorite Charity

*A*bram waited for Beniah's revenge. He felt not only cast out of the Eden of serenity that he had hoped for in middle age, but as if the thorns that had started to grow after the fall pierced outward from everywhere under his own skin, and the beasts, as they fell upon one another, wreaked their blood-spilling carnage in his breast. He did not feel simple hatred for Beniah; he had created his own nemesis—almost, he saw now, courted him. Abram thought of killing the man many times. Picturing the final act, though, he always saw his own face.

At last, the message he expected came, with a strange reminder of his better intentions, his former spiritual quest, for Beniah included a newspaper article from *The Pennsylvania Gazette*, dated September 7, 1770.

OUR APOSTLE'S LAST JOURNEY?

The great evangelist, the Reverend Mr. George Whitefield, has come to this colony again. I had the good fortune to attend his preaching this past Thursday in a simple field outside our town near Bryn Mawr. He spoke of the New Birth and the great God of the Universe, the God of both slave and freeman. I received this message with the continual Amazement that his much affecting and always suitable Theatricality inspires.

As my readers know, I am a longtime friend of the good Gentleman, and have often found myself so pleased to be among the throngs in his open fields that I have left these places with my pockets empty. On Thursday he took up a Collection for the sake of his beloved orphanage Bethesda and his late mission to the slaves outside of our municipality.

After playing the parts of the Rich Man and Poor Lazarus, and reminding us all that our good deeds shall be rewarded and our evil punished, if not here, then hereafter, the good Mr. Whitefield looked forward to his own reckoning with the Deity. "I soon shall be in a world where time, age, pain, and sorrow are unknown," he said. "My body fails, my spirit expands. How willingly would I live for ever to preach Christ! But I die to be with Him."

These colonies' Apostle Paul may see his death as gain, but no friend of true religion or morality can. I am reminded of my time at the court of St. James and the fashion then of producing plays, such as the famous Gareth's "Dr. Squintum," which essayed that all such as George Whitefield must be mountebanks intent on little but their own financial gain and the attentions of fainting ladies.

No doubt there are some such, and have been, much to his disappointment, among Whitefield's associates.

After a friendship of such longstanding, though, I may say without fear of any contradiction that George Whitefield is the true article who so many counterfeit. If I cannot believe that the Lord takes so active a role in the affairs of men, I cannot doubt that George Whitefield acts as His hands in these same matters. His painstaking labors and indefatigable perambulations in the Mother Country and on our own shores have resulted in more than 10,000 pounds being donated to his Georgia orphanage, Bethesda. He has never taken anything for himself but has always lived simply, on a chaplain's salary. My good friends in Georgia have made it plain that the entire colony found its anchor in Mr. Whitefield, as his many acts of mercy on first arrival there made a community out of what had been only scattered wilderness settlements.

George Whitefield took to his horse as soon as he finished this last open-field "exhortation," a term he used on this occasion in preference to "sermon" since his remarks only proceeded for about an hour: barely time enough, he felt, to work up a good "preaching sweat." I can only hope I have not seen or heard the last of my Reverend Friend, for what credit I may have with his Lord depends, I must assume, on the good George Whitefield's kindness towards me.

While dogma seems to be a subject used most often to divide men and puff up with pride otherwise negligible figures, Whitefield made it the good tidings of harmony and accord betwixt God and Man that another Open Field Preacher once proclaimed. We wish him well on his journey north and counsel our New England neighbors to see to his wants and comforts as much as he will allow. In such a world, at such a time, the colonies have most need of their apostle and greatest friend.

                                                    —Benjamin Franklin

Appended to this article, this letter:

September 15, 1770

To Our Own Missionary,
    I could not help but find the parallels between the colonies' Apostle and our own Missionary striking, especially when Reverend Parsons announced that Whitefield himself plans to make Newburyport a stop on his itinerary. What could be more fitting, I thought, then a meeting between these two Great Men? What an occasion for them to compare their Acts of Mercy!
    But then there seemed to be an unhappy disparity between a man who has created and endowed this institution, Bethesda, and one who has only created, as of this writing, another orphan child to fill it. This caused me much anguish of spirit. How to meet this difficulty?
    We certainly have Urchins and Abandoned Young Miscreants enough to fill our own Institution in the Points. This presents no difficulty. For many have done good work in this enterprise, fathering children they have no intention of owning and have sometimes even taken pains to put away from them. Yet we have in this Newburyport—in the whole of Essex County—no such orphanage, and indeed the almshouse, which does a little along this line, is so badly administered by the Overseers of the Poor that children receive the least part of its mercies.
    I am in much perplexity over this matter, and so I am venturing to bring it to the attention of "Our Missionary," whose efforts have been inspired, I am informed, by George Whitefield's example. Could it be possible that you would not merely shadow this Type, following his example in a stealthy way, but actually come into the fullness of that same Charity? Are you worthy of this? Do you desire it?

I can only hope that this goads your conscience with a prick that you will not be able to kick against or otherwise abuse. As I am more and more drawn to think upon your welfare, I am coming to believe that your Salvation depends upon it. How strange that in the end, I should prove,
　　　Your Guardian Angel,
　　　Beniah Lynch

Before Abram could adequately discern how quickly Lynch meant to expose him, for the missive surely meant this at least, the Reverend Jonathan Parsons appeared at his door—within the same morning hour, in fact, as Beniah's letter.

Rev. Parsons shook Abram's hand—*pumped* it—as the captain greeted him in the foyer, with a suspicious enthusiasm. The minister's lantern jaw was hanging open, and the two front teeth of his jack-o'-lantern grin were much in evidence. He moved around on his feet, even as they greeted each other, as if still in a hurry to get somewhere.

"Come into the sitting room," Abram said. "Please."

The Reverend Parsons took the Chinese yellow upholstered chair, with its ribbed and fanning back—the best chair in the room. Abram used his mother's old rocker.

The minister threw up his hands, a gesture of benediction and cheering gladness. "Ho-ho! You are such a puppet face! Innocent as your morning's meal. How long will you feign such ignorance?"

"I feign nothing, sir," Abram said. "What have I to tell?"

The minister folded his hands together and prepared himself, it seemed, to deliver a solemn yet glad little speech on whatever consummate occasion he believed himself to be attending. "I have just received, printed in the hand of a professional calligrapher, the note of one Anonymous Donor, volunteering to provide an Orphanage in this Essex County, to be built in our own town."

Beniah's letter.

"An *Anonymous Donor*," the minister said, as if teaching children the answer to what should have been an obvious school exam question. "Who else but 'Our Missionary' would be such, would do such? Think not overmuch of the Scripture that counsels prayers in closets, good man. The celebration of such examples is the last and perhaps most important part of tremendous benefactions, for there will be derision and jealousy enough among those of your class. Your generosity will make them uncomfortable, and like so many geese with their long craning necks and pinching bills, they will pick whatever feathers you might be tempted to add. Complete the work through this! Complete it! Say that you are the man and let the Almighty judge whether your gift is the widow's mite or only a satrap's dropping of coins in the street. I think I know that the Lord shall judge aright."

"I thought I would do something," Abram said, stalling.

"An institution of this nature is more than something," the Reverend Parsons said. "It has taken my good friend George Whitefield the whole of his life and crossing the waters four times now to keep his Bethesda in Georgia. Have you sold your lands? The dimensions of such an enterprise!"

"I'm not sure the Anonymous Donor promised so much. Others should add to the work. It can only be effective in that way."

"Indeed, indeed," Rev. Parsons said. "The original building and the lands—which the Anonymous Donor has indeed promised—must inspire others to their keeping." He turned back to Abram. "We can be sure the cost of this particular Tower should run to 10,000 pounds, can we not?"

"The plans should determine the cost," Abram said, fearing he could not conceal his alarm. "I may have to think again if the plans prove your estimate. I cannot ruin myself. That would be the end of my capacity for doing further good."

"Good sir, you are already committed to more than anyone else might venture, so I cannot think anyone shall demand a greater dimension to the project than you can supply. We are already in your debt."

"I am beginning to feel that word 'debt' acutely, reverend sir," Abram said and tried to laugh.

The minister stood up abruptly. "I must go. I must spread this good news to the Overseers and the town council. This is a project not only for South Presbyterian and our sister churches, but for the town and the county, at least in terms of the recognition that is due. You know your own example, George Whitefield, is due to speak at South on his way north into the reaches of Massachusetts. It brings to mind certain pairings, certain dual possibilities!"

"I want nothing of George Whitefield's glory," said Abram, with a sudden heat that turned Rev. Parsons back to him as he was heading out.

The pastor shook and circled his upturned finger in the air, the tail end of a whirlwind disappearing into the heavens. "The Lord's glory! All for the Lord's glory! And we shall be so pleased as to see more than our portion of God's own *Shekinah* light in this day!"

CHAPTER 36

—

Two Heads

The Overseers liked doing business at Wolfe's Tavern, because then their informal meetings were not subject even to the casual scrutiny of keeping minutes. Still, Abram would meet there with Theophilus Parsons, Patrick Tracy, and Tristram Dalton and discuss what the whole town now knew as the Orphan House. Abram noticed how his steps dragged as he walked over from Federal Street to Market Square; it was almost as if he had to pull himself along.

Fortunately, he had quickly concluded that Beniah Lynch had miscalculated in an odd way—his plan made more poetry than sense. Abram could tie up the process for years, through requests that others, including the counties and towns themselves, participate, holding out the gold ring of a never-specified gift, while running through multiple plans that could be rejected on the grounds of being either inadequate or grandiose. If he simply meant to expose Abram he could do so; Abram was even then preparing himself for the experience. Abram would not be ruined by the scandal, but building an orphanage entire and keeping it going would indeed ruin him; Beniah had not miscalculated in that. Abram knew enough of George Whitefield's life and work to understand that only a peripatetic world celebrity could raise sufficient funds for such an operation, apart from direct levies, and he doubted the Overseers would hear of any addition to taxes in these times.

As he neared the tavern, with its carved wooden sign out front, an oversized hollow "O" in "Wolfe's," he thought of being discovered, and he knew that the world would not hate him for bedding a maid. Most of the celebrated men of his time, even George Whitefield's own friend Ben Franklin, were famous for the practice; Franklin's illegitimate son was now Governor of New Jersey. No, Abram would be hated for the very thing that so galled Beniah—his pretended virtue. He thought of the whole town regarding him as Beniah did, and that brought the same wild animal impulses to escape that the hunger of his childhood had. He reminded himself of his age and went through the tavern's door.

The three men actually stood and applauded as he came in, and it seemed that every other customer at least raised a hand in greeting.

"Theophilus," he said. "Mr. Tracy. Dalton." He shook each hand.

"These outfittings must have quite a margin," Patrick Tracy said. "Perhaps those contracts need renegotiating."

"Now, now," the elder Theophilus said, "the sum required must be a man's life, not a season's work. Let us have no nay-saying, even in jest."

"You have given us all an example to consider," Tracy said, beginning again. "I would never have thought of any such thing in these times, but then I would never have thought of any such thing at any time. What I admire," he said, "is audacity, and you have it in the service of others. A swashbuckling saint."

"Oh, I am none, as to that," Abram said.

"Sit, sit," Tristram Dalton said. "We have our own plans to share with you."

Abram sat reluctantly, for at the mention of plans he felt another burst of that quicksilver fear that had almost driven him past the door.

"Theophilus," Dalton said, urging the epicene man to take the lead.

"But the tribute was your idea," Theophilus said, smiling like an old aunt.

"I had a discussion or two . . ." Dalton said, stuttering, "then to it, we imagine . . . you know, of course, of George Whitefield's visit at the end of this month. You have already made his likeness such a familiar one that we thought to preserve these resemblances. We are commissioning two busts, one of Whitefield, one of you, and will be presenting them at the Town Hall on the Monday following Whitefield's services here. He will not stay but for the morning, but that should be time enough. We know you have much to consider, but perhaps you will have made sufficient progress by that time in your calculations to specify whatever particulars of the Orphan House have become clear. We are certainly at your disposal as to what you may expect of the town, and Theophilus will be communicating our intents to the county commissioners as well. We would, though, prefer this to be seen mainly as the town's venture, since your work has really been here among us."

"I still say," Tracy put in, "that the county's participation is important, since we do not breed all the homeless children, although there's many a country girl that comes and abandons hers in this place."

"What say you?" Theophilus said, putting an end to the presentation.

"There cannot be time for such art works."

"The artist is at it already, a Mr. Quentin, the local engraver, and if we do say, he is the man to do a fine work with any metal or piece of stone."

Abram looked at them quizzically.

"They'll be fashioned out of granite. They'll be resting some place long after the Town Hall is gone."

"He wants me to sit for him?" Abram asked.

"He is working from the sketches that have appeared in the *Essex County Gazette* and his own memories of seeing you in church for these years. It shall be Mr. Whitefield who may test his fancy."

"This cannot be," Abram said, as decisively as he might.

"This is to be," Theophilus said in his judicial way. "This must be."

"And why is that?" Abram asked, his tone heating.

"You would have given the gift anonymously, we know," Theophilus said. "And you would have denied Tracy and others, myself included, if I may say, Patrick, a chance to supply some symbolic repayment. Grace, pure grace from our own kind, is too difficult for us to live with, Captain. I believe that the Reverend Parsons told you that your reception of our thanks must complete the gift. This is why. We must be able to receive the gift in a way that allows us to accept it."

"I have given nothing as yet," Abram said.

"We know you of all people to be a man of your word," Dalton said.

"I cannot say I will do this," Abram said.

Patrick Tracy suddenly displayed a completely unexpected sensitivity. "I have a horror of public occasions myself," he said. "Is that your objection?"

"There is something in that . . ."

"Think of your wedding, man," Tracy said. "You thought the world would pass before it was over, and it took but a quarter of an hour of one single day."

Dalton and Parsons sat back and exchanged glances, which Abram saw, and he knew they were thinking of how unhappy his marriage was and regretting Tracy's analogy. Abram himself would have liked to be feeling the precious sentiments they were suspecting.

"I told Rev. Parsons I do not want any of Whitefield's glory. My sentiments are neither too feeling nor too humble. I would not appear absurd."

"We do not think our notions absurd," Tracy said.

"And I am sure," Theophilus said, pouring oil on the waters, "that Captain White did not mean to accuse. You must remember that George Whitefield's life has been devoted to urging men to emulate his example. As I do after my Lord, so you do after me—as the Apostle Paul wrote and as Whitefield has in effect reiterated through his every action. Think what satisfaction he will find that his message has been so received in a place where one of his earliest friends, Jonathan Parsons, ministers to God's people."

"This one speech has more religion in it than any I have ever heard from you, Theophilus," Abram said. "What a barrister you are—you will argue the Lord's case."

"I do find my education a deep well that is a constant pleasure to draw on," Theophilus said, and then gave his double chins a stroking squeeze. "For all that, what schoolboy does not know the Scriptures?"

"Are you reconciled, then?" Dalton asked.

As Abram thought of what it would mean for him to be "reconciled," he felt too staggered to quit his tactic of stall and delay. "I shall think upon it."

"Think not overmuch," Theophilus said.

"I doubt I shall have any specifics of our plans by that time," Abram said.

"This is not at issue," Tracy said. "Give us then our quarter of an hour, good Christian, and we shall not trouble more. Those, like me, who are mere flesh—as Theophilus rightly argues—will feel much the easier."

"And I shall feel?" Abram laughed to himself. "I do not know what I shall ever feel or think looking at this bust of yours except that the material was well chosen as regards my head."

CHAPTER 37

Ropes of Sand to the Moon

For the past day, a dust bowl had surrounded Newburyport, a brown perimeter that hung in the sky like the outer wall of a floating city. By horse, cart, wagon, mule, and on foot, the county farmers and more far-flung visitors—who inhabited the triangle from southern Rhode Island to the Berkshire frontiers in the west to Bangor in the north—gathered together in this new Joppa, the seaport of Jerusalem. The evangelist George Whitefield had arrived, and the town's population had suddenly doubled. There were encampments on the Mall, in the Points, on the wharves, and everywhere on the way to Plum Island. Spontaneous choirs formed in these places, and hymns floated on the wind. Abram had the feeling that someone, whom he could not quite hear, was always speaking to him.

Toward five o'clock, the hour of the coach's arrival, Abram was standing outside of Wolfe's. Behind pewterish clouds, the sun lit a diffused shield, which was lowering now onto the ramparts of the brown wall. The cloud by day, the pillar of fire by night, or a stockade? Were they Israelites bound for a Promised Land, an intermediate heaven, or a martial gathering in a hostile land? State Street was thronged, but few greeted him. He kept dodging to get a look up toward High Street, where the coach would appear.

Finally, he saw its four black horses bobbing toward him, the driver up high swinging his whip. He began to distinguish the clopping hooves of the team; their thunder shook his feet. He had never felt an earthquake, but some power magnified this approach. He thought of the horsemen of the apocalypse. Were these the steeds of his own?

Sarah, so prolific in her epistolary revenge, had now sent only the briefest of letters. She meant to return. Gaylord and Submit would be traveling with her.

Submit wrote with more details of the fire and what, he thought, must be a euphemistic description of Sarah's disfigurement.

Anne had chosen to return as well, and he guessed that Beniah's bribery must have played a part in her earlier surreptitious entry into the town. By letter she had invited him to visit with her that evening at Mrs. Fiddich's shanty. He had sent no reply as yet; any would constitute an admission.

And for that fourth horseman, Death, he thought of his mother, who rested in the graveyard behind the Mall and its present encampment of enthusiasts. That he had not spoken the full truth to her before her passing had cut her off from him, he felt, even more absolutely than death itself. Every time he started to remember their talks together, his lies intruded. He had not been able to picture her in his mind's eye since last spring.

As the first coach waited for the street to clear a hundred yards off, another rounded the corner, and then a third.

He barged up the street and tried to peer inside each coach and could spy his party in none of them. He turned round and saw a dark-haired woman step off the first coach, then a clergyman with a double-linen collar, and a bonneted ancient dame.

"Abram!"

He turned and saw Submit, who had stepped off the middle coach. Gaylord came off, then Sarah. She was turned away from him as yet.

He rushed forward, and she turned and he saw her. Still the same person, but how changed. He embraced her quickly. She was small in his arms, as he remembered—despite himself—Anne's impression in his arms as well.

He broke away to shake Gaylord's hand and bow to Submit. "I've never seen it this way," Sarah said. "The world has come to Newburyport."

"My world has," Abram said, conscious that he wasn't looking directly at Sarah, as he should have been to bring the remark off, but rather at the bottom of the ladies' skirts, where their boots were hiding.

"Shall we go directly up to the house, Captain? I think it would serve us all," Gaylord said. "These ladies have shown a remarkable patience with the carriage ride already."

"In truth, all we did was complain," Submit said.

"We shan't now, though," Gaylord said, "not with such prospects of inspiration before us."

Abram took a deep breath and swallowed. "The town behaves as if the Lord had come," he said and tried to laugh, and quickly wondered why he had said so much.

"Only Mr. Whitefield, not the Lord, I fear," said Submit. "Though our host's countenance approaches those looks of stark fear the Lord's own appearance might inspire. Are you well, sir? You look as if you had ridden with us here, but atop the horses."

"Submit," Gaylord said.

"I have not seen my wife these many months, cousin," Abram said. "This shows itself in my appearance, I'm sure. If we are not receiving the Lord himself, it remains a marvelous thing to receive again so much of His bounty to me." Then Abram did look at Sarah, and he tried to hold her eyes and will his expression right.

"Shall we go up to the house, then?" Gaylord asked again, always helpful.

———

The travelers only had time to change into fresh clothes, when they had to set out for Whitefield's arrival at the parsonage. Their neighbors and the town's visitors walked with the quick determination of people rushing to see a fireworks display, something splendid yet fleeting. Their pace quickened, too, as they weaved through the crowd. They were disappointed at finding themselves at the back of a shoulder-to-shoulder crowd while still several doors from Rev. Parsons' steps.

It appeared that George Whitefield himself was standing on the steps next to Rev. Parsons, his muff-eared wig, his wall-eyed look, and his jowls recognizable from so many newspaper drawings. Rev. Parsons was turning to one member of the crowd or another, leaning forward and making remarks, while Whitefield looked over the throng, his hands holding his Bible at his chest.

"Captain White! Captain White!" Rev. Parsons was calling for him in a voice that competed with Whitefield's own for range in the open field. "Is he here, good people? Does anyone know if he's here? Captain White!"

"I am," Abram tried to call. He held up his hand and waved it. "I'm . . ."

"Let him through, then—let him through!" Rev. Parsons shouted. "Let the good captain come up."

Abram turned back to those he was with. He looked at Sarah and Submit and Gaylord, and they actually closed on him, turning him, pushing him forward. "Go on," they said. "He will have you up there. Hurry."

As he made his way, people began to pat him on the back and shake his hand.

Abram stood at last on the bottom step with Whitefield and Parsons above him, staring down. Rev. Parsons took a step down and tried to make introductions, but he could not sufficiently distract Whitefield's attention from the members of the crowd who felt familiar enough to shout out their questions.

"Let's go in," Rev. Parsons said. "We'll go in now," he said to Whitefield.

"Jonathan, they will be in after us. Your house is strong enough?"

"We have no galleries to fall," Rev. Parsons said, alluding rather lightly to a tragic incident—the one that had sent Whitefield into the open fields. "We can open the windows and let you speak from the stairway. The parlors will accommodate some."

"I thought to rest." Whitefield was breathing heavily.

"We might meet later in private," Abram said, without being heard.

"This multitude will have a word, won't they?" Whitefield asked rhetorically. "A short exhortation, then, from your stairs."

Rev. Parsons took Abram by the elbow and pulled him up and ushered the three of them through the door. They had only a moment before Whitefield's prophecy as to the crowd would be fulfilled.

"George, this is Captain Abram White, the man who means to start an orphanage in Essex County. Your example has been his inspiration. I wrote to you of him. We are planning that ceremony on the day of your departure."

Whitefield listened to the explanation a moment too long, and yet, in the next moment, his hearty, if sweaty-faced, greeting made Abram feel approved.

"Captain White," Whitefield said, "there is nothing like acts of mercy for the spreading of the Gospel. 'If we say we love God and yet not our neighbor . . .' " He wagged his finger.

The men laughed together as Abram thought of how soon he would be classed a liar.

"You can only do much in the winning of souls," George Whitefield said decisively, "when you have first demonstrated your love to their hearts. I have always found this, and learned most acutely of this truth in my first years in Georgia."

Up close, Whitefield had a houndish sag to his cheeks and a liverish coloring under his eyes. His cockeyed look became more pronounced; the left eye level, directed outward, earnest; the right turned inward, ironic, as if looking across the bridge of his long nose back toward an unworldly purpose. That nose, with its cavernous nostrils, and his sensual mouth, its lower lip curled out and under like the rim of a goblet, looked greedy for the air.

Abram hurried to speak, to bridge the awkward silence his rapt attention had introduced. "I have read of your work in Georgia, Bethesda. I have a collection of your writings and articles about you," Abram said, surprised and hating himself for fawning.

Before he had finished, Whitefield was looking around again, as people now stood in the open doorway, and the three of them had edged back toward the stairs in the central hallway. The people appeared ready to crowd in like a mass of worker bees following the queen into the hive.

Abram realized he would not be able to say anything more to Whitefield. The way his own breathing was swelling and making him light-headed told him how much he wanted to speak further with him. Unconsciously, he had been harboring a reservoir of expectation that the great man might somehow say the words he needed to hear.

The hubbub conquered. He already found himself fighting his resentment of Whitefield's obliging his admirers, suiting his theatrical self.

Whitefield took several heavy steps midway up the stairs. Then Parsons opened his double parlors up to the crowd, who covered the floors backing against and up along the walls, as children were hoisted up on shoulders. Abram clung to the newel post of the banisters, keeping his place. The windows in the parlor were opened so that the people who could not get in could hear.

Whitefield requested a candle to read his Bible by, since the light outside had faded and the interior of the house was nearly as dark now as at midevening.

The light of the candle, as Whitefield stood on the steps, seemed to cradle his chin in its long fingers. His eyes were mostly lost in the shadows, but then for an instant the one that turned inward peered directly through the small light, and Whitefield looked like a visionary creature ablaze with the celestial fire.

He was having trouble juggling the candle and the book, and he ended by putting the Bible back in his pocket.

The evangelist pushed the candle out at arm's length before him, looked directly once more into its flame, and spoke as if his words would pass through the fire and be cleansed.

" 'Ye are the light of the world,' " he quoted. " 'Ye . . . are the light of the world . . . a city that is set on a hill cannot be hid. Neither do men light a candle, and put it under a bushel, but on a candlestick; and it giveth light unto all that are in the house. Let your light so shine before men, that they may see your good works, and glorify your Father which is in heaven . . . The light of the body is the eye: if therefore thine eye be single, thy whole body shall be full of light. But if thine eye be evil, thy whole body shall be full of darkness. If therefore the light that is in thee be darkness, how great is that darkness! . . . Ye are the light of the world.'

"I have been wont to say," Whitefield continued in his own words, "that *the world is my parish*. But if the Lord had seen fit to place me down in a particular locale, surely He could not have supplied a more commodious seat than this Newburyport of yours. 'A city set on a hill' indeed. As I have often remarked to my friend of long standing, your pastor, Jonathan Parsons, if the Lord sees me to my end on these shores, then I would be buried here amongst this people."

The crowd reacted with an even humming, not knowing how hospitable in this the speaker wished them to be.

"When I think what a light of holiness burns here, what an example of charity your good works are to the whole of this commonwealth of Massachusetts, how dedicated you are to the things of God, my heart rejoices in God my Savior."

More pleasant murmurings to this.

"You have your champion in the excellent Captain White, I understand. May the Lord pour out on all the people of South Presbyterian and this Newburyport a double portion of the blessing with which you bless others."

Abram gave a grimacing smile and felt the prickle of a rash start along the back of his neck.

"For some forty years now," Whitefield said, "we have been a minister of the Gospel. The Lord, by His grace, has prospered the work of our hands; yea, He has prospered our handiwork. The revivals of these past years, this Awakening, as it is called, is known throughout the world and in every corner of the globe. Many have been called. Many have responded.

"And now this Awakening to the things of God is undergoing a supreme test. The tyranny being visited upon this land is no less foreign for being initiated by the Mother Country. Such ill-usage, such a dictatorial spirit, can only be foreign to an English people who have labored for centuries to be men born into the legal possession of God-given rights. For the Mother Country to deny these same rights to its own colonists shows a family, a house, divided against itself, and this cannot and must not stand."

The crowd began to cheer, so much so that Whitefield almost looked startled. He labored to get his breath again.

"In such political times," he said, "there shall be many temptations to forget the things of God. To let slip the gains the Awakening has brought. To see the seeds that have been planted spring up only to wither and die for lack of cultivation.

"So now, more particularly than ever before, 'Examine yourself, whether ye be in faith.' By their fruits ye shall know them. Will you then be distracted from your great calling, as a city set upon a hill, an example of freedom and Christian charity to the world, or turn and become the mirror image of those who would oppress you? Our works are to be an example to the world, so that men may see them and glorify the Father.

"But do we rely upon good works for salvation? By no means!

"Works! Works! Can a man get to heaven by works? I would as soon think of climbing to the moon on a rope of sand. No, no, 'he that believeth on him.' I am trusting in the New Birth and God's sovereign election for my salvation. Nothing else shall suffice. For there is none righteous, no, not one. What I have done in this life, I have done by His grace. It is all grace! His grace is sufficient for me, for it is perfected in weakness. So then I rejoice in my infirmity, for when I am weak, it is then and only then that I am strong. By His grace, He holds me secure in the palm of His hand, and nothing can remove me from it."

Suddenly, the candle Whitefield had been holding went out. Abram was standing close enough to see that the man had deliberately puffed it away, but the crowd gasped.

"No one move, please!" Whitefield called.

Abram had tried not to meet anyone's eyes directly, and he had little idea who surrounded him. Now it was suddenly so dark within the house that he could not see beyond those immediately next to him. Whitefield himself was nearly invisible, the darkest among the shadows filling the house, and listening to him now was like listening to an intruder or a ghost.

"I soon shall be in a world," Whitefield said, "where time, age, pain, and sorrow are unknown. My body fails, my spirit expands. How willingly would I live forever to preach Christ! But I die to be *with* Him."

Then his voice broke out with a new emphasis. "*Ye* are the light of the world. I am a flickering candle, a flame that the least puff of breath can put out. *Ye* are the light of the world!

"This light of which we speak is not a light that is added to one's life, as the flame may be added to the candle. This light must be within you. Your whole life must be filled with this light. And it cannot be if you are filled with the darkness of evil imaginings and evil deeds.

" 'If your eye be single, your life shall be filled with life.' But, 'if therefore the light that is in thee be darkness, how great is that darkness.' Far greater than the one we stand in now. The physical darkness here, at this moment, would hinder any exertion on our own or others' behalf. So that darkness of evil imaginings, of hypocrisy, and deceit hinders whatever efforts we make to secure for ourselves and our neighbors a better life. Examine yourselves!

"For '*Ye* are the light of the world.'

"I have seen my time to witness to that light pass away, even as I now, with a good hope of His appearing, await that final day when His light will search me through and through. I pray that whatever in me be dark, His light will illumine, and whatever in me be double, His strength shall join and make one. Pray my brothers and sisters that we may all be one, even as the Father and the Son and the Holy Ghost are one. Amen."

With that, Whitefield turned and went up to his room. The crowd called after him, but he only turned, nodded, and went higher.

For a while longer the crowd remained, waiting, perhaps, for Rev. Parsons to dismiss them—wanting, it seemed, to have the event they had just witnessed acknowledged. Abram still hung by the newel post. When no one came forward to address the crowd further, the people reluctantly began to make their way out of the house, bumping elbows, muttering apologies, squeezing past one another and through the doors.

Eventually, Abram turned to go. Someone leaned in to him in the darkness and whispered, "Evil loves the night, don't it, Abram?" His devil was quoting the Scriptures—how had he made his way to him?

Abram walked up the heels of his neighbor before he could escape Beniah's voice. Yet he kept expecting that voice to rise behind him and give chase.

CHAPTER 38

———

Truer Lives

*A*bram waited downstairs in the parlor until he thought Sarah would be asleep. He had dozed off in his chair reading—that would be his excuse, he decided, as he made his way up the complaining wooden stairs. He left the candles in the center hall luminaries burning, in case he should need to retreat.

When he made the landing, he was still carrying his book in both hands, and his shoulders were pinched high, as if preparing to duck. He put the book in his coat pocket, set himself again, and opened the door.

He saw her immediately, sitting at her dressing table, staring into its oval mirror. She was wearing a fine silvery dressing gown with a gathered bodice, whose close folds showed nearly white by the candles on the table. Its skirts of many sheer layers flashed sterling. He could see the least damaged side of her face clearly in the glass, and he thought of the portrait and what Mr. Copley had seen—that future the world would never realize.

He closed the door and took two steps into the room. As yet, she had not moved. From this angle, only a slight veering of the tip of her nose broke the illusion of symmetry. The groove of crescent scar from her nose into her cheek and the whorl of burned skin along and below her ear were in shadow. He could not look at her without thinking of her scars, though, which she seemed to be gauging as she let him look at her. Was he ashamed of her?

Yes, embarrased, too. And yet from the moment Sarah stepped off the coach and he had seen her disfigured appearance, he had detected something even more unsettling. Strangely, this new quality about her did realize what the artist glimpsed—met up with it at such a distance that Abram could not understand his own sense of its presence. The artist had framed what he saw or foreknew in beauty and yet it existed now, in life, beyond that mere beauty.

He had come in dreading confrontation, and now he felt almost calm, although her image in the mirror had imparted no reprieve from judgment.

"Sarah," he said. "Are you well?"

"Yes."

"Shouldn't you be sleeping?"

Her eyes in the mirror looked at his.

"It must be one o'clock."

At last, she turned toward him. "I didn't know whether you would come up."

"For being so long married," he said, trying to keep his tone light, "we know so little of each other now."

She bowed her head and put her hands on her knees. She raised her head and met his eyes, very slowly. "I know what you cannot say. That Titus is your son. That Anne loves you and feels you should be hers. And I can understand why, if I cannot excuse it."

He seized up so much that he waited for a word, any word, to come to him. "So," he said.

"The truth need not be an accusation," she said. "It can just be," and she gestured with her hands, "what it is."

He could have blessed her for that. "There is a terrible factuality to some things, at which the mind rebels, so . . . uselessly." He went and sat in the chair by the window. He found he had to say the words. "Yes. Yes. Yes. Titus is mine." He tried to think of how to describe his relationship with Anne, without saying too much, without lying. "I thought I could keep the world to that cottage. For a time, I wanted to."

"And I," Sarah said, "I tried to invent a world, or several. Are you worried that I am a madwoman?"

"Your letters always seemed to have their purposes."

He waited for how this was to go on, feeling the tensions and the shared experience of their life together coming back. Yet the quiet felt unhurried.

She pivoted around and faced him and turned her face from side to side. "What do you think of what the fiery blast has made me?"

"I cannot see that you have changed so much."

"No. Look. Look now and say." Again, slowly, she showed him one profile, then the other, the sisters of an unflattering comparison.

"I see something else. What guided Mr. Copley. That spirit now belongs less to appearance and more to you alone."

"A spirit?"

"What you have learned—or become. I do not know that spirit fully as yet, but I can sense the change. And it may be what I have longed for, although I cannot name it."

"Call it hideous."

"Sarah, that is not . . ."

"No. The truth about me is ugly, and I have become so."

He turned to the side, crossed his legs, could not get comfortable now in his chair.

"Did you know that the fire killed a child? His name was John. A lovely young lad, not quite a man. Perhaps I should say the fire killed two children. For we may safely say that Sarah the Innocent is no longer."

"What, who, are you, then?"

"Truer," she said. "As you must be."

For all the mystery, he grew hopeful. "The fire did not take away your spiritual gifts," he said.

"Those," she said, dismissively.

"What shall I do to be 'truer'?"

"You are trying to escape the trap Beniah has laid for you. Spring it, instead."

He questioned her by waiting.

"You know of my letter and Anne's. He has surely used them by now. Submit explained the planned ceremonies. He means to destroy you publicly."

Abram blew out a breath and stretched back in his chair. "I am not an innocent, either—only the town's baby. A helpless idiot."

"Listen to me, then, Abram. You cannot really be caught in this snare except through cowardice and stupidity. But these are the hand-maids, to use a figure, of guilt."

"I must have that ceremony stopped."

"And to do so you must choose what you will give up, and you had better renounce what's least important—your dignity."

"What should I do, then?"

"Speak the truth. Go to Rev. Parsons privately tomorrow and tell him, quite early, before services. He can make some excuse, or announce your infidelity to the congregation; in either case, the matter will be at an end."

"My life here as well."

"You cannot know that. 'Twill take some time for the town to forgive your seeming virtue. If you stay, though, accepting their condemnation, their judgment should finally turn to mercy."

"Would you see this accomplished with me? What *have* you come here to say? Tell me now. I know you have made your resolutions."

Sarah stood up and leaned back against her table, with her hands clenching its sharp edge. "I want you to live, as we have said, a truer life. For us both to do so. I would have you recognize Titus and give him part of your fortune. He is the first orphan that must be cared for. And then I would have us live in peace together and fidelity."

This sounded too simple. "As man and wife? *Truly*, as man and wife?"

"I have come back to ask that of you, good husband." She nodded and raised her eyebrows. "But there is a condition. A necessary limit, however unhappy. You must never again meet with or see Anne. Or your child. Not until Titus is grown."

He hesitated for one moment before he could tell her. "She is here."

"Anne?"

"In the Points. Staying with Mrs. Fiddich."

"Have you seen her?"

"Not as yet."

"You will, then, and it shall be for the last time. Since you say you care for me."

Now that he had been given the chance he longed for, he found it almost too hard, too difficult. "You would have me recognize a child I shall not see?"

Before she would have turned back around to the mirror, but now she simply nodded.

He felt his stomach clench. "If that is the price, then."

"I wear mine," she said. "You shall have to carry yours in your heart."

"Until he is grown."

"Never until then. Never."

He waited to see if his sudden exhaustion would pass.

"Except for tonight. Go now and tell her."

"This night?"

"She is not sleeping."

The way Sarah spoke, everything she said sounded true.

"I'll go, then." He stood up. He wanted to acknowledge their new accord in some way, receive some token. He went to Sarah's side and bent down and kissed her on the cheek where the fire had whipped her skin. It was sickly smooth and yet stringy like boiled cheese. He kept his head close to hers for a moment more, willing the affection back. As he breathed, he remembered her scent.

"Anne is before you," Sarah said. "Go quickly. And return as soon."

CHAPTER 39

Declarations in Whispers

As Abram walked down to Five Points in the predawn cold, he reminded himself of his efforts to separate from Anne. Why did he feel that this dank morning hour—an hour of fog and shipwreck—would see her true abandonment? He hunched his shoulders forward under his greatcoat and carried his arms with each hand clasping the opposite forearm—a fender for the heart's cold ashes.

As he approached Mrs. Fiddich's door, he became excited at the prospect of seeing Anne again, and was horrified. He wondered whether he should really knock and awaken her at such an hour.

The door opened as if by itself, and Anne, shivering and huddled in her nightdress, opened the door and withdrew behind it. A pallet lay just inside. She had been sleeping there—or keeping watch. She put her finger to her lips and led him up the stairs, away from her hostess's family.

In the single upstairs room, Anne lit a lamp and set it on a central table. Theo lay at the outer boundary of its light, in his accustomed corner, on another pallet. Abram could not find Titus at first, and then saw the basket on the floor at the foot of the simple wooden bed.

Abram expected Anne to keep her distance, but she came close and said, "I have had your child. Cannot you welcome me? Won't you touch me?"

He tried to give her a bent-over hug with his arms and shoulders, but she clung to him, pulling him against her.

"Anne," he said, breaking off the embrace.

"Why have you come out to me?"

"Were you awake? You seem to have been."

"I have been watching. I knew, in the end, you would not disappoint me."

He wanted to leave then, as he already felt pushed. He tried for a quick reversal. "Why didn't you marry Sean Murray?"

She came a step closer. "I have committed many faults, practiced deception, as have you, Abram. Yet I have been true in this love. If only in this, true. Why would you have me sin against it?"

He had not thought through to an answer, when she said, "You have been talking to Sarah tonight."

"Yes."

"She wants you to name Titus as your own."

"Yes."

"Not I. That's too little, and, as you see"—she gestured toward the baby—"helpless. I am not helpless. I would have you recognize your true affections."

She came close to him again and laced her hands around his neck. Her thumbs massaged the tight muscles under the ribbon tie of his long hair. "I would do anything for you. Except for staying away. That I cannot. I won't."

"Anne . . ." he said. "I have told Sarah the truth."

"Sarah thinks she knows what happened. A poor handmaid, doing her master's bidding—in which her mistress half conspired. Does she?"

"What do you mean?"

"Does she know how your body declares its love for me. At a touch? A thought? Do you know anything like this with her? Have you, ever?" She pulled him back into her embrace, holding him yet closer, moving her hands over his shoulders and up to his face. "And now that she has destroyed her own beauty . . ." She kissed him so intensely and with such desire that he felt as much as seduced.

He broke off from her and set her away from him. He waited, counting his breaths. "Bring our child to me," he said.

She went to the crib and picked up his son. She looked so pleased as she brought Titus and laid him in his arms.

He held his sleeping child, no longer an infant but a baby nearing one year in age, dark-haired, with the cleft chin his mother had written of and already a long nose, like his father's. Abram fumbled in the blankets and picked out the child's hand—put his finger in its reflexive clutch. Even in the dim light, he could see the baby's fingernails, and they were, exactly, his: miniature replicas entire from the longer, thinner rectangle at the little finger to the oval over his index.

"My son," he said. "Titus. Your father welcomes you at last into this world and parts from you."

Anne rushed to him and tried to take the baby. "You cannot say such a thing. Give him to me."

He had to shove her away, rudely. "I would have a moment more," he said. "This is what Sarah and I have agreed. That I will support this child as mine but never see him again until he is grown."

Anne began to moan. She put her hands to her face and raked her cheeks.

"Dear Titus," Abram said, "when you are grown, if you should hate me, you are forgiven. Even if you should take my life, you are forgiven. And yet I beg you to live well, for yourself, for your mother, for the God who has not abandoned you, nor ever will."

Anne was sobbing.

The baby opened his icy blue eyes and they grew bigger as he looked at his father.

Abram shut his own and turned away his face as he handed the child back. "You will always be provided for," he said.

"No!" she cried.

"You will live in comfort, and Titus shall have any opportunity I can provide."

"No," Anne said. "Do not speak." She rushed at him and tried to cover his mouth with her hands. "Do not speak again. Do not speak."

He caught her wrists. "I did love you," he said, "which was the most grievous fault. What a power it has."

He went toward the stairs, pushing her away as she tried to wrap the three of them into a last familial embrace. They were in danger of toppling down the stairs when, to catch the child from falling, she finally let go and clutched the banisters with her free hand.

As he escaped the shanty, the door banged closed, and its shotlike report seemed to strike him through the shoulder blade. He took a quick step and his boot swiveled on the sloppy street and he sprang away to keep his balance. He had not slept, and he wanted to lie down, but he drove on toward the parsonage to keep that night's pledges—to finish.

Abram expected a surprised welcome at Rev. Parsons' home. Instead, the maid came to the door already dressed in her apron, as if he were expected. She showed Abram into the back, past the double parlors and the stairs from which George Whitefield had spoken, to a small bedroom that the minister used as a study.

Rev. Parsons looked up at him from his chair, his mouth open, his eyes appealing for information, news. His head fell, and his elbows and forearms dropped onto his thighs.

"Abram," he said quietly, as if he were reminding himself of who Abram was and why he should be there. Then he turned round fully and asked, "How did you hear? You are good to come."

"I've not heard . . ." Abram said. "Something has happened?"

The Reverend Parsons raised up staring, blank eyes. "Mr. Whitefield is dead. My friend, George Whitefield, is dead."

"He is?"

"He could not get his breath all last evening. Mr. Winter and Mr. Smith, who are journeying with him, rubbed him, put spirits to his nose. I called in Dr. Smithers. All hope is gone. He is as cold as frost."

Abram went over and put his hand on Rev. Parsons' shoulder. The minister grumbled in sympathy as Abram said, "He leaves us too soon, this chaplain of the Colonies. Your friend. I'm sorry for your loss."

Then Rev. Parsons seized his upper right arm, pulling on it so hard that Abram wondered whether the man meant him to kneel by his side. "I tell you, Abram, you could not have selected a more worthy model to emulate. Some thought of him as an actor, a comedian, but in all that he did, howsoever rehearsed and theatrical, he had but one thought, and that the Lord."

Parsons broke down, weeping, muffling his cries with the handkerchief he put to his mouth.

Abram took the other chair close by him. He could not say what he had come to say and felt the simplicity of Sarah's recommended course dissolving.

Rev. Parsons cleared his eyes and rubbed his brow with the handkerchief. "Pardon my emotion. I am sure the Lord sent you here to take it from me, for I will have need of every strength to assuage the grief of others. You have appeared like Ananias to Saul, to deliver him from his blindness. I see that I must comfort with the charity by which I am comforted." Rev. Parsons leaned over and clapped his hand on Abram's shoulder. "But say, why did you come? It's hardly daylight."

He was being given a chance, after all—the chance to disappoint. "I came to say that there must be no ceremony."

"As to that," Rev. Parsons said, and his upper lip almost raised over his prominent front teeth, "there can be no question. We shall have other ceremonies to attend. Sad ones. The town will have to content itself with another occasion." He patted his lips once more and doubled the handkerchief over. "But you were not aware of . . . why did you come?"

"I am not fit . . ."

"To fasten the laces of his sandals?" Rev. Parson asked, interrupting.

"The orphanage was not my conception. It was Beniah's."

"Beniah Lynch? The other ship builder? Beniah?"

"He discovered me . . . he learned of my hypocrisy. The untruths that I told about Anne's circumstances."

"The maid you sent away."

"She was not assaulted in the Points."

Rev. Parsons had begun to nod his head and suck in his withered cheeks. "Her child is yours."

"Beniah thought to embarrass me and I . . . cooperated."

"The lie will be hardest to forgive," Rev. Parsons said and pinched his closed eyes, the lids scaly with his lack of sleep.

"That was my thought. I must understand if people cannot."

"You should not have let this go on. You must recognize the child."

"Yes, I plan to."

"You must not plan to, you must do it." The pastor waved his handkerchief in the air, semaphoring his distress at not being allowed to grieve.

"Yes, I will."

"Did not I see that your wife has returned? I thought she was in the crowd today."

"She has. We have spent this night resolving to do what you ask."

"I am not asking anything of you. I am presenting your plain Christian duty."

"Yes, yes."

"At such a time!" Rev. Parsons said, warming in his anger, his lips drawn and thin. "I am glad, then, that there can be no question of a ceremony. That, at least, will give us both opportunity to account for this at more leisure."

"I will follow whatever you advise."

"It is not a question of my advice!" Rev. Parsons said, vexed.

"Consider this the beginning, then, of my making amends," Abram said.

"We shall," Rev. Parsons said. "Tell me—and in a short space, for the time could not be more . . . incommodious—tell me how Beniah maneuvered you."

Unsure what the man meant exactly, Abram tried to supply a generous answer. "Sarah, Anne, they admitted what they knew."

"He went to visit them?"

"Beniah persuaded them to sign letters."

"He has what amounts to affidavits in his pocket?"

"I'm afraid."

"He will ruin you. We must not let that happen. You are not the first . . . not even among the clergy, but *go to* with that! Let me only say that the good that you have done should not be utterly vitiated by this offense and your means of compounding it. What the Lord may offer you as amendment, I cannot say. I shall give you what attention I can."

"I wanted you to know. I wanted to stop the ceremony."

Rev. Parsons stood up. "God in heaven, what a mortal day!"

"I will be going, then," Abram said. "We will be having services this morning?"

Rev. Parsons nodded his head. "Of course, of course, how else shall the people know of Whitefield? I'm thinking of announcing a vigil. You may attend all of this. I would most heartily advise you to do so."

Abram wanted to thank him for his kindness, but the minister had so little wanted to be kind, Abram thought, that he might regard this as an impertinence.

"I would not have burdened you," Abram said finally. "But the falsehood would have grown so contemptible under the circumstances. I'm glad I spoke, albeit at an unpropitious time."

"The thing itself is contemptible, and I would 'advise,' since you ask for me to play a role in this, that you meditate on its odious character. Excuse me now, Captain. The rest of this dark world will be here presently, I'm sure, with all of its iniquity!"

Rev. Parsons left him alone, and he could hardly feel glad about the interview. George Whitefield dead. He wished he could feel the import of that great matter; instead, he worried.

CHAPTER 40

The Words of the Dead

At services on the morrow, amid gasps and cries and against one nakedly angry shout, the Reverend Parsons announced an all-night vigil at the parsonage beside the death bed. Leaning forward on the pulpit he was gripping tightly, the minister rushed into a shout of his own.

"Pray . . . come and pray. Not for this saint, who even now rejoices in God's glory with the angels. Pray that you will remember your own end and come to it, like Mr. Whitefield, hearing the Lord's 'well-done thou good and faithful servant.' " He leaned back, raised his eyes, and seemed to envision his lost friend. "Pray for our infirmities of spirit, the meanness of pride, the losses of neglect. Pray that we all might be found worthy of this grievous sign of our election in the Almighty's greater purposes."

Abram had not slept the past night, and he did not sleep as that Sunday night wore on. Without undressing entirely, only taking off his coat, waistcoat, and shoes, Abram lay beside Sarah for a while—

awkwardly, as they could still only mimic reconciliation. He tried to ask her about Elysia and her sisters. Then the unrestful silence of their bed, in which they counted each other's breaths, suggested how difficult their truce would be to keep.

After an hour or so, Abram rose again, re-dressed, and went down to the parlor where he looked at Whitefield's *Journals* and paged through Law's *A Serious Call To A Devout And Holy Life*. These still had the power to remind him of his former enthusiasm, and the remembrance distressed him. He thought of his son. Ishmael set aside by his mother to die: but the Lord made His own promise to them. Would He again, or was this sin's presumption?

Abram waited until none but the sea captains would be capable of keeping watch. Then he picked up his old snail-shaped hat from the foyer's shallow closet and went out into the street and starting walking toward the parsonage.

He entered the house with the sense of how recently he had been there and crept up the stairs to the bedroom where George Whitefield lay. He kept his knees bent, his shoulders hunched—stealthy as a thief, hoping he would not meet up with Rev. Parsons. He remembered Whitefield preaching from the stairs, the cupping hand of flame holding his chin, and Abram went cold as if he were walking through Whitefield's ghost. Turning back for a moment, his hand on the banister, he thought of himself at the newel post, receiving the great man's words of commendation. He started up once more as if fleeing that embarrassing horror.

From the hallway, Abram saw one of the old church women, Mrs. Bostock, sitting in a bedroom, her rocker drawn close to what must be the still-unseen bed where Whitefield lay. She had on her bonnet, and her head was bowed as she nodded in prayer or reverent slumber. Coming closer, he heard her snoutlike nose sniffle back her own humming snore.

Whitefield lay in the bed to her right under a down comforter. The silk coverlet had a pearly sheen, which softly mirrored the flames in the fireplace across the room. The evangelist was wearing his white powdered wig with its mufflike curls, and his legs had been straightened. The toes pointed stiffly upward. His hands, clasped at his breast, held a small Bible. His nose and chin pointed as straight into the air as his toes, projecting him into the only world where his interests lay.

Still, the corpse asked to be attended; Whitefield remained the focus of attention even in death. Abram could say what he had been meaning to, even if Whitefield could not reply.

Impatient for Mrs. Bostock to wake up, Abram touched her shoulder at last, and she snorted awake.

"Captain White," she said.

"Mrs. Bostock."

She was suddenly the sentimental grandmother. "Look at the dear, great man. He's in the heavenlies, you can certainly see. With his God and our Maker. Wasn't it nice the things he said of you in his last words?"

Abram nodded.

"You will treasure that memory."

"I will."

Mrs. Bostock looked about her. "You must, to come at such an hour. I wasn't much praying, was I, though I thought to keep him company. You'll do much better as the light comes. 'Ye are the light of the world'—those were his words. But we wait in such a darkness tonight, don't we?"

"Mrs. Bostock," Abram said, annoyed at her chattiness, and even more so at the points she made that echoed his own thinking.

"Yes?" she asked.

"I'll be taking the watch now."

"Of course, that's why you've come."

"That's why I've come."

The woman pulled at her skirts as if unbinding her legs and ankles. She gave a bobbing nod and shuffled out, bent over as if leaning into a wind.

Abram was finally alone in the room. He half closed the door and sat in the rocker, suddenly unsure why he had come, despite his anxiety that Mrs. Bostock leave him alone there.

He looked at Whitefield. The evangelist's eyes were closed; somehow he had imagined the gray eyes would be open and clear. The complexion had darkened, the ruddy shadows at the cheeks and underneath the curling lower lip had become kidneyish. A jaundiced pallor reigned elsewhere, contrasting with the fresh powder of the wig. The body wore these colorings like a wooden marionette its paint.

Abram thought of his eagerness to hear Whitefield's exhortation from the stairs and of that moment when his hopes expanded at the thought of a private conference with the gentleman. He still would have liked such a talk. Sarah, Anne, and Rev. Parsons had heard his resolutions. Yet something remained undone.

Works! Works! Abram remembered Whitefield saying, *a rope of sand to the moon.*

His had become an inverted Jacob's ladder, a gangway to Sheol.

He looked at the corpse again, holding its Bible, and presumably the truth of all its secrets. One word now. From such a vantage point, any word that Whitefield might utter.

Even if Abraham were to come back from the dead, for a greater one than he . . .

Yes, he knew this, he almost told the corpse.

If I tell you things of this earth, and ye believe not, how shall I speak of things above?

"I do not require that," he said, whispering.

Behold I go to prepare a place for you. In my house there are many mansions. If it were not so I would have told you.

Hope, wild hope, fit like a key into that softest of locked mechanisms, and his heart turned over; it gave a crushing thump. He knelt down by the bed, shoving the rocker back. Thinking of his cries and the public spectacle he had made of himself in church, he hesitated. But the words strangled themselves out of his throat.

"I am dead," he prayed. "Why has this death come to me?" He waited, almost expecting an answer. "Where is the day I ran from the church in Glenwhirry to follow where You led? Where is the man who once heard Your voice?"

Neither height nor depth . . . nor any living creature.

He looked across the coverlet to Whitefield. *"Ye are the light of the world."* He remembered the asthmatic rasp of Whitefield's voice.

" 'But if the light that is in thee be darkness, how great is the darkness. But if thy eye is single, thy whole body shall be filled with light.' I know this. But what must I do?"

Sell all thou hast and give it to the poor.

He felt his resistance, his leaning against that door; how he put his shoulder into it. As soon as he knew the pressure there, he felt his confinement. "It is more blessed . . . one might even say, more pleasant." His own prayer closet turned out to be a well-fitted casket. He had taken what he had been given and built such cramped quarters. Balky desk drawers and an aging fear.

The silence demanded its answer.

"*I will,*" Abram said.

Ye are the light of the world. The words seemed to register in the same voice he had heard before aboard *The Apostle*. This time he heard it more clearly, its timbre, inflection, which proved strangely multiple. For it was his father's stern voice, his childhood champion Mr. Leach's as well—the Rev. Innis in his dedication as he led his congregation to the New World, and even his mother's at her catechetical exertions. A chorus of voices and yet one.

The taste of his mother's tea cakes was in his mouth, the savor going right down to the root of his tongue. His childhood surprise on the day of his first pastor's healing returned, and that running, sailing gratitude.

He lifted his eyes to the bedroom window and saw the sun rising outside its crosshatched panes. Flanking clouds winged it with a translucent vibrancy, a butterfly stain. The rays of the sun needling his eyes made him want to cry out, "Holy, Holy, Holy," as he heard the world's hymn. For a time—he did not know how long—he seemed to join in. To be asked. He thought of the Apostle Paul's third heaven, and the day of Christ's Transfiguration, as daybreak came.

As the calm of the morning gradually sifted into his soul, Abram took a last look at George Whitefield. *We are eternal until our life's work is done*, he remembered the man writing in lament. *You enjoyed it*, Abram replied. *You enjoyed every day on horseback, every exhortation, every sermon. You love the Lord's work. So much so He gave you this last miracle. What conceit! Quel type! as Maman would have said.*

Then he was perfectly glad to be gone from the corpse, as its occupying soul must have been, and he went down the stairs, his step quick and light.

He did not hesitate when he saw Rev. Parsons talking with a group of a dozen men in front of the house, but came up to the minister's side and stood at his elbow.

Parsons was saying, "His wishes were very well expressed."

Abram noticed that nearly the entire group wore swallow-tailed collars beneath their overcoats. Their eyes looked as baggy as the valises on the overnight coaches they must have taken.

"Think, man," said an elderly gentleman with a long patrician nose, distant eyes, and deep-rutted gums about his lower teeth. "Mr. Whitefield's expectations may have been modest, but the world's grief will not be. It is more fitting that the funeral be held in Boston, where such a great sadness can be countenanced. You will not be able to contain it here."

"Rev. Sargent, my brethren, the wishes of the dead are sacred. You may have as many memorial services in Boston as the churches you command. But George Whitefield shall have his funeral said here, and be buried here, just as he wished."

Rev. Parsons waited for the next counter, but he had already shown himself sufficiently resolved. "I recommend Wolfe's Tavern for your lodging, holy sirs," Parsons said. "I plan a funeral procession from the parsonage to the church, commencing at ten o'clock of tomorrow morning. Until that time, you will excuse me, as there are the arrangements."

Parsons pivoted around and bumped into Abram. His look said, *You? Again!*

Abram turned to the company. "Gentlemen, I will show you to Wolfe's, and those he cannot accommodate may come home with me."

Parsons gave him a quick and cutting glance. Then, literally throwing up his hands, Abram's pastor made off toward Water Street, where the carpenter would be making the casket.

Abram and a host of Boston's prominent clergy went toward Wolfe's.

———

On Tuesday, October 2, 1770, six thousand mourners stepped heavy and slow from Rev. Parsons' house to South Presbyterian Church on Federal Street. The town had swelled with the evangelist's arrival. Now that the visitors' apocalyptic dust had swept up Whitefield's own, the town's population tripled.

A hivelike cluster swarmed in and around South Presbyterian, but Submit and Gaylord were able to find seats inside.

Abram and Sarah's smallest weave from the Chaunceys took them to the crowd's farthest edge. The skies were piercingly bright, with big low clouds that were heavy and dark—the occasion's crepe. A few near Abram and Sarah cried, some talked too loud, and others held themselves as quietly as trout in a stream's current.

The mostly unheard orations drifted back. Whitefield's entombment in a crypt below the pulpit began.

One of their neighbors kept muttering, "In such a time as this."

CHAPTER 41

The Quality of Mercy

*A*bram stood high up in South Presbyterian's crowned pulpit. The huge sanctuary and the oval contours of the balcony were filled. After Whitefield's death, the town feared leaving an empty seat, even at this Thursday night service. He thought of that captain from his childhood, the one who had collaborated with the Reverend Innis to take the people of Glenwhirry away. He felt as stiff and unable to speak as that man had been, before the captain found Abram's eager face in the congregants and his courage.

Gaylord and Submit sat with Sarah in their front square pew. He could see Beniah as well, in the back row on Abram's left. The man had been shadowing Abram's steps, frustrated at the delay of his infernal ceremony.

Rev. Parsons, sitting opposite the family, finally prompted him, "Speak on, man!"

"You are my neighbors," Abram said, hurrying, his voice strange to him. "I have asked Rev. Parsons if I might address you this night, as your neighbor, as a fellow Christian, and"—he trotted out the formula for a public confession—"as one who has sinned against God and this community."

He saw people looking from him to his family.

"Mr. Lynch, if you please—stand up," Abram said, in as much of a commanding voice as he could muster.

Beniah bulged up, a hunched, wary plug.

"Mr. Lynch it was who volunteered my fortune for the orphanage. He knew I would not deny being the 'anonymous donor,' because he carries with him letters attesting to my shame."

The murmuring went clearly against Beniah.

"Are you going to speak to that?" Beniah asked in a sudden, loud voice.

"If you will take your seat again, you will not be disappointed, Beniah," Abram said.

The gopher went down.

" 'Against thee, thee only, have I sinned,' sang King David," Abram said, "and I plead first of all to the 'God of the universe, who surely will do right.' And I plead to the same God, His Son, whom I face now in this body of Christ. And to the Holy Spirit, who has long cried out in the groanings of my soul against the travesty I have made of the Gospel.

"For like David, I took a woman, Anne Farmington, and slept with her and we have had a child."

The talk lifted the congregation so much that a number rose in their pews to make comments to their neighbors.

"Yes, and as you know, I blamed this on the violence of an unknown criminal—who was, indeed, all along the unknown man, the criminal before you. I even let you think, when I wept here so publicly in this pew, that I did so out of sadness for my mother's loss. But I was weeping for my lost and illegitimate child."

"Despicable!" he heard from one man. The women's voices sounded like sparrows quarreling in a tree.

"I stand this night first to acknowledge my paternity of Titus Farmington. From this day he shall be known as my child, and the same shall be officially recorded so that he and his may have all the rights of full legal heirs. And I shall give to Anne and Theo Farmington and my son Titus sufficient properties from among my holdings to support them in comfort from this day throughout their lives."

The people all seemed to sit back together as they considered what it would be to receive such a windfall.

"Now as to the orphanage, let us speak the truth here, for this is a matter I have closely considered since Beniah Lynch thought to entrap me. Many among us, I'm sure, have read the late Mr. Whitefield's journals and know that only his solicitations in behalf of his Bethesda have enabled it to survive and serve its proper ends. The whole of my wealth would not be sufficient to support such an institution."

Sharp doubting protests: "So he says now," and "Believe that!"

"I shall, however—listen to me now—I shall devote nearly the *whole* of my remaining wealth to founding such an institution. I shall sell my lands, build up a fund, and give nine-tenths of the revenue to the orphanage. Following Mr. Law's example, I shall live on a tenth. In addition, all profits from my shipyard from this day shall go to that same end. What business I shall have must be determined by your own judgments and the necessities of an increasingly strained time. The Lord and you have my commitment, though, and it shall be prospered however so He wills."

The continual throbbing of reactions died down. Had this ended in a challenge?

"God is so good," Abram said, his voice nearly breaking with a cry, "that I am permitted no doubt of His forgiveness. I have given, though, permanent injury to my dear wife, Sarah. She has promised to forgive, and for that mercy I am truly grateful.

"If, as the body of Christ, this community, this church, can extend our Lord's acceptance to me, I shall be doubly grateful. If the greater wisdom is to do so without conferring the trust of public responsibilities, without entering into joint enterprises such as the orphanage, that is a judgment against which I can hardly protest. Do what you think is right. I cannot say more."

Abram went to his front pew and sat down by Sarah and felt the entire congregation perching on his shoulders.

Rev. Parsons stood up to go to the pulpit.

"One moment, good people!" they heard from the back.

Beniah left his pew and came to stand under the overhang of the balcony at the central aisle.

"One moment!" he called. "This good man, our Missionary, has made his confession to you—a most sincere and earnest plea. A prayer filled with thoughts of forgiveness and mercy and benevolences as balm for every wound. He is always impressive, this man, even in his betrayals and rank infidelities.

"Shall we not take him then again to our hearts and souls? How can we not?"

"Mr. Lynch," Rev. Parsons said from where he stood by the side of the pulpit steps, "you have not been given leave to address this assembly."

Abram stood up and said to Rev. Parsons, "Let him speak." He turned round to the congregation. "Let us hear, Beniah. Speak on." He settled again.

"The great Captain White wants to hear me, and so he shall. For if I kept him in suspense these days, I did so knowing that a time such as this must come. And I suspected that when the time did come we would have such a scene, an altar provided with the knife of judgment—but only for the sake of slaughtering any remembrance of his goatishness. That's his blood of mercy and forgiveness.

"But I would have you notice, good people, that our captain's sacrifices are still nothing but contingency. The orphanage is beyond his means. He will join his means with yours if you will do your part. If you will allow him to be responsible for a 'joint enterprise.'

"What part can you have in times such as these? With the non-importation order, our ships bottled in the harbor, and the town retreating to country neighbors and relatives to share their gardens' bounty. Will Captain White give over the fitting work of his shipyard to others? What will he do with this profiteering if his impoverished neighbors cannot meet his challenge? Sleep well and long in his manse, reconciled, he believes, to his wife, with his illegitimate child and the woman he abused at a safe distance—that is what he will do! And we will probably complement this ultimate swindle through feeling that *we* have failed. While he may again stand at our cleric's elbow and read out the Gospel that he has given the lie to."

"Enough! Enough!" people cried.

"No, you will hear me this time, for if, as is well-known, I have no belief in the Gospel here espoused, if I can only see its forgiveness and mercy, its balm of Gilead, as the ambergris that lights the lamps of the wealthy and is made into scent for the gentry's ladies—the fuel and fancy of the good life, but by no means good and virtuous living. If I can only regard what is preached here as the rationalizing of a ridiculous and sentimental self-regard, a dog's mess of pride twice consumed, it is because, good people, you conspire so diligently to betray common decency and replace it with a 'supernatural' and sentimental injustice.

"Captain White posed as 'Our Missionary,' and in the guise of charity did quite other loving work. He has obliged Mrs. Farmington and her Titus to live in a despicable exile.

"But that is so difficult to think about, and we would rather not. We would rather not. In this instance, you shall. You shall not forget.

Justice must be served. Captain White must be punished and severely, or you shall give me and all your secretly doubting neighbors more cause to despise your Gospel.

"Let the law handle Captain White. The Justice of the Peace must be informed and the laws against adultery enforced!"

Beniah continued to stand at the back, and it was clear that he would not quit his field until his own challenge had been answered.

Abram felt his shoulder brushed, and he saw Sarah standing and then exiting their pew. She went to stand beside Rev. Parsons, where he remained on the pulpit steps, and whispered in his ear. He nodded to her.

"In these extraordinary circumstances . . . not so much a worship service as a time of public confession and *community reconciliation*, Mrs. White has asked leave to speak. I think it fitting." He turned and gave Sarah's upper arm a clumsy shake of reassurance with both hands and stepped a little away from her.

The congregation "oohed" in a pained way when they saw Sarah standing before them, her face twisted by scars that reminded everyone of the beauty she had been so recently.

"If I were to speak out my own shame . . ." She stopped and opened her palms. "But you see I bear its marks."

The congregation grew powerfully silent.

"So I say I know the law and its exacting retribution. And I agree that Abram is not qualified to plead for mercy. Someone must plead for all of us in that. And now, it is given to me, I think, to plead for my husband."

Sarah extended her hand toward Beniah at the back. "What justice should there be, Mr. Lynch," she said, "for a man who finds a woman in weakness and sorrow—her faculties clouded—and uses the occasion to assault her?" She waited for an answer. "Would you insist on punishment, swift and severe? How severe, Mr. Lynch? Tar 'n feathers? With a cart ride through town and then the stocks? Imprisonment? Mutilation? How severe would you have this judgment be?"

Sarah once again wore that mask of anger and pain. Then her expression became as searching and yet impersonal as judgment itself.

Beniah unfolded his arms and dropped them dead at his sides. He yawed for a moment or two on his feet, then turned slowly and went out into the night.

Voices rose in a querulous satisfaction.

"No, no," Sarah said, quieting them, "that's not the end of it. For if Mr. Lynch had answered my question, I would have acknowledged the justice of his remarks. This town must think of its survival in these times. It is not the time for certain joint ventures . . . except for those who are so joined.

" 'To whom much is given, much is expected.' I have been given a great fortune." Sarah took two or three steps closer to Abram's pew, lowered her gaze, and spoke to him. "I have been given a great fortune, and now I give it to you, or to this orphanage and, I think, school—which there must be as well? Yes, an orphanage and school for the poor children in this county. Even in these times a third of the best lands on the Long Island should fetch a sufficient price. We will undertake this mission together, and as was told to us many years ago, we shall have children, spiritual children, aplenty."

Sarah looked up at the congregation. "Thank you," she said and stepped back into the pew, where Abram gave her as warm an embrace as he dared in public.

Rev. Parsons went back up into his pulpit. "What we have witnessed here tonight," he said, "is a proper and needful beginning. Only that. I caution you. Do not expect our trust, Abram and Sarah White. I, too, have to agree with much of what Mr. Lynch has said. Abram has been guilty of using the good offices of the church to abet his iniquity. He has shown himself unfit for the Lord's service. It took a Reformation to right the historical sin of simony, and it shall take much personal reformation before the Lord can use the Whites for His purpose. Work out your salvation then in fear and trembling. We shall watch and pray."

Rev. Parsons composed his hands, preparing to lead the congregation in prayer.

"If I may! If I may!"

Submit was standing, turning from the pastor to the congregation and back again, attracting attention. "I would speak a word in due season," she said.

"This season?" Parsons asked, scowling.

"I mean to say this. What we have seen here today is the very drama of the world. Evil subverts the good. And the consequences of evil, even when repented, go on. This broken world itself groans for its deliverance. Yet we live in hope, which is all that makes such sorrow endurable. For if Christ be not raised. If Christ be not raised! That is our glorious hope. And so we pray, 'Even so come, Lord Jesus.' "

Parsons waited a moment. "Amen," he said.

CHAPTER 42

———

North of Paradise

Latitude 32.30 N. Longitude 65.45 W.

A cloud of white bubbles explodes around the granite head as Abram's commemorative bust weights the anchor, taking it down ten fathoms to the sandy ocean floor.

The yacht rests in a becalmed sea. A fish's tail thumps it like a tub. Close at hand, the water is irradiated by thin shafts of light; at a distance, it is a quicksilver reflection of the aquamarine sky spread out with lazy clouds.

Abram sits by the wheel, presses down with his hands and stretches his back. He put up the mainsail at daybreak, but the trade winds never came up. They are in no trouble, but they are not going anywhere, having reached this subtropical latitude, ten nautical miles north of the island of Bermuda, where they have anchored close to a palm-studded atoll. Sarah slept below while Abram kept watch, and she continues sleeping.

Abram decides to stretch out, and lies on the fantail's deck, its laminated boards smooth as calfskin from his hours of sanding. He feels the morning sun on his face and hands and bare feet and in the weave of his light duck trousers and shirt. Why did he ever leave the sea? He feels much younger than he has in the landed years, even as the extra weight in his shoulders, upper arms, and at his middle reminds him of the time away.

Of course, if he lived at sea, he would not be spending his time cruising down to Bermuda. Still, Abram can hardly think why there should ever have been so much need of such business; he does not want to, not now. After all, he handed along any new refittings to Beniah, becoming ever more glad to have done so, as he started to build this yacht himself, the good *Hopeworth*. They would not keep her, but the last of the shipyard's lumber would contribute best in this form to the orphanage and school.

He hears Sarah's steps on the ladder. He looks up to see her looming, a cloud the garland of her hair. The sky is so bright that he can only see her as a statuesque shadow, and he shades his eyes with his hand, shifts his position, and the sun appears to the right of her head, uncovering from the cloud, and blinds him. He feels and hears her step, and the deck shifts as she jumps into the sea. He opens and closes his eyes, clearing the mercurial after-images.

She is swimming underneath the clear, radiant water, her long hair waving and pulsing with her strokes. Until two days ago, when the wind dropped and they anchored here, he had not known her to be such an enthusiastic swimmer, although she claimed to have told him during their courtship visits to the Long Island Sound. She breaks the surface, takes a breath, and dives again, diving deeper with three hard strokes and kicks. Green, finger-length fish flit after her. She lengthens out again and pulls her arms wide, scissor kicks as she turns around the back of the boat, and Abram has to shift his weight onto his right elbow to keep watch. But for the linen undergarment she wears, from her neck to her knees, she might be a mermaid, she moves so easily. The linen as it waves about her adds an impression of sea lily.

She surfaces again, takes several breaths, pinches her nose, clears her eyes, treads water. She drifts a little more than he would have thought, the current carrying her toward the atoll.

"Abram," she says. "This is the day the Lord . . ." She gulps a breath and throws out her arms, sending off a fanning shower of drops. "You might join me."

That's all the invitation she gives—her first—but Abram needs only the one word. He removes his shirt and jumps. He strokes forward of the prow and swims along beside her, keeping his head above water, watching for her eye as she turns her head to take a breath.

They swim together until he feels his own breaths coming much harder and remembers the current, his age, and thinks of the patch of rigging over the side. He leaves her to her swim, and after several hard strokes and a scrambling grasping at the rigging with chilled hands, he climbs aboard.

The water sluices off him as he sits on deck, and his breathing becomes easier as he warms up. He has a sensation of rising into the air as the water dries from his skin. He stands and looks out over the flat glistening sea and senses care and protection—the spirit of his mother. He salutes her, grateful to have experienced the sea as a loving hand.

Sarah is thirty yards from the yacht now. "Are you going on to Bermuda without me, then?" Abram calls out.

She takes another two strokes away, turns on her back and keeps going, but with her head up like an otter, watching him. He says nothing else and she turns and heads in.

Abram gives her a hand up, and before she thinks to ask for the towel, he puts one around her shoulders and begins rubbing her dry. Quickly, he pulls it over her head and fluffs her hair, moving behind her. Her long dark hair has taken the weight of the water and proves heavier than he could have imagined. He keeps drying her, though, going on to her calves and feet when the ends of her hair begin to spiral into ringlets. She feels cold, wet, unbelievably fresh in the warm morning.

"That's fine, then," she says, her voice bright. "I suppose I'll dress."

Still, she does not move away from him. He looks into her damaged face and suddenly wants to touch her nose, the place at her cheek that is scarred, the smeared skin.

He searches for the old resistance, their habitual unhappiness, and cannot find it.

Sarah half closes her eyes and breathes in the morning air.

He reaches out and touches her scarred cheek. His touch is tenuous, uncertain, easily broken, easily refused, easily withdrawn.

Then he says, foolishly, "You will want something dry."

"Will I?" she asks. She presses his hand against her cheek with her own. "You can never look at me again as you used to. But can you look at me?"

He swallows and nearly panics, for suddenly all of the wanted desire makes his heart flutter. In the next moment, though, the shade of the past returns, or at least another heartfelt aspiration deeper than desire. "What if we cannot have children?"

She sniffs and gives the smallest clearing shake of her head. "We will most certainly have many children now," she says.

"These are not just brave words?" he says.

"It is not that I am resigned," she says. "I do not feel the same urgency. I have searched for it. Perhaps I am free."

"For the time?"

"What would you have, then, promises for life? We've made those."

"So unsatisfactorily," he says.

"Yes," she says and kisses him.

He brings her close. The linen is wet against his chest. He likes it. "Is this satisfactory?" he asks.

"A little wanting," she says. "A little . . ."

He holds her closer.

"Better," she says. "Bet . . ."

He gathers her as close as can be. Familiarity, absence, and willingness braid together into a nest that hangs upon the air. Everything is warm and soft in this nest. A knitting of balky straw that holds the sea's power, the sky's glory, and the closeness of this world and the next.

In this old and new marriage, this union of souls, life comes again. This once, Sarah's second sight has failed her. A greater urgency or purpose exists than either she or Abram can feel. Love's voice utters a name. In nine months—as people sometimes do who adopt children—Abram and Sarah have a son of their own, whom they call Izak.

NOTES FROM THE AUTHOR

1. A few words about my use of Newburyport and its history. I am indebted, as are all writers who treat this topic, to John J. Currier's two-volume work, *The History of Newburyport, Mass. 1764–1909* (republished by the New Hampshire Publishing Company, Somersworth, 1977); as well as his *Ould Newbury.*

   Much of the town's actual history comes into the narrative, and my minor characters tend (as noted below) to be real historical figures.

   At the same time, "use" must be the word, since for a number of purposes I have superimposed a few of my own metaphoric structures—the most notable of which is the slum Five Points. Geographically, Five Points corresponds most closely to the area known as Joppa, the old fishing village close to the estuary, which retains some of its original character today. Five Points is made up of my research, guesses, and most importantly, creative intentions.

   In some cases, I have washed in both original street names and their current ones, as with King and Federal Street.

   I have also inserted my fictional character Abram White into the history, and in so doing greatly simplified community structures and their cast of characters.

   I make this admission readily because there are many students of Newburyport's history, and it's a rich one. *Daybreak* is not meant to be an exact recounting of the town's past any more than *The Merchant of Venice* is meant to be a guide to trading practices.

2. The case of the Acadians is drawn from the town's history. In the early months of 1767 Joseph Dorsett did petition the town for relief, in behalf of himself and his family. The selectmen authorized the Overseers of the Poor to see what could be done about the matter. Mr. Ebenezer Little, Capt. James Hudson, Tristram Dalton,

Esq., Mr. Jacob Boardman, and Mr. Stephen Hooper were appointed a committee on May 19, 1767, to consider the matter. The petitioners were granted assistance, and Currier reports that during the following summer "most of the Acadians found their way to Canada." (See Currier, vol. I, p. 39.)

3. For my own Overseers, I selected three figures from that period who particularly appealed to me, and they are used throughout this novel to represent the town's inhabitants in colonial times. It's unlikely that these three men ever served together on the Overseers, although all three would have been acquainted with the topics discussed and approached these, I think, from the points-of-view ascribed to them.

Tristram Dalton was graduated from Harvard in 1755. Before the Revolutionary War, he did have farmlands and interests in various businesses. He was elected representative from Newburyport to the General Court, and then, after the adoption of the Constitution of the United States, he became a senator from Massachusetts. He moved to Washington, D.C., but in 1815, after suffering financial reversals, he came back to Massachusetts and accepted a clerkship in the Boston Custom House. He died in Boston on May 30, 1817, and was buried in St. Paul's churchyard, in Newburyport. (See Currier, vol. II, p. 214.)

Patrick Tracy was born in Ireland in 1711 and came to Newburyport early in his life. He was one of the petitioners of the General Court for the incorporation of the town in 1763. A prominent ship-master and ship owner, he was an active supporter of the Revolutionary War effort. The Tracy family did go into the business of privateering, although it's Patrick's son Nathaniel who is best known for this. Currier tells us that a memorial to Congress presented in Nathaniel's name claims that from the beginning of the Revolutionary War until peace was declared in 1783, Nathaniel owned one hundred ten merchant vessels, which with their cargoes were worth $2,733,300. Twenty-three of these vessels were "letters of marque": ships that were authorized to seize others, although their primary business was trade. Nathaniel also owned twenty-four cruising ships, carrying three hundred and forty guns and twenty-eight hundred men. Although almost all of Nathaniel's merchant vessels were lost or captured, his cruisers captured cargoes of $3,950,000. He reimbursed the government $167,219 for supplies and merchandise. (See Currier, vol. I, p. 624, footnote 2.) Unfortunately, these profits did not sustain his fortune thereafter.

The great days of Clipper ships and new fortunes were still to come in Newburyport.

Patrick may be "jumping the gun" here a bit historically, in terms of discussing privateering, although smuggling and privateering were more a mainstay of many respectable fortunes of the time than we colonists would like to admit.

An important note: The Newburyport Public Library currently occupies Nathaniel's old home on State Street. Some of my researches were carried on in that building among the special collections there, for which I thank the library and its staff.

Theophilus Parsons is frankly my favorite Newburyporter, and I have juggled some dates here, making him a somewhat older man, in order to give him his role. He was in fact born in 1750 and was graduated from Harvard just as these events unfold in 1769. Admitted to the bar in 1774, he opened a law office in Newburyport in 1777. He was known as the polymath he is represented as being here, and he played a key role in the adoption of the U.S. Constitution by Massachusetts. In these discussions, he worked tirelessly behind the scenes to enable passage. In 1806, he was appointed chief-justice of the state supreme court; before that, John Quincy Adams clerked in his Newburyport law office. He died in 1813. (See Currier, vol. II, p. 262, and also vol. I, pp. 92–101.)

4. Although the Bowditch navigational guide was quite real, the ship architect "Herman Bowditch" is purely fictitious.

5. The god Cupid fell in love with the mortal Psyche, who was sworn never to try to see his face. She broke that rule and had to endure many trials in order to be reunited with him. She was finally made a goddess and Aphrodite allowed them to marry. John Singleton Copley's original letter to Sarah includes then a fairly stern warning to keep away from him for the present. It also offers an impossible ultimate promise.

6. The details as to John Singleton Copley's work and his marriage are accurate. The portraits of the Smiths exist; that of Sarah most closely resembles a portrait of Elizabeth Oliver, painted in 1758. The painter was not known as a womanizer, but his letters make clear his propensity to flatter. Like many artists, he was simultaneously ambitious, vain, and self-doubting. He spoiled much of the latter part of his career in England through overreaching and being difficult. His early letters repeatedly refer to his frustrations with "little Boston."

7. Benjamin Franklin and George Whitefield were longtime friends. The article that appears here from Franklin is ghost-written, but

it fairly represents his sentiments and his experiences with Whitefield.

8. George Whitefield died on September 30, 1770, and was buried in
   South Presbyterian Church on Federal Street. Apart from Abram's
   presence and the notion of the vigil (which is entirely invented, if
   a possibility), Whitefield's death and his entombment took place
   as described. I have drawn some of Whitefield's last exhortation
   from quoted remarks of that day. Those interested in Whitefield
   should see especially Harry S. Stout's *The Divine Dramatist* (Eerd-
   mans, 1991), an outstanding work of scholarship and highly read-
   able.